How Does Your Garde

P·A·M·E·L·A J·O·N·E·S

HOW DOES YOUR GARDEN GROW?

The Essential Home Garden Book

ILLUSTRATIONS BY BOB JOHNSON

VIKING

VIKING
Published by the Penguin Group
Viking Penguin Inc., 40 West 23rd Street,
New York, New York 10010, U.S.A.
Penguin Books Ltd, 27 Wrights Lane,
London W8 5TZ, England
Penguin Books Australia Ltd, Ringwood,
Victoria, Australia
Penguin Books Canada Ltd, 2801 John Street,
Markham, Ontario, Canada L3R 1B4
Penguin Books (N.Z.) Ltd, 182–190 Wairau Road,
Auckland 10, New Zealand

Penguin Books Ltd, Registered Offices:
Harmondsworth, Middlesex, England

First published in 1989 by Viking Penguin Inc.
Published simultaneously in Canada

1   3   5   7   9   10   8   6   4   2

LIBRARY OF CONGRESS CATALOGING IN PUBLICATION DATA
Jones, Pamela.
How does your garden grow? : the essential home garden book/
Pamela Jones.
p.   cm.
Bibliography: p.
Includes index.
ISBN 0-670-82636-7
1. Gardening.   I. Title.
SB453.J66 1989
635—dc 19   88-40289

Printed in the United States of America by
Arcata Graphics, Fairfield, Pennsylvania
Set in Perpetua and Caslon Open Face
Designed by Liney Li

*With love
for my sisters, Helen and Anne,
for their sense of possibilities
and beauty*

ACKNOWLEDGMENTS

NOT A GARDENER has crossed my path whose work or advice has not in some way enriched me, and each encounter has created an indelible bond of friendship, of experience shared. Little did I suspect that it would be the same with this book. What began with a casual comment, a seed, from my sister Anne, germinated instantly in the exuberant, fertile mind of my dear friend and literary agent, Charlotte Sheedy. Tirelessly, she nurtured and cajoled the seedling into growth, until she deemed it ready to transplant into the care of my editor, Amanda Vaill. With unabated enthusiasm, Amanda examined every leaf for texture and form, weeding, feeding, and grooming her charge. At the same time, Joel Allen cast his horticultural eye over it, to avert potential flaws. And finally, when the book-plant reached maturity, Bob Johnson prepared it for show with his magic brush.

To all these friends, old and new, my most heartfelt thanks.

CONTENTS

Introduction **xi**

1. A Garden? A Yard? **1**

2. N-E-W-S **7**

3. Know Your Soil **17**

4. Basic Tools **27**

5. Planning Your Garden **43**

6. Compost and Fertilizers **53**

7. Preparing the Beds **69**

8. Buying Your Plants **81**

9. Planting **93**

10. Watering Your Plants **119**

11. Mulching **131**

12. Weeding **141**

13. Pests and Pals **151**

14. Simple Propagation **163**

15. Garden Maintenance **181**

16. Winterizing Your Garden **193**

Appendix I: 150 Herbaceous Perennials **201**

Appendix II: Thirty Common Weeds **213**

Useful Readings **222**

USDA Plant Hardiness Zone Map **224–25**

Index **227**

INTRODUCTION

THE BEAUTY OF GARDENING is that it speaks all languages and crosses all borders. It makes no social, geographical, or political distinctions. It is impervious to poverty and to wealth. It is art and commerce, science and solitude—whatever you want it to be. It brings out not only our passions but also our sense of possibilities. It creates both a universal greed for and a need to share knowledge. It lets us experience both the force and the playfulness of nature, to recognize our own place in it. A garden can never be fully subjugated to our will, and yet always it promises us beauty and joy; always, it is forgiving.

To begin with, there is no such thing as a "born" gardener. Even the most famous and accomplished gardeners had to start at the beginning, and all gardeners are perpetual students. The only qualifications you need to enter this "school" are an interest in plants and the desire to learn. The only *real* rules are of nature's devising: climate and seasons, soil and stamina—yours and the plants'. Your tests consist of your own capacity to adapt to, or to bend, these rules, as long as you always know that nature has the last word. Nor is there an art in gardening as such. The art of a garden lies in the personality it projects—your personality. This is quite inevitable, because your garden will be determined by your personal tastes and habits, by your likes and dislikes.

There are gardens that are pictures of exquisite, orderly perfection, and there are gardens that burst with color and movement; there are serene and wooded gardens, expansive, lazy, generous gardens, and there are seemingly spontaneous gardens, which look as if they had simply "happened." The possibilities are as endlessly varied as are the people who create them. The simple fact of the matter is that *all* gardens are successful if they please and satisfy their creator.

The magic of watching things grow has always been a central part of my life. Even now, in summer, I often lie in the warm grass and "listen" to the earth, to the hum of life. Among my earliest memories are Mother's gooseberry trees—yes, trees, not the usual shrubs—one uncle's London garden filled with prize-winning roses, another London uncle's prize-winning chrysanthemums the size of footballs, and my grandfather's storybook Impressionist garden near Strasbourg. An old photograph shows me earnestly studying an unidentifiable plant, like some learned and wizened professor. By the time I was five years old, I already owned my very own miniature set of gardening tools. The fact that my younger sister soon afterward wielded the hoe on my skull, as an inducement to let her have one of my dolls, may of course be the underlying reason why I've never much cared to use hoes.

Not much later, as it was wartime and food was scarce, Mother sent us into the fields all around us, where we lived in the country, to pick the plants that grew wild. Dandelions, nettles, and purslane; wild mustard, sorrel, and cress. With these she made delicious and nourishing soups, or vegetables, or salads. Wild strawberries, raspberries, bilberries, and a kind of cranberry became jams and jellied desserts. There were chestnuts, hazelnuts, and beechnuts, and all the peaceful happy hours we spent shelling these. Two for the pot and one for us. And all the time, unwittingly, we were learning, as we roamed among the fields and pastures, along the edge of woods and a nearby brook.

Later still, glorious schooldays were spent away from the classroom, on daylong field trips, to pick wild herbs for medicinal use. Lady's-mantle, potentilla, elderberry, pine needles, clover, and all the others. My favorite was lady's-mantle, because of the dewdrops that nestled like little diamonds in the centers of its frilled and fluted leaves.

It is from all those long-ago days that I have carried with me an almost religious love for all the myriad marvels of the soil, their textures and colors, aromas and uses. What began with a little patch of my own in my childhood gardens developed over the years into ever more structured, thoughtful plantings, on both sides of the Atlantic.

In New York City, my indoor garden became so dense that my husband often feared he would be seized and devoured by some man-eating plant. There was one time when I perhaps tested his patience beyond endurance. Accidentally, I had knocked a philodendron off the windowsill, and there it lay, mangled and twisted, four floors below, in a tiny, dark, and inaccessibly walled-in courtyard behind our West Side apartment. I had just begun to experiment with talking and playing music to my plants. Seizing on this accident as a first *real* opportunity to test the validity of communicating with plants, I begged and pleaded and cajoled, until finally my beleaguered husband capitulated reluctantly. An hour, a torn shirt, grubby jeans, bleeding hands, and numerous suspicious neighbors later, he wearily trudged up the stairs, bearing the mutilated victim. Of course, I didn't know at the time that it is virtually impossible to kill a philodendron, so it might well have recovered without my ministrations, music, and small talk. Years later, the morning after we had decided to separate, some twenty magnificent coleus plants of every imaginable hue, all of them healthy, thriving specimens, were dead—all of them totally, irretrievably dead. Makes one wonder!

A series of small city gardens followed—yards they were

when I began, gardens they were when I left. For the past several years of living in upstate New York, I have finally been able to give full vent to my insatiable greed for a glut of all the color and variety which nature has to offer. I still talk to plants, although not so overtly that anybody can overhear me. The uninitiated would probably judge me to be a certifiable lunatic. They don't know that the carbon dioxide I exhale acts as a stimulant to the plants' growth—that's *our* secret.

Now you are about to join this fellowship of plants and gardeners. You have just acquired your very first, very own piece of property. The land around your new house may be large or small. It's what you dreamed about. In the first flush of excitement at all the possibilities you envision, all the beauty and perfection within your grasp, a typical scenario may continue as follows: Depending upon your nature and the season, you (a) rush out and buy every plant at the nearest nursery, or (b) rush out and buy every gardening book you can find. In the case of (a), the plants will be dead within a week or two, because you suddenly realize that you do not know what to do with them, or how or where to do it—nor do you have any tools. In the case of (b), between unpacking and settling into your new home, you study the color illustrations of hundreds of plants. You try to memorize the plants' botanic and common names, only to find that many of the former are unpronounceable and many of the latter are not listed in the index.

You discover that descriptions and planting guides might as well be written in a foreign language, for all the sense they make, with phrases like "bud union," "pH value," and "hardiness zone." In catalogues, a proliferation of blazing color photographs promises easy care, vivid (purple, red, yellow, bronze, etc.) foliage, masses of blooms from May to October. You want them all. Of course, the catalogues do not make it too clear that, should you order seeds, it may take several weeks before you see the first green sprout—provided you planted them at the right time. And if you order some of the plants so beautifully illustrated at the peak of blossom time, you will receive a shipment of pitifully small seedlings, or a twig with roots at one end, which is supposed to be that gorgeous flowering crabapple shown on page 47 of the catalogue.

No, the books and catalogues are not lying or trying to deceive you. What they are doing is to assume that you, the reader, already have a basic knowledge of plants and gardening. But to you, it all seems suddenly too daunting, and you may begin to think that you don't have time for a garden anyway, that mowing the lawn will be work enough.

My purpose, therefore, in writing this book is to introduce you, the first-time home gardener, to a basic knowledge of gardening and plants. I have made the assumption that, although you have no gardening knowledge at present, you are armed with both the desire to have a garden and the willingness to learn.

Without being scientific or technical about it, I have attempted to guide you through the proper sequence of procedures. Inevitably of course, some of these overlap, while others coincide; some are necessary throughout the growing season, others only once. I have included the reasons for doing certain things in a particular order or manner at the moment these apply. I have defined such strange-sounding terms as "deadheading," "double-digging," and "water regularly" at the moment you will be doing them, and explained *why* they are necessary or desirable. Most of all, I have tried to show you how to relax and enjoy the versatility of gardening, and to avoid the anxieties we all feel at the beginning, of being permanently "stuck" with our inevitable mistakes and clumsiness, our failures and plant losses. Bear in mind that even the most practiced gardeners experience these, too.

There is only one point I cannot stress enough: do please learn the botanic *and* common names of all your plants. Not doing so can lead to frustration and misunderstandings.

Take, for instance, only one single example and you will quickly see how invaluable this knowledge is. In my garden, I keep a plant whose botanic name is *Monarda didyma*. Monarda is a genus that includes seventeen species of herbs, and derives its name from Nicolas Monardes, a physician of Seville, Spain, who in 1569 wrote a book about the New World's medicinal plants. Because it is a fragrant herb, I have grown *M. didyma* in my herb garden; because of its showy, dark scarlet flowers, I also have it in my perennial bed. The plant as such is indigenous to North America. It is sold through some catalogues and nurseries under any one of its several names, with or without cross-reference, so that if you don't know all the names it goes by, you may not recognize it. And here begins the fun. Its common names are bergamot, because its fragrance is reminiscent of the bergamot orange grown in Spain, from which English marmalade is made— except that the bergamot orange's botanic name is really *Citrus bergama*, and it is a tree into the bargain; bee balm, simply enough, because it attracts bees (hummingbirds are also drawn to the flower's bright color); and, finally, Oswego tea, because it was discovered in the region inhabited by the Oswego Indians, from where it was introduced into England during the 1700s, reaching the Continent under the name of gold Melissa, among others, which is not to be confused with *Melissa officinalis*, also known as lemon balm. To add to the confusion, *all seventeen* monardas are called bergamot—and horsemint. *Horsemint?!* Now you look under the mints (botanic name *Mentha*), where you discover that only the American horsemint is a monarda *(M. punctata)*. But lo, what's this? There's also a bergamot mint, except that its botanic name is *Mentha citrata*, or *Mentha odorata*. Oy vey!

The fact remains that, if you want that fragrant, scarlet-flowered plant I described above, it's the *specific* name, *"didyma,"* in its botanic name which unequivocally identifies the exact *Monarda* variety I have. So I urge you, no matter how many charming, quaint names you read or hear, like cardinal flower, coral-bells, dutchman's breeches, or orange glory flower, please take the time to learn their botanic appellations. It's the only way you can ever be sure of what you have or what you're buying. The above, incidentally, are in turn botanically named *Lobelia cardinalis, Heuchera sanguinea, Dicentra cucullaria,* and *Asclepias tuberosa.* I know they sound like a mouthful, but knowing them, you will be understood by professional nurserymen and ardent gardeners everywhere, whose own regions, or countries, undoubtedly have common names of their own for each of these examples. To help you get accustomed to this "bilingualism," as you will see later on in this book, I have been deliberately inconsistent at times about using the botanic and common names in reference to one or another plant. In this way, while your eye sees "digitalis," for example, your brain will instinctively say "foxglove." And vice versa, of course.

Lastly, there is another point I wish to make. Crucial as water is to your garden, not a single gardening book I have ever read has been explicit about how much water is "enough," either at planting time or thereafter. The nearest I've come upon is the advice that if the top one inch of soil is moist, your plants have sufficient water. Alas, this leaves the way open for many unanswered questions. As you will see yourself, in Chapter 10, there is good reason for this reluctance to stipulate specific amounts of water for your plants. However, because I believe that, until you have an understanding of the intertwining factors governing your garden, until you develop a "feel" for your garden's needs, you cannot be expected to judge how much water is enough for your plants, I've decided to stretch my neck across the chopping block by suggesting some specific amounts. In return, I ask you to understand that I've based these suggestions on *my* kind of soil, *my* weather conditions, and *my* hardiness zone. Depending on where you live, your garden's needs may be less or more, but my recommendations will be a general guide, near enough to the right amount.

Once you are familiar and comfortable with the basic aspects of gardening I have put before you in the following pages, you will automatically "graduate" to the many specialized and sophisticated gardening books that are available everywhere. For the present, however, if you've decided that you do have an interest in plants, the next most important ingredients are perseverance, patience, and the necessary skills. You must provide the first two. I will help you to learn the skills. There's no denying that some gardening activities are hard work, but the satisfaction is immediate and the rewards can be infinite. The basic tools are available everywhere. And some of the most useful things you will need are already in your house, wherever you live—you have undoubtedly been throwing them into the garbage for years. Just remember, as long as you breathe—literally—your garden will benefit. (Of course, you will, too!)

A Garden? A Yard?

Essentially, the use of either "garden" or "yard" is a matter of semantics. Both words have their origins in the Greek *chortos,* an enclosure, although it does appear that "garden" is a derivative of "yard." In any case, the Greeks did not invent gardening—only the word for it. But as *chortos* traveled through the centuries and was adopted into various European cultures, it came to give distinctly separate meanings to "garden" and "yard." What modern English calls a "garden" became an Italian *giardino,* a French *jardin,* a German *Garten,* and a Danish *have,* for example. Only the Spanish made still a further distinction between a vegetable garden, *huerto,* and a flower garden, *jardín.* "Yard" became an Italian *corte,* a French *cour,* a German *Hof,* and a Danish *gård.* Once again, the Spanish further distinguished among *patio, corral,* and *cercado*—the last an enclosed field.

In the course of time, a "garden" came to mean an enclosed piece of land that is cultivated for the growing of flowers, fruits, vegetables, and herbs; a "yard" came to denote a *paved* enclosure, as in courtyard, stockyard, barnyard, shipyard, etc.

Despite the evolution of these separate meanings, however, many Americans continue to say "yard" when they really mean "garden." I've never been able to decide whether this is due to a lingering linguistic purism or because people think that "garden" applies only to *famous* or *foreign* gardens. Frequently, somebody has said to me how much he or she would love to have a cottage garden, or a wild English garden, or a formal garden. Shown a variety of colored photographs, the individual will automatically respond with something like "That's exactly the kind of garden I had in mind." However, when actually visiting some beautiful American home gardens, that same person almost invariably exclaims, albeit with genuine enthusiasm, "Oh, what a lovely yard."

Nevertheless, "garden" is rapidly gaining coinage. Mind you, with that deliciously irrepressible capacity and drive for getting things done, some Americans do think they can decide in June to have a garden and find it ready-made a few weeks later. They can, of course, if they're willing to part with a suitable amount of legal tender. It happened to me on a relatively small scale. A client told me in May that she wanted to unveil an instant garden on the occasion of a huge July Fourth party she planned to give. There were to be shrubs in full bloom, massed to look as though they had been there for years, flowers everywhere, planters, window boxes, hanging baskets. Colors were to explode and cascade everywhere. The show wasn't bad when I was done, but I believe now, as I believed then, that a practiced eye could quickly see through the artifice of this set design.

In any case, whatever the nomenclature, the key word governing both garden and yard is "enclosed," although I prefer to use the word "framed." Therefore, if a garden is your "painting," then an enclosure is the frame that provides both focus on and enhancement of that painting. For example, a few flowers planted alone in the middle of a large expanse of lawn appear like little lost waifs in a grassy sea—*if* they can be seen at all from even a modest distance. The "frame" of lawn in such an instance is too overpowering for the "picture" of flowers. It is like pinning a small black-and-white snapshot on the bare wall of a church hall. However, the moment you add a handsome rock near the flowers, or a small grouping of shrubs, or a flowering tree, the eye is drawn automatically to your flowers. Their "frame" contains them, and acts against their being visually swallowed up by the green sea around them.

Not for a moment am I suggesting that a garden should be fully enclosed on all four sides (unless you want this), or by one type of device, such as a wooden fence, a stone wall, or conifers standing parade-ground fashion all around. On the contrary, I personally believe that the *suggestion* of frame is often more attractive, and also allows greater latitude in design. A partial wall or fence then can not only define a boundary but also become a secondary frame for a special-interest planting; a grouping of trees can suggest property line and also act as pointer to a large flower bed, or become the visual interruption to a surprise behind it.

Whether your property is confined by neighboring houses, by city lot, or by distant landscapes, a garden always radiates from the building(s) it wholly or partially surrounds. Simultaneously, the garden itself serves to focus on the building(s). As often as not, the style of your house will influence the style of your garden. Both are determined by your personal preferences.

If you have bought a large, imposing house at the top of a hillside, it is more than likely that your garden design will include elegantly articulate sweeps, startling vistas, to emphasize the location's intrinsic drama, its sense of grandeur, as well as its insularity. If that same house is set deep in the woods, you will perhaps lead to it along quiet winding paths, past sun-dappled woodland gardens, the house glimpsed here and there, both mystery and safe haven. An architecturally insignificant, small house along a narrow stream, surrounded by open fields and a few clumps of trees, can become a cuddly cherub nestling in a wildly exuberant embrace of flowers. Similarly, a suburban, or even the tiniest city, garden, can be visually stretched beyond its confines through a sense of movement, destination, and height created by curves and undulations. As easily, the same garden, the fences or walls around it densely overgrown by vines, can outwardly proclaim privacy, while bursting with radiance within. Some small gardens are ornate, or serene, or starkly surrealistic; some are comfortable outdoor living rooms, flagstoned patios surrounded by flowers and vegetables, shrubs, and even a tree or two; some small gardens amble and ramble among clumps of berries and wild grasses, clusters of flowers and fragrant herbs; some bristle with corn and tomatoes and peppers and lettuce, and some are evergreen, peaceful retreats.

A garden may be large or small, even on a large property. It may consist of a series of individual gardens, each framed or linked by hedges, paths, fences, a stream's winding course, a rocky outcropping, woodlands, or arbors. It may be parkland with groupings of uncommon or delicately flowering trees that seemingly happen to meander through various flower beds; it may be a cobbled plaza surrounding a fountain or statuary, with only a few potted plants at its base. A garden may be no more than a grassy path amid flowering shrubs, leading to a solitary bench or a distant mountain view. A garden may be a small patch of space in front of, or behind, a building, artfully planted to create a moment's exuberance or serenity. Even a tiny paved or flagstoned enclosure—a yard—may become a garden, with the help of hanging baskets, graduated plant stands and screens, lattices, or planter benches. Holes chiseled into the cement or stone can be filled with rock-garden plants or fragrant herbs, as can the spaces between flagstones. A few potted plants grouped around the periphery of the enclosure, or hung on its surrounding fence or walls, will instantly transform what seemed to be a hopeless area into one of welcoming charm. In fact, no more than an otherwise offending high wall can become a garden, a vertical garden. Its starkness can be interrupted by a series of graduated supports, even iron gratings or trellises, at varying heights, to accommodate pots and planters, window boxes, vines, and roses.

In short, a garden is anything you want it to be, limited only by your imagination—and its physical dimensions. I fervently believe that the truly satisfying, happy garden is the one that is looked upon as a living organism, an extension of home and family. The reason is simple. A garden has decided needs; it grows or rests, it expands and changes, it thrives and fades, and it is proportionately dependent on its environment and on the care it receives. Different plants, like people, respond differently to sun and wind, to soil, cold, and water. To varying degrees, plants reach for light and sun and water, and if they are entirely deprived of these, like people, they become listless and frail. Above all, like people, plants need to breathe free. They do best when there is a little space around each of them, when the air can circulate among them, when the soil in which they stand offers them stable conditions and balanced nutrition. Like members of a family, plants provide much joy and moments of sorrow or disappointment. And if some of them get a little out of hand now and then, they must be gently but firmly disciplined, or coaxed, ignored, or "grounded," until they are ready again to participate in family life—or else leave home.

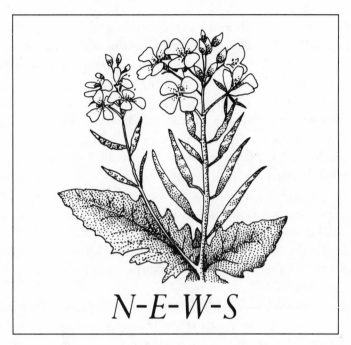

N-E-W-S

There is something unique in the human experience about owning a plot of land. Whether it be large or small, bare or overgrown, on a hilltop or by the sea, in the city or country, that plot is a dream fulfilled. Yet although we carefully poke through every nook and cranny of a new house, to acquaint ourselves with its idiosyncrasies and foibles, many of us give not even a passing thought to the fact that the land around our house has characteristics of its own. And *not* knowing these can lead to serious trouble, if you plan to have a garden. It means learning the **North**, **East**, **West**, and **South** of your property, and becoming familiar with the subsurface conditions of your land and with the hardiness zone in which it is situated. Not only is this information crucial, because it will likely spare you potential plant losses and needless work and expense, but gathering it can become a voyage of discovery for you. So arm yourself with a compass and a camera.

Among other odds and ends, I usually carry a small compass around with me. I always like to know in which direction I'm aimed, no matter where I am, to get my bearings. If I also happen to be looking at somebody's garden, or where a garden might be, a quick compass reading in my own region immediately makes me privy to some crucial information. Once north is fixed, it tells me at what angle the house is positioned, and which are its sunny and shaded sides. Many houses are so situated that they present one entirely north-facing side. As often as not, that side happens to face the front—the very side we would like to present at its best. The sun, however, never directly reaches a true north side, and so this is a major factor to consider. Just as there are few human beings who genuinely prefer to live without any light or sun at all, so there are few plants that are happy in such an environment.

The compass also lets me determine the direction of prevailing winds, and which garden areas are likely to be windblown. Even if what I'm looking at isn't a garden yet, the compass tells me where one *might* be. To know about sun and wind exposures is most important for any gardener. They could make the difference between a happy and an unhappy garden. In this way, that little magnetic needle literally, if indirectly, forms the basis of your garden plan.

Prevailing winds generally come from different directions in summer and winter. They tend to be strong and gusty, whether they carry moist or frigid air, or whether they are hot and dry off the desert. Especially if your area is flat and exposed, and your garden lies unsheltered in their path, these winds can cause serious damage.

In my corner of the country, for example, the winds are either out of the northwest, Canada, or from the southeast. In summer, that wonderful dry, cool air from Canada is a delicious relief for us humans, particularly after a humid siege. Such a cool frontal system and its accompanying winds can, however, send anguished shudders down the spines of our flowers, particularly in early spring. On the other hand, our rolling thunderstorms of summer, whipped along by blustery gales, usually come from the southeast. These are just as uncharitable, by bruising, battering, and bending the flowers, until many of them are too dazed to stand up again.

In winter, the northwest winds tend to be mercilessly icy blasts of arctic air, while southeast winds often bring wet snows that weight tree branches well past breaking point. These winds also frequently bring warming trends, a false promise of spring. Under these fluctuating conditions, your perennials could suffer beyond endurance. Although they are frozen back to the ground and may look dead to you, they are merely in a dormant condition. Their barely visible crowns, in fact, hold next year's growth. If these are not insulated by a cover of snow (always a bit iffy), or by a cover of mulch, the plants' dormant buds could first be duped into awakening, only to be seared soon afterward by a lethal dose of windburn. Literally nipped in the bud. Although, clearly, the compass reading doesn't specifically tell you all this, a fix on north allows you to fill in much of the rest.

Wherever you may live, you can easily find out about the prevailing winds in your own region by telephoning the local airport or weather station or the Cooperative Extension Association—unless you're in luck and have a meteorologist living next door. If none of the above is available, then ask a nearby farmer, a gardening friend or neighbor, or an area nursery. And if *that* leads to naught, you'd better try a windsock to learn which way the wind blows.

Because it's safe to say that your house and property have at least four sides, the type and scope of your garden design will, in large measure, rely on the amount of sun reaching both, and on how exposed they are to wind. If you are on an open hilltop, subject to unremitting sun and sweeping breezes, you will do best to stay away from delicate shade-loving plants, unless you first create the necessary protective environment. In a small forest clearing, reached only by dappled sunlight, although protected against powerful winds, you'd best avoid setting out plantdom's sun worshippers. High flat and open surroundings would demand some kind of windscreen, and a deep hollow at the foot of a north-facing mountainside might well be a frost pocket, where the growing season is shorter than on the other side of the same mountain.

The mention of frost pockets brings me to the next piece of vital information with which you should arm yourself before planning your garden. It concerns the hardiness zone in which you live. If you have done any visual wandering through the maze of gardening catalogues, you've undoubtedly encountered the mention of zones. Descriptive paragraphs under the colored plant illustrations may begin or end with the words "Zones 4–9," or "Hardy in Zones 4–9." Alas, not all catalogues include zone information, in which case it's a good idea to check with your local nursery whether or not certain plants can grow in your area.

Just what are these zones, and what do they mean? Very simply, the U.S. Department of Agriculture (USDA) has developed a map that divides the North American continent into ten so-called hardiness zones (see pages 224–25). These zones are based on long-term Weather Bureau observations of the *average* minimum temperature of the coldest month, with Zone 1 representing the coldest. This means that certain plants which can grow in one zone cannot live through the average lowest winter cold in the zone north of that.

You'll notice that each zone traverses the continent in meandering and often jagged bands. Within each band, from east to west, the lowest mean temperature range is the same. Nevertheless, not all the plants considered hardy for a given zone can grow there; all they have in common is their survival rate in the winters of their particular hardiness zone. That is due to the many other factors that play a role in plant growth, such as soil type, amount of rainfall (or lack of it), altitude, and shelter. Consequently, moisture-loving plants that feel right at home with all the rainfall in the northeastern portion of USDA Zone 5 would die of thirst in the arid conditions of the same zone's southwestern desert portions. The lowest average temperature during the coldest month is, however, perhaps the most decisive factor in plant growth.

The operative word here is "average." Hardiness zone maps, of which there are several varieties, serve as a general plant hardiness guide *only,* and not as an indicator of your local weather conditions. Only *you* can know these. For example, officially I live in USDA Zone 5, although not too terribly far from USDA Zone 4. The lowest average temperature in USDA Zone 5 ranges between −20° F. and −10° F. Yet, more than once in recent years, nature has seen fit to let fly with some ferociously frigid blasts that made −20° seem almost like a heat wave. True, if an insulating layer of snow or mulch covers the ground during such uncommon assaults, some plant losses may be avoided, but that's entirely too circumstantial and risky for my taste. The plain fact is that such occasional climatic deviations *do* occur, and must be expected in this region. So I prefer to play it safe, by selecting as many plants as possible which are hardy in USDA Zone 4.

Therefore, before you become too enchanted by some of the plants you see, read, or hear about, I urge you to learn the temperature range for your area and to observe the vagaries of your local weather conditions. Neglecting to do so could prove a costly—not to mention disappointing—oversight. If you live, as I do, near the border between two zones, it's always wise to select plants that are hardy in the colder of the two. Naturally, as with so much else in this business of gardening, there are possible exceptions. Suppose you live in USDA Zone 5, according to the chart, but your land is on a well-protected lower portion of a south-facing slope. In such a spot, you might well be able to venture to have plants that are described as hardy only in the next warmer USDA Zone 6, provided you protect them with a thick layer of mulch (see Chapter 11). On the other hand, if your land is on the other side of the same slope, high up and facing north, you'd be well advised to look to plants that are hardy in the next colder USDA Zone 4. My sister and I experienced such different conditions—her garden lay at the bottom of a north-facing hill; mine, below the top on the other side of the same hill. Her growing season regularly began and ended up to two weeks later and earlier, respectively, than mine. Yet the exact distance between us was 1.2 miles.

Once you've determined your hardiness zone, as well as the directions of sun and prevailing winds, you'll begin to have a better understanding of your land. No matter how close it may be to a neighbor's, or how similar, you'll slowly discover the characteristics that are peculiar only to yours. In this sense, your land might be described as an entirely unique micro-universe. Therefore, the more you know about it, the more satisfying will be your garden.

For this reason, perhaps one of the most rewarding and inspiring things you'll ever do for your garden is to walk around it slowly, thoughtfully, before you do anything else at all. Armed with compass and camera, as well as a shovel or digging fork, crisscross your land, get a feel for it, familiarize yourself with every inch. I can't tell you how many people I know who have never seen or walked through *all* their property. They have no idea what landscape treasures may be around them. They often don't even know their exact boundaries. Consequently, their pleasure has been boundless when I've introduced them variously to such delightful surprises as a tucked-away spring house, positively afloat in a sea of watercress, a woodland raspberry bed, an old apple orchard, a vast field of sky-blue Louisiana iris, and so on.

I can't urge you enough to take the time to find out what surprises await *you*. These might well become a deciding factor in your garden plan, a focal point, a destination. As you walk about, you may see undulations you hadn't noticed before; dramatic outcroppings of rock; a little stream meandering through a meadow; the ruins of an old wall; a single magnificent tree next door, or a handsome skyline—or even a jungle of overgrown brush.

In this last instance, I suggest you wait before rushing out with your machete, especially if you're visited by a variety of birds. Some of these like to nest in such jungles. A wood thrush taught me that one early spring morning. All through the winter months, that messy clump of leafless growth had been an eyesore, and I couldn't wait to cut it down. Until that morning. From somewhere in the midst of the brush came a song so exquisitely pure, its phrases flute-like, melodious, so filled with both longing and joy, that it was almost unbearable. In all the years since then, I have never seen the bird, but whenever I hear his song, I know it's spring. Subsequently I learned that wood thrushes live in such thickets. It goes without saying that from that moment on I would sooner have walked on hot coals than destroy it.

Of course, if your house is completely surrounded by a jungle of brush and overgrown weeds, you'll have to reach some agreement with the birds. In such a case, you could perhaps leave them a patch of their own, not too near the house, in deference to their shyness and sense of privacy; the rest you could chop down with a weed or brush cutter, to create a patch of *your* own for your future garden. That kind of clearance, by the way, is hard work!

Your stroll may also reveal all kinds of features—or even just one—that lie beyond your property's boundary. There might be rolling hills in the distance, a craggy tor, or a clump of birches in the middle distance, a picturesque barn or farm. Visually, these, too, can be included in your garden. Approach such a view from different directions, find the way that offers it as the most delightful surprise. If your land is flat, and such a view is visible wherever you are, then begin to think in terms of a possible foreground planting that will guide you around it for the surprise. Similarly, although you may be less than thrilled with the dominance of your neighbor's stockade fence or garage wall, especially if these are in the direct line of vision from your living-room window, think about how you might *use* such an intrusion. There's no point in developing ulcers over it. It won't go away, you can't ignore it, and there's a good chance that you also can't hide it completely. However, you *can* incorporate it as a part of your own garden, by making it the background of an interesting group of flowering shrubs, for example, or by echoing the fence line in a foreground border planting. In brief, try to find the many ways in which you can utilize existing surroundings—yours as well as other people's—to create a visually harmonious landscape from your perspective.

During your walkabout, take periodic compass readings and

snapshots, get your bearings, study the arc of the sun, the shadows cast by trees. And make periodic probes with your shovel or digging fork, by digging them into the ground, to the full depth of blade or tines, so that you can discover any major rock obstructions that might lurk directly under the surface. If these are present, you will know that it is impractical to plant anything there.

Don't forget to look back frequently toward the house, to observe its features from a distance. Does it look comfortable in its immediate surroundings? Could a grouping of shrubs near one corner soften, or interrupt the stark whiteness of two walls? Would a flower bed beside the front entrance mute the angularity of the porch? Would a second set of steps from the terrace provide access to the pond?

If you have outbuildings, how do they fit into the overall picture? Are they too dominant, too intrusive? Would a few apple trees add perspective or provide a more rural look from where you're standing now? Or perhaps a clematis climbing to the low eaves would add the splash of color that's needed to relieve the flatness of the wall.

By the time you track your muddy boots back to the house, you'll suddenly realize that you've ended up with more questions than when you started. Cheer up, it's only the beginning. For some time to come, there will be two questions for every answer you find. That's part of gardening, too. The time to worry comes when you *stop* ruminating.

So scrape the mud off your boots, because you're not finished yet. You have a general idea now about what the outside looks like—and that includes the outside looking beyond your boundaries, as well as the outside looking back to the house. It's time to find out what is visible from within. As you look through each window and door, refresh your memory with an occasional compass reading. And I do encourage you to look out of *each* window and door, because these will act as frames for each view. Try to visualize these views in winter, when the trees are bare, when the landscape consists of grays and browns and white. You might want to relieve the monotony with an evergreen planting, or shrubs whose red berries will liven the winter scene and also attract birds.

During your tour, both indoors and outdoors, make notes about the things you like or dislike outside. Write down your various observations, because you know you can't remember them all. These notes, together with your snapshots, will become very useful once you sit down to plan in earnest (see Chapter 5). Remember, too, that the view most often looked at is through the kitchen window, so it's important to give careful thought to what would be most pleasing to see there. The herb garden? Perhaps fruit bushes or dwarf fruit trees? Or a patio garden? And don't forget your sundeck, patio, terrace, or other summer lounge-chair area.

Finally, there is the matter of foot traffic. Nine times out of ten, foot traffic follows the shortest route between two points, and all *you* have to do is follow your dog or children to find it. I learned about this "science" soon after I moved into my first house in the country. There, neatly wrapped around the building, at sharp right angles, was a path made of heavy slate. It would have been perfect for a one-man army in parade-ground drill, but as we didn't have one of these, the path was never used. Instead, we had a far more practical streak diagonally across the lawn. A similar thin brown line swept across my future mini-orchard. Regrettably, I ignored its message and went ahead with planting a windscreen around the area. Three days of hard work, and when I finally sat back to gloat, blow me down if a band of neighborhood kids didn't come flying out of nowhere, careening over the lawn and through my new hedge on their bikes. Hooligans, thugs, delinquents, nihilists! Hell had no fury to match mine, but I was too tired to commit murder. So I cried. The lesson is, if you want to have paths or hedges, first consult your progeny and pooches.

R · E · C · A · P

1. Take compass reading to find north in relation to your house and property.

2. Determine prevailing wind directions.

3. Learn the hardiness zone of your area; observe local weather conditons.

4. In a walkabout through your property and house, observe special features, landscape characteristics; take compass readings and snapshots; probe for subsurface rock.

5. Find pleasing distant views to include into your garden plan; think in terms of incorporating into your plan those views that cannot be changed.

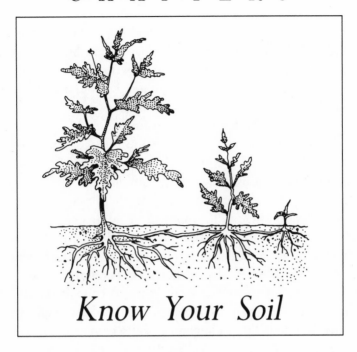

Know Your Soil

$\mathbb{F}$or me, few things are so exquisite, so fundamental, as the sight of freshly plowed fields in early spring. Warmed by the sun and brushed by mellow breezes, they have a special stillness about them that comes only in spring, a stillness full of sounds, a pulse so vibrant and all-engulfing that it becomes almost unbearable. Moist and glistening, the rich black soil seems to throb. The air is suffused with an aromatic nuttiness, a mixture of wet leaves, rotted hay, and manure. Earth and air become as one, filled to bursting with promise and expectation. Life itself seems momentarily suspended in a surge of indescribable energy and strength.

That kind of rich black soil is what gardeners dream about, what most of them will work tirelessly to attain. Few of them can resist touching it. If only a small part of your garden is blessed with such soil, consider yourself within sight of gardeners' heaven.

So don't be shy; pick up a handful, feel it between your fingers, smell it, and sense the wonder of what you're holding—a part of the great mystery and riches of the universe: without soil, there can be no life. Directly and indirectly, soil provides a large portion of our own and our plants' sustenance; the better the quality of soil, the better the sustenance.

In broadest terms, soils are divided into three groups—sandy soils, loamy soils, and clayey soils—and your garden may have any or all of these soils, singly or in combination. The three basic groups are further divided according to the proportions of sand, silt, and clay in them. The more sand your soil contains, the smaller is its moisture-retention capacity; the more clay the soil contains, the better is its moisture retention, but the harder it is to work that soil. An ideal soil, therefore, is referred to as "sandy loam." It contains plenty of sand, but also enough silt and clay so that, squeezed when it's moist, it will hold its shape when it is lightly handled. Depending on a soil's composition, its color may range anywhere from a deep brown, near black, to a light beige, or yellowish tan. The darker the color of your soil, the richer it is in organic matter, in humus (see Chapters 6 and 11).

As it happens, one of my own gardens ran the full gamut of the three basic soil groups. The house and garden were set in a granite-infested area, so much so that the rocky outcroppings formed about one-third of the house foundation. Daunted as I was by the prospect of difficult digging amid so much rock, at least I could be sure that the soil would be quite sweet (perhaps even too much so), thanks to the lime content of stone. But I was less than thrilled when I also frequently struck clay at various levels. In fact, in some parts of the garden there was so much clay that I entertained serious ideas of going into the pottery supply business. A yellowish tan color, it came up in large slimy clods, dense and doughy, clinging to the shovel and having to be scraped off the blade and hacked into pieces.

Other parts of the garden turned up a coarse, gravelly sand, mixed with dark humus and caramel-colored silt. As there was no shortage of lush green grass and strapping trees in these areas,

I seemed to have little to worry about here. In still another part, I discovered a predominantly sandy soil, grayish brown and seemingly "poor," judging from the sparse and yellowish grass, even in spring, after a thorough soaking from rain and thawing snow.

I soon realized that, before I could do any serious gardening, I first had to do some serious work on most of the soil around me.

Then, quite by chance, I came upon a gold mine. Because I felt crowded by dense growth too near the house, preventing easy access to the wooded hill behind, I decided to break into this, open it up a little, to create more open space, as well as a meandering, eventually surprise-filled way to the woods. That's when I discovered a small, low-lying swampy area, totally impenetrable with underbrush, dead tree stumps, and reeds. In short, a mess. Moreover, when it rained, water spilled from the swamp into areas I had already designated as future garden beds. These water spills also made the woods inaccessible for prolonged periods. Not least, there was the problem of prime real estate being wasted on the merrily lustful breeding practices of mosquitoes.

So I undertook to clear the entire swampy area over a period of weeks. With the help of some heavy machinery and strong friends, I dug what I called my horsehoe ditch around it, for drainage. Until then, I had had no particular plans for this spot—already I was considerably overextending my energies in other parts of the garden. But when I saw the color of the soil revealed by the clearance, I nearly wept for joy. There it was, the richest, blackest earth imaginable, thanks to decades, perhaps centuries, of undisturbed leaf mold rotting in the swamp. I was beside myself with happiness, and in a flash, my vegetable bed was born. The trees all around sheltered it from winds, and also focused the sun's warmth. And the vegetables were assured of always having "wet feet," no matter how great or prolonged the summer heat might be, thanks to the underlying water level that was kept in check by the horseshoe drainage.

Of course, not everyone has all three soil groups—sand, loam, and clay—so separately defined. Therefore, if you're interested in learning more about your own soil, a great deal of information is available about soil types, classes, and textures, especially from the U.S. Department of Agriculture. Much of it makes fascinating reading from the standpoint of pure scientific knowledge, for a better understanding of the earth's diversity. For the purpose of this book, however, all that really matters is whether your piece of earth will respond to gardening. The answer to that is a guarded yes, no matter what kind of soil you have, because you can do something about it. Guarded, because the rescue of landfill and most swampy areas requires considerable time, effort, and, often, expense.

If I had to make a quick choice, I would say that a slightly sandy loam is the most desirable soil to have in a garden. This mellow, warm brown soil is easy to work and weed, its texture not unlike finely ground, barely moist bread crumbs. It holds nutrients and moisture well, and also provides good drainage. A handful of this soil, when dry, does not sift through the fingers like sand but momentarily holds its shape when it is squeezed. Moist, a squeezed handful can be handled quite well without crumbling. Roots can establish themselves firmly in such a soil, without being held in a stranglehold, as in clay, or finding little support, as in sand. Repeated digging, tilling, composting, mulching, and raking of this soil, over just two or three years, gives it an almost silky texture that remains firm, but not dense, when you tamp it down.

My second choice would be the grayish tan sandy soils, although in this instance I would quickly begin a process of soil improvement. Because they dry out more quickly and warm up both earlier and more intensely than others, sandy soils lend themselves best to early crops, like radishes, peas, lettuce, or to root crops like carrots and parsnips. However, because of their loose texture, sandy soils are quickly leached of nutrients, which therefore leaves them relatively infertile. That's why they need some improvement (see Chapters 6, 7, and 11). Of course, digging in sandy soils is like slicing through butter, but there's not much satisfaction in that if nothing much will grow in them. Generous applications of soil-enriching materials, working these in deeply and thoroughly, do wonders for these soils, both for their moisture and nutrient content and retention and for improving their texture throughout. If you have a severe case of sandy soil, an effective treatment is to seed it thickly with buckwheat in early spring, let this grow to about 5 or 6 inches, dig or rototill it into the soil, wait a week, then seed another buckwheat crop and repeat the cycle until mid-September. At that point, turn under the last buckwheat crop, wait a week, then thickly sow winter rye. Although this will grow before winter, leave it, and the following spring, dig or rototill it when the rye reaches a height of about 6 inches. By then, this repeated and inexpensive "green manuring" process will have introduced a considerable amount of humus and necessary microorganisms into your soil, to allow you to proceed with your garden. To accelerate this soil improvement, either buy or ask your own or somebody else's children to find you plenty of earthworms. Add these to your newly worked soil, where they will perform wonders not only in digesting all the compost created by the green manure but also in aerating and mixing the soil—and in multiplying at an incredible rate. Always bear in mind, no matter how *you* feel about them, there is no doubt that earthworms are among the best friends your garden can have.

Clay is a soil type for which I simply can't work up much passion. When it's wet, it is a yellowish-tan lump of plastic, although quite silky in texture. When you squeeze a little bit between your fingers, it forms a kind of adhesive, slimy skin. And when clay dries, it becomes a hard clump that is difficult to splinter even with a shovel blade. Clay is so dense that it has virtually no drainage at all, and if there is a lot of it, a heavy rainfall will produce some long-standing puddles. The best time to work on this soil is when it is moist, not wet—but even then it's heavy going. In fact, to add insult to injury, predominantly clayey soil isn't even suited to gardening! However, with proper care and perseverance, heavy mulching and composting, it can be persuaded to become very productive in time. On a positive note, clay does have the advantage of holding moisture well, which is a definite plus if it lies fairly deep below the surface. If it is at the top, however, or even close to the top, smack where you wanted to plant your lupines, then you'd be well advised to hold off on the lupines (or whatever else you had in mind) until you've reached some acceptable agreement with the clay: once delicate little roots have wormed their way into clay for a foothold, they're doomed. Not even you can pry them out of the vise-like grip of the clay without breaking them.

As I mentioned before, I had a lot of clay in one of my gardens. Naturally, it was exactly where I intended to put one of my perennial beds. Instead, I had to put that bed on hold for a year and work on the clay. First, I double-dug (see Chapter 7) the bed, carting the largest clay clods into the woods and replacing them with aged manure. Lesser clods I broke up and loosened as much as possible. I also dug in a thick layer of rotted leaf mold from the woods and let the bed rest until late summer. At that point, I dug it twice more (by hand—didn't have a rototiller then), each time breaking up more clay lumps, and in the late autumn, I seeded it with winter rye. The following spring, I hired a local boy with a rototiller and asked him to go over this bed at least four times. By the time he was finished, the last of the near-surface clay lumps had been decimated and blended into the rich black humus of the bed, which was now ready for planting. There's no denying that all this was painstaking work, especially as the bed wasn't even particularly large, but the results were well worth it. That bed, with continued applications of mulch and compost materials over the years, probably had the finest, richest soil in my entire garden in the end—except for the vegetable bed!

In addition to discovering the type of soil in your future garden area, it is a good idea to determine the overall alkalinity (sweetness) or acidity of your soil. In reading gardening books, you have undoubtedly come across the admonition that certain plants "prefer acid soil." Or a gardening friend may have asked, "What pH is your soil?"

"Oh my God," I hear some of you wail. "I don't even know what that means. And I threw out my chemistry books."

Relax. You don't need those books—the answer is quite simple. The pH measures the full range of acidity and alkalinity in the soil, on a scale from 0 (extreme acidity) to 14 (extreme alkalinity). However, the only range that need concern gardeners is a scale from 4.0 to 9.0, which is the entire range within which plants can grow. Within this range, 7.0 is neutral—neither acid nor alkaline. A divergence from this point, in either direction, is universally described by the symbol "pH." Therefore, if your soil test reveals a pH value between 6.0 and 7.5, your soil is "normal" and anything you plant should thrive. If your pH value is below 6.0, or above 7.5, you can either limit your garden to plants which prefer acid or alkaline soils, respectively, or else adjust the pH through regular applications of compost, mulch, or packaged minerals, available at garden centers and nurseries. Even so, most plants are extraordinarily good sports, resilient. Unless they're provoked to death (literally) by extremely uncharitable soil conditions, they'll grow, provided you at least make an effort to give them what they need. Look at it this way: you may be happier with whole-wheat bread or green socks, but you'll adjust to rye or blue socks if that's all there is. It's the same with plants. They adapt.

After having said all that, I now must confess that I myself have never chemically tested my various garden soils. It's not so much that I'm stubborn or arrogant about it; rather, it's that I enjoy the challenge and sharpening of my observational powers by reading nature's own signs. Thus, if the grass is thick and juicy green; if there are healthy fruit trees about; if there is an abundance of wildflowers or lush weed growth; if there are plenty of various deciduous trees or open fields close by, and a handful of soil reveals a medium-coarse texture that briefly holds its shape when I squeeze it, and a shovelful of soil exposes several worms diving for cover—then I can be pretty sure I have a happy mix of acid and alkali soils, a "normal" reading. If, on the other hand, I am surrounded by conifers and oaks, and the grass is sparse, interwoven with mossy patches, or overrun by wild strawberries;

if the soil is packed down densely, a dull drab brown, a little slimy-looking when it's wet, poorly drained, then I know I have some work ahead of me to sweeten that soil. This doesn't mean the soil is bad; it simply means it is too acid for most garden plants. Extremely alkaline soil in the home garden is comparatively rare, as it occurs mostly in salt marshes, the alkali deserts of the West, and in limestone regions—or in soils to which too much lime has been applied (see Chapter 6). However, if your soil indicates a pH value above 7.0, just where you want to plant a show of conifers, you can compensate with applications of aluminum sulphate to make the soil more acid. Recommended amounts appear on the packages.

There *are* some soils that can be described as "poor." These occur frequently in heavily populated areas, where sun and light have trouble penetrating, where years and years of neglect have discouraged even the hardiest weeds. As often as not, these are areas where one can find an impoverished-looking silver maple, box elder, or ailanthus (tree of heaven) hanging on for dear life from among cracks in a building's foundations. The soil in such an area, likely as not, turns into a slimy thick mud when it rains, and into hard-baked, almost white dust during a drought. But let a kind and willing soul dig up such a patch, green manure, mulch, and fertilize it—and keep the neighborhood cats and dogs out!—and within a year, that patch can become a tiny garden. All soil, even the most deprived, can be rescued with humus. It's simply that some soils require more time and effort than others.

Before I digress too much, back to acid and alkali soils. If you feel safer with a more formal approach to testing your soil, test kits are available from many garden centers and suppliers, from some nurseries, even from certain department stores, and from major seed and plant catalogues. Soil-test kits are also available in several price ranges, depending on how much detailed chemical analysis you wish to obtain. All kits include instructions for use, and it is a perfectly straightforward procedure. To obtain the most comprehensive reading of your soil, I advise that you test samples from each separate area you plan to develop. If this seems like too much bother, however, then gather small soil samples from each area, mix them all thoroughly, and proceed with the test, in order to obtain an average reading.

There is yet another possibility, especially if you're uneasy about, or unwilling to use, a soil-test kit. That is to take your soil sample(s) to the nearest county agent (you can find him/her listed under U.S. Department of Agriculture, or under your County Cooperative Extension, in the telephone directory) and request a pH test.

But no matter what the pH value of your soil, or the type of soil it is, if the piece of property you have acquired already features an established, thriving garden, you will probably have to concern yourself less with improving the soil than with nourishing it on a continuing basis (see Chapter 15). On the other hand, if yours is essentially "virgin territory," then I suggest you learn as much as you can about the soil you have before you plant anything. It may save you a lot of unnecessary labor, expense, and heartache.

R · E · C · A · P

1. Check type of soil in your garden:

   a. *Loam*—mellow warm brown; slightly gritty feel; when squeezed dry, will loosely hold shape, then crumble; when squeezed moist, can be handled gently before breaking; moisture and nutrient retentive, good drainage.

   b. *Sand*—grayish tan; fine to coarse grainy feel; when squeezed dry, will sift through fingers; when squeezed moist, will briefly hold shape, crumble when touched; not moisture or nutrient retentive, excellent drainage.

   c. *Clay*—yellowish tan; dense texture; when squeezed wet, feels sticky, elastic, slightly slimy; when dry, is hard as rock; not suited to gardening on its own; very moisture-retentive; puddles badly when left unbroken.

2. Buy soil-test kit or take soil samples to county agent, to learn pH value of your soil: *normal:* pH 6.0–7.5; *acid:* pH 4.0–6.0; *alkaline:* pH 7.5–9.0.

Basic Tools

Up to now, in theory, your only serious investment in gardening has been a small compass and, possibly, a soil-test kit. (I say "serious" because I won't be held responsible for all the gardening books you've bought.) Now it's time to get down to brass tacks—the tools you will need to make your dream garden become reality.

Although it does not, strictly speaking, qualify as a tool, the kind of clothing you wear for gardening work is of great importance. *Comfort* should be top priority. At the head of the list are sturdy shoes that protect your feet against mud, rough terrain, and injury, and also against feeling pressure and strain when you're digging for a prolonged period. Blue jeans, slacks, or skirt; blouses, shirts, or knitted tops should all fit loosely and be old enough, so that it doesn't matter if they become soiled or stained. If you're fair-skinned especially, I suggest that you wear loose-fitting long sleeves. Some kind of lightweight head covering—a brimmed hat or visored cap, or a scarf—is essential, to protect eyes, scalp, and hair from too much sun, while also allowing air to circulate on your head. For cool spring or autumn days, I suggest that you dress in several lightweight layers, so that you can peel these off as the warmth of the day increases.

As for conventional tools, the whole subject is a gray area, because not only does every gardener have his or her own way of doing things but most gardeners have also acquired two of everything over the years, plus a shed full of accessories. Be forewarned. Gardeners tend to be hoarders (I'm no exception). They save bits of string and burlap, empty milk and egg cartons, coffee cans, broken clay pots, as well as handles of old brooms, and much, much more. In time, you probably will, too.

Long before that time, however, there have to be the basic tools of the trade. A walk through a garden center, or the study of a catalogue, can be quite overwhelming if you are unsure of what you need. Many tools, you will find, are specially designed and ideal for just one function. And if you bought them all, you could be in the poorhouse before you ever planted a single daisy. Apart from that, you'd soon be confused over which tool to use when. Frankly, many are not necessary. Fun perhaps, but not necessary.

Here is a list of the most essential tools for any garden, large or small. Please note, this does not include lawn mowers, roto-tillers, chain saws, or other heavy-duty equipment. The first six tools are, in my opinion, the most indispensable for any garden. Eventually, you may want all the others as well, plus some that aren't on the list, but even if you do not, you're bound to end up with more than the first six.

Basic tools:
1. Shovel or spade
2. Garden rake
3. Trowel
4. Hand grubber

5. Watering can
6. Sharp pocket knife

To these you may shortly want to add:
7. Digging or spading fork
8. Wheelbarrow or garden cart
9. Hand pruners

Before long, you will find yourself in need of:
10. Folding handsaw
11. Cultivator or hoe
12. Leaf rake
13. Watering hose
14. Tree pruners
15. Hedge clippers

In addition to these, I also always keep on hand (a) a handled fruit or other basket, (b) a handled plastic bucket, (c) a few covered plastic kitchen waste bins. I use (a) to carry my hand tools about the garden. Compartmented bags of canvas, leather, and vinyl *are* available for this purpose, as are polypropylene containers. But I personally find the former too prone to being used to transport such other things as plant cuttings, debris, or lunch, and the latter are generally bulky and can't be slipped over the wrist, thereby freeing the hand for other things. And (b) is particularly useful when I work on a new bed. Into the bucket I put such debris as bits of glass or plastic, rusty nails, tin cans, or horseshoes, which turn up in digging. Old farmland is particularly subject to this sort of thing. Similarly, my digging up of a city garden unearthed such divers "antiquities" as a 1940s radio, light fixtures, a toilet seat, and several unmatched shoes. I use (c) to store such adjuncts to gardening as potting soil, lime, fertilizers, and bone meal. Be sure to keep your buckwheat and winter rye seeds in these covered bins, so that mice can't get at them. I forgot to do that one year, and a month later, five pounds of seed were gone, with a fat dead mouse at the bottom of the uncovered bin!

Below are full descriptions, with illustrations, of all the official basic tools.

1. Shovel or spade

Right away, it's a matter of personal preference. Shovels usually come with long handles, although some are available with the so-called YD handle. Because of their rounded blade, which tapers into a slight point, shovels can penetrate even gravelly soil easily, cut into clay, and bypass or dislodge medium-sized rocks. Their

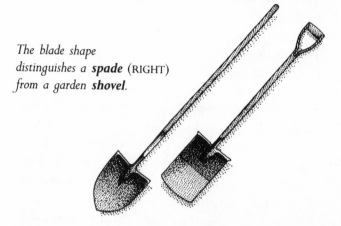

*The blade shape distinguishes a **spade** (RIGHT) from a garden **shovel**.*

blades are wide enough and also slightly concave, to make it possible to dig up a decent amount of soil without half of it slipping off. Especially when working on an entirely new bed, in an area that hasn't been previously cultivated, I prefer to use a shovel with a long handle (or a digging fork, see #7), because this gives me better leverage. To counteract the minor inconvenience of slightly curved cuts when I dig a straight line, because of the concave blade, I overlap the cuts.

Spades, too, are available with long handles; however, more often they are offered with the YD handle. This usually comes in three different lengths, to suit the user's height. It is therefore important to test all three, to find the length that's just right for you. Spades have slightly concave rectangular blades, with a sharp, straight cutting edge. They are wonderful to use, especially in cultivated, friable soil. Although I find spades less persuasive than shovels in dislodging rocks under the surface, they do a much better job in cutting cleanly through, say, a one-inch tree root. Nevertheless, it really *is* a matter of personal preference—shovel or spade.

2. Garden rake

This is a most versatile tool that comes only with a long handle (about 5 feet). The teeth of a rake may be straight, perpendicular to the handle, or they may have a slight inward curve. This makes no particular difference to the tool's efficiency—I have one of each. Frankly, a gardener without a rake is like a cook without

Curved or uncurved, a garden **rake**'s *teeth serve many uses.*

a saucepan. Rakes are incredibly useful. Teeth down, and with a hacking motion, the rake can be used to break up clods of soil. In the same position, its most common use is to level freshly dug earth and to rake off any large stones from the bed's surface. With the teeth facing up, you can smooth the surface, to remove any remaining "wrinkles" in the soil. With the teeth held vertically, the rake makes excellent furrows for planting vegetable seeds. And to cover the seeds, I hold the rake straight up and down, and with the back of the teeth, I gently move the soil over the seeds and level the ground again. Finally, still holding the rake upright, I use it to firm the soil over the seeds, by double-tamping it in an X pattern. The rake is also convenient for removing broken branches from trees, for picking those perfect apples that are always just out of reach, for "combing" dead growth out of deciduous shrubs and herbs in early spring—and for getting giant lumps on the head, if you forget to lay it on the ground *teeth down!*

3. Trowel

There are valid arguments for having one each of a wide- and narrow-bladed trowel, with or without "elbows" between handle and blade. I have several of each—heaven knows why, because I only use the same favorite, wide-bladed, unelbowed trowel. This tool digs holes for seedlings and bulbs; it loosens soil around

Wide or narrow, elbowed or not, **trowels** *are indispensable.*

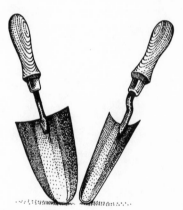

plants and helps to dislodge hard-to-pull weeds; it's a wizard at planting bulbs; it scrapes mulch aside in early spring, when you want to see if your perennials are coming up, and it doles out fertilizer at planting time; it also cuts through small roots if you forgot to bring along your pocket knife or pruners. Not least, a trowel is good for scraping the mud off your other tools.

4. Hand grubber

In essence, this is a miniature cultivator. It's another handy, versatile little helper in the garden which performs a variety of tasks. It loosens and aerates soil around the roots of young plants, without damaging their roots; it also helps you weed, even lets

*The **grubber** can work
in places most other tools
cannot even reach.*

you dig holes for your small plants or seedlings. With the grubber, you can also gently scrape loose and remove last year's dead growth from among such plant clumps as iris, and many others.

5. Watering can

Watering cans come in all kinds of designs, made of all sorts of materials. For practical purposes, I find the plain old-fashioned design best, except that I like it made of heavy plastic, because it is lighter in weight than the galvanized metal cans. In addition to its usefulness, with or without the sprinkler nozzle, for your indoor plants, as well as outdoor window boxes, pots, and planters, you will need this tool to water in all your newly planted seeds, seedlings, flowers, shrubs, and trees. When I transplant some things, I also use the watering can to keep roots cool and wet. And on hot days, a full watering can nearby provides *me* with a cool splash. In fact, more than once, I've emptied the whole thing over my head.

6. Pocket knife

The best kind is the army knife, with a variety of attachments and *very* sharp blades. With the latter, you can make clean cuts, whether you're pruning a small shrub or perennial or picking a bunch of roses. Such a knife will also help loosen a carrot from the soil when you get a bit peckish in late summer. It will slit open your seed packets and fertilizer bags, cut string, tape, or thin wire, and even open cans.

7. Digging or spading fork

This is a most useful tool, with four flat tines that come to a point, and either a long or a YD-shaped handle, most frequently the latter. It is also available in three lengths to suit your height. (The digging fork is not to be confused with the hay fork, whose tines are thin, round, and curved—and lethally sharp.) This fork

The **digging fork** is undoubtedly among a gardener's staunchest helpers.

is excellent for digging up grass or overgrown areas, for prying loose underground obstructions or loosening soil among tree roots. It's also ideal for transporting plant clumps, even small trees, to which dense root balls are attached. To do this, I simply spike the clumps on the ends of the tines. I also use this tool for spreading compost, manure, and mulch. And because I prefer the YD handle for this tool, I use it to prop up my other tools, to save me having to bend down more than I have to.

8. Wheelbarrow or garden cart

Quite honestly, I'd be hard-pressed to give preference to either of these. I've had one of each for many years. Both are durable, stalwart workhorses, and both are easy to use for transporting a broad variety of items and materials. Wheelbarrows are one-wheelers with two handles and legs at the back, supporting a U-shaped, load-bearing body made either of metal (in which case

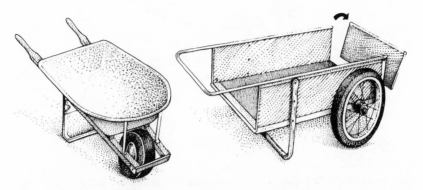

Wheelbarrows or **garden carts,** *whatever their minor design variations, are essential.*

it's called a contractor's wheelbarrow) or of sturdy plywood, with removable side panels (in which case it's called a garden wheel-barrow). Either kind is good. Wheelbarrows may be pushed or pulled, and are most useful for maneuvering small loads through awkward, narrow, or rough terrain. Garden carts are spoke-wheeled two-wheelers balanced over an axle, with two legs and a handlebar at the back and a high-sided, metal-trimmed plywood body, with or without a removable front panel. They, too, may be pushed or pulled, but carts are capable of carrying much larger, heavier, and bulkier loads than wheelbarrows. Because of their two large wheels, garden carts are more stable; they are available in several sizes. Both vehicles can be easily stored up-ended. I wouldn't be without either one of them.

9. Hand pruners
Now this is a tool about which most gardeners have very strong feelings. In fact, some of them get downright belligerent on the subject. There are those who swear by the superiority of the

"anvil" type of pruning shears, whose straight blade comes down on a wide base, an anvil; and there are those who argue for the

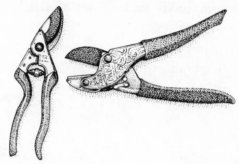

Your choice of **hand pruners** *is entirely personal.*

far more superior superiority of shears that sport a curved blade and hook. Having given both types a fair chance, over a long period of time, I must say that my vote goes with the latter type—for several reasons. One of these is that the hook allows me to get in close to the axils of plant limbs; it lets me cut twigs and small branches with ease, because the hook holds these, whereas the anvil pruner often tends to slide off; the handles are shaped to conform to the hand, and the blades rarely need sharpening. In my case, as I'm a southpaw, there is the added advantage that the pruners I have are available in left-handed as well as right-handed models. But as I said, it's a tool that elicits strong feelings.

10. Folding handsaw

A friend introduced me to this tool just a few years ago. How I ever managed without it is a wonder now. The one I have is lightweight, with a sturdy plastic handle, into which the saw blade folds. At first, I was suspicious that it might be a bit flimsy, but after years of truly heroic work, often cutting down even small trees, that saw has proved invaluable. Most impressive is the fact that its teeth seem to have lost none of their original bite. This tool is particularly handy when you're clearing dead wood out of overgrown shrubs, or if you want to cut branches near the ground. I also use it to clean up dead branches in conifers, or to cut suckers at ground level. The length of the handle adds practically a foot to your height, which helps if you happen to be short, and the negligible weight lets you use all your energy for sawing instead of supporting the tool. The blade is quite flexible, which means you can get into awkward places, or flat on the ground. On top of all that, it's also inexpensive.

11. Cultivator or hoe

These are tools which I must confess I rarely use. Except that they have long handles, which avoids the need for bending down, they do nothing I can't do just as well with trowel, grubber, or spade. But that is strictly my own feeling. The cultivator loosens soil and weeds around trees and shrubs, among herbaceous per-

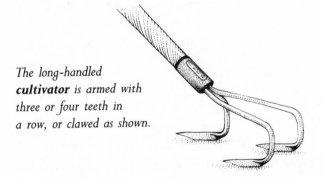

The long-handled **cultivator** *is armed with three or four teeth in a row, or clawed as shown.*

ennial plants and vegetables; the hoe cuts through small roots and is very good at digging into heavy, compacted soils, and at trenching. While hoes consist of a roughly 4-by-7-inch sharp-edged blade, cultivators are available either with four curved prongs in a row, about one inch apart, or with only three prongs in a claw formation. Although I have used both types of cultivators, my chief objection to the four-prong head is that I've found it not nearly as efficient in penetrating hard soil as the three-prong claw type. Also, its width has more than once caused me to damage a plant. As for the three-pronged type, if the prongs are separately screwed into the shaft that is attached to the handle, repeated hoeing action can loosen and dislodge the prongs. So be sure to look for a cultivator whose prongs are jointly affixed to the handle.

12. Leaf rake

If there are deciduous trees anywhere near you, you are bound to need a leaf rake in the autumn. Whether or not you wish to keep your lawn free of fallen leaves, for the sake of neatness, this tool will let you rake them for mulch purposes at least. Leaf rakes are manufactured with tines made of metal, plastic, bamboo, or rubber. Again, I've tried them all. Unless the metal heads are constructed of top-quality steel, I would opt for a sturdy plastic or rubber head. Poor-quality steel tends to bend before long, or rust; bamboo tines often break, and inexpensive plastic heads and their handles, I've discovered, soon part company. Although this tool's high season is generally regarded as being only in autumn, it is, in fact, most useful as well in raking up weeds, cuttings, and debris.

13. Watering hose

This is essential, once your garden consists of several beds or extends over a large area. Without a nozzle or sprinkler attachment, a hose may be terrific for washing the car, but for the garden, I urge you to buy at least a hand-pressured spray gun nozzle, although I also like to use the hand-held sprinkler. The first allows you to spray over a considerable distance, while simultaneously adjusting the pressure of the jetstream. The latter is a gentler method of watering, best suited to flowers and vegetables. Still other watering attachments are available, of course, such as the stationary sprinklers that provide a variety of whirling, arching, and oscillating water streams. I do not care for these, because they waste water by also soaking unplanted areas, whereas a gentle "direct hit" guided by the hand will better assure the water reaching the plants that need it. It's best not to leave watering hoses in the sun for prolonged periods, as this will gradually weaken or crack them. Finally, of course, watering hoses are an excellent aid in the layout of new garden beds (see Chapter 7).

14. Tree pruners

The same arguments pertain to these as to the hand pruners— anvil or hook. Again I prefer the hook. The major difference between tree and hand pruners is the length of the handles, and they are used mostly for cutting somewhat thicker branches and thick roots. Here I should add that it's never a good idea to go

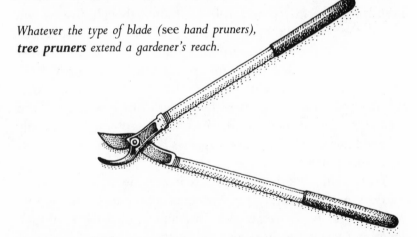

Whatever the type of blade (see hand pruners), **tree pruners** *extend a gardener's reach.*

haywire on cutting tree roots. If you find that a proposed flower bed has a root the size of your arm running through it, it would be best to leave the root, or else to move the bed somewhere else. Trees don't mind losing a few minor connections to the earth, but they might well object to being seriously mutilated.

15. Hedge clippers

Unless your property already sports a hedge, it'll be a few years before a hedge planted by you will be large enough to need pruning and shaping. But when it does, it's worthwhile having shears that will trim and shape without damaging your plants. For this purpose, I suggest shears of the best quality, with razor-sharp steel blades and a so-called sap groove. This all but eliminates the inevitable pulling and tearing friction between blade and sap-filled branches, and also minimizes the impact of the cutting action on your shoulders.

In time, you may wish to add to this list, or you may substitute one implement for another. Only you can know what feels comfortable and right, and fortunately, there are usually several options on the market. As with everything else about gardening, there are no hard-and-fast rules.

Except one: Always buy top quality. This does not necessarily mean most expensive. As a rule of thumb, though, just as you wouldn't expect to find genuine Limoges china in a five-and-ten-cent store, so the chances are slim that you'll find top-quality garden tools there. The prices may be tempting, but shortly you'll be replacing such bargains. One of the most valuable lessons I ever learned came from a wealthy friend many moons ago. "I'm not rich enough to buy cheap," he told me. Although he is only a blurred memory, what he said springs vividly to mind whenever I open my purse.

There is no one brand name that is better than all others, nor does any one manufacturer produce all the tools. Prices, too, may vary greatly. There are also variations in the weights of such things as shovels, for instance, and in the lengths and shapes of handles. Trowels may be broad or narrow; pruning shears, as I said above, may have curved blades or straight; and so on. Bearing in mind all these variables, don't feel that you must buy all your tools at once, or at one source. Pick them up, lift them in one hand; find out if you can do so quite easily, without feeling as though your shoulders will be dislocated. Go through the motions of using the tools in the store. Is the handle too long, too short; is it securely attached to the tool? If at all possible, ask an experienced gardener friend to accompany you on this shopping trip; get his or her suggestions. Ask questions. If it's a toss-up, for instance, between a top-quality, too heavy shovel with a lifetime guarantee and a less expensive, lighter weight shovel without a guarantee, then you might be wise to sacrifice a modicum of quality for comfort. After all, there's not much point in having a tool if you need a derrick to hoist it.

It's always a good idea to learn about a store's policy regarding replacements of, or refunds for, faulty tools. A few years ago, I bought a three-pronged claw cultivator from a reputable store. Twice, one of the prongs fell off, and twice the store replaced the cultivator. When it happened a third time, however, I asked for and received a refund, and the store returned the remaining stock of this tool to the manufacturer.

My own tools bear the imprint of various manufacturers. I am not concerned that they look pretty on my garden shed wall, all matched like bathroom accessories; rather, I want to know whether or not they will be capable of lasting service, and suited to my height and personal strength, as well as to my needs.

As your initial tools will represent a small investment—nothing, of course, like the cost of a car, but certainly more than a week's groceries—you should make your selections with careful thought, so that you get your money's worth. It's also a good idea to treat your tools with a bit of respect.

And how can you do that? Well, I myself, my family, and my friends are the first to confess that I'm not the tidiest person in the world, especially during gardening season. But when it comes to my tools, I'm meticulous. First of all, I always clean them after every use—scraping off soil, mud, and matted grass, or hosing them down. I never leave them outdoors overnight, so that neither rain nor dew can get at them, which would, in time, rust the metal portions and warp the wooden handles. And I always return the tools to their own places.

Many gardeners I know lean their tools, all together, in the corner of a shed, or keep them in a wooden crate, still all bunched together. Personally, I find my method more efficient, because at any given moment I can see whether or not they're all present and accounted for, and I can always reach for the right one, without having to rummage through a forest of handles. To do this, I screw a row of U-shaped hooks into the wall of the shed, barn, garage, or basement—wherever I choose to keep all gardening paraphernalia. To accommodate the varying lengths of the handles, I place the hooks at different heights, so that all the full-sized tools are just off the ground. Long-handled shovels and rakes hang upside down, YD-handled tools hang by the handle. Small tools hang at eye level. If you can't find U-shaped hooks, you can use very large, sturdy nails, two per tool.

On the other hand, if you prefer not to use this system and decide to lean all your tools in a corner, then please always make sure that the teeth and blades are turned toward the wall. Being viciously attacked by wooden handles, and knocked senseless on numerous occasions, after *not* doing so and accidentally stepping on those teeth and blades, was undoubtedly a major contributing factor to my meticulous neatness!

At the end of the gardening season, after you've closed down the garden, do take the time to clean your tools thoroughly. Wipe the handles to rid them of crusted soil. Scrub and wash all the metal parts, and oil these, before storing the tools away in a dry location. This extra care will protect your tools through the inevitable dampness of most winters—whether or not you live in a cold zone. And they'll be ready to work for you again at the first sign of a new spring.

R · E · C · A · P

1. Buy only top-quality tools.

2. Test tools in store, for weight and comfort.

3. Clean tools after every use; never leave them outdoors.

4. Store them neatly to avoid accidents.

5. During winter, store cleaned, oiled tools in dry location.

Planning Your Garden

Planning is undoubtedly one of the most enjoyable aspects of gardening, because it actually lets you take your daydreams seriously. Planning and designing your garden brings out all your hidden talents, your sense of color and form. It lets you be daring, if that's what you want, without being made to feel like a fool if it doesn't work out after all. Unlike so many other things we do in life, we never need to feel stuck with anything we do in the garden. If what we thought was a terrific idea turns out to be less than inspiring, we simply change it. That's the beauty of gardening—it need never be approached as though it were about to be cast in bronze.

By now, you've probably bought or borrowed, or at least browsed through, numerous gardening books, and come to realize the infinite possibilities that await you, both in design and in available plants. You've come to know your soil, and you know what kind of terrain you will have to work with and where the prevailing winds strike most severely. You've taken note of some areas you would like to highlight; others you'd just as soon obscure.

Of course, your new house may already have a garden, in which case you may simply want to wait a year or two before changing any of it, to see what comes up. After all, although it may not have been the major reason why you bought the house, the garden, its contours and flow, undoubtedly influenced your choice. In that case, especially during the first year, practically every day will bring you the joy of new surprises as the garden reveals its treasures. By the end of that year, you'll have a good idea of what you want to keep, or even enlarge, and what you definitely do not like.

On the other side of the coin is the house whose land has been left almost entirely to nature's own devices. Perhaps there are some trees, a few shrubs, and a lot of lawn. Here, the sky's the limit—with a few practical reservations. First of all, if the smooth running of your household depends on well water and a septic system, start out by clearly marking the access to both. You could quickly age ten years and become bald from tearing out your hair if you needed work done on either one after you'd painstakingly put your classic medieval knotted herb garden over them. True, the grass really is greener over the septic tank— actually, over the leach field near the tank—and that's quite a temptation for the eager gardener: all that fertile soil going to grass. However, I don't recommend planting anything serious, like trees or shrubs, directly over the septic tank or septic drainage field, because the roots would soon invade buried pipes in search of water. Instead, you can either have a plain lawn there or a bed of annuals, or your vegetable garden. Or you can create a "field" of spring bulbs, as I did. I planted dozens of daffodils, crocus, scilla, and grape hyacinths throughout the grass over my septic area. These will bloom and die before the grass grows completely out of control; they'll quickly multiply, to provide a sea of color in early spring; and they won't get hysterical if they

If you plan to have roses, it's good to remember that these usually not only look best but also grow best if they're on their own, rather than amid a lot of other flowers. More and more roses are being developed which can tolerate the colder climes of Zone 4. Even so, they require winter protection and do best if they're planted in a reasonably sheltered, sunny area, bedded down with plenty of mulch. They can be a bit temperamental, but given the slightly acid soil they like, protection against wind, and no serious competition for the nutrients in their soil, they'll reward you amply for your extra care. So put them in a spot where you can savor their colors and fragrances. Among other acid soil lovers are rhododendrons and azaleas, conifers and ferns. Artfully grouped together, these four can produce a most handsome show, as long as especially the rhododendrons, azaleas, and ferns are shielded from icy blasts and too much sun (see Chapter 16).

Annuals tend to use up more nutrients in the soil than do perennials, because their growth cycle begins and ends within a single year, so that they need a heavy dose of energy. If you're interested in sports, you might equate annuals with sprinters and perennials with long-distance runners. Of course, this doesn't mean you can't plant mixtures of annuals and perennials in the same bed; on the contrary, such a mixture will infinitely enhance the color range of your plantings. It's just that annuals need watering more often. Because their roots are often shallower than those of the perennials, they use up surface moisture quickly and lack the capacity for reaching deeper for more. Do keep that in mind. Three annuals that come immediately to mind, which are more heat-and-drought tolerant than some others, especially if they're planted directly into the garden, are geraniums, petunias, and marigolds. This list can be lengthened if you provide a thick layer of mulch and plenty of compost (see Chapters 6 and 11). On the other hand, if you love impatiens as much as I do, no matter how mulched and composted they are, they're always thirsty and need to be watered daily during the height of summer.

The shapes of your beds, no matter what you intend to plant, is an entirely personal matter, whether they're angular, round, oval, or free-form. A general guideline, however, might be not to make them wider than 5 feet. This is not to say you *can't* have wider beds, but if you do, it's a good idea to make some provision, like stepping stones, for reaching the center. A 5-foot-wide bed lets you just about reach the far side at a stretch (literally), or the center comfortably from both sides, in a freestanding bed. On the whole, life is so much less complicated if you don't have to tiptoe through a 10-foot-wide bed, trying not to step on plants, as though you were picking your way through a minefield.

This rule for bed widths does not, of course, apply to vegetables, because vegetables are usually planted in rows of narrow beds, with paths between each. If you intend to have vegetables, be sure to give them an area that receives full sun—all day long, if possible. The ideal vegetable bed lies north-south, with rows running east-west; the taller vegetables, such as corn, standing at the north end, the others graded downward, according to their optimal heights, toward the southern end of the bed. The reason is that with this layout, all your vegetables receive an even amount of sun, the corn doesn't shade the lettuce, one end of the broccoli row isn't half the size of the other end (see Chapter 9).

Plan to plant spring bloomers like crocus, daffodils, scilla, and early tulips fairly near the house, so that you can relish their wonderful colors to the fullest. Although many people plant these bulbs along the walls of their houses, I personally don't, because then I can see them only when I'm outside. I prefer, instead, to look at them through my windows as well. There's nothing quite like the thrill of a yellow sea of daffodils in early spring—in my neck of the woods that can frequently happen when snow still covers the ground. As I mentioned above, these bulb plants can be put in the lawn; they don't *have* to have a bed (see Chapter 16).

To outline all or some of the borders of your vegetable bed, you might want to plant fruit bushes, such as currants, gooseberries, blueberries, or beach plums. All of these are wonderful to eat fresh, cooked, frozen, or bottled. Or, at a somewhat greater distance from the bed's perimeter, you might like to group some dwarf fruit trees—delicate, fragrant blossoms in spring, full-sized fruit easy to reach at harvest time. Or flowers. There's only one thing to keep in mind.

If your proposed vegetable garden happens to be right across an ancient deer path, you might be better off planting your yummies elsewhere. Why? Have you ever noticed those yellow highway signs showing a leaping buck and the words 1 MILE, and wondered how deer are supposed to read these? Or asked yourself how the Highways Department can be so sure that deer read English, or that they'll obey? Those signs are, in fact, an official concession to the power of nature, notwithstanding *Homo sapiens* and all his technology. It's most of humankind that can't "read": it keeps thinking that deer can be diverted in the same way as water. Well, deer can't. Deer are genetically programmed, generation upon generation, to follow their own ancient, traditional trails. Like you perhaps, my sister and her husband didn't believe it either at first. For several years. They tried old folk remedies like onions, mothballs, and dried blood, modern contrivances like electrified fences—and the deer simply walked around or over the onions, mothballs, and blood, and jumped over the charged wires. They tried a six-foot fence, and the deer took a flying leap over that. They planted a "deer garden" outside the fence, and the deer ate that and *then* jumped over the fence. The deer adjusted to bells and tinfoil strips and scarecrows and lights and loud music. After two or three years of sleepless summers and empty freezers in winter, my sister moved the vegetable bed elsewhere, and spent quiet evenings watching the deer snort and snuffle peacefully across the new lawn (see Chapter 13).

An important consideration in planning your garden is to keep in mind the differing heights and widths of the plants you want, as well as their colors and textures. Study all these elements carefully in catalogues and books, well ahead of buying time, so that you can have a rough idea of where you should plant which. Many descriptions give approximate heights, such as "1–2 ft." or "up to 3 ft." If you wonder about the vagueness of these, it's because several factors play a role in how tall (or wide) *your* plants will be at maturity—soil composition, its humus content and nutrients, moisture retention; climate, amount of sun and rainfall, exposure to wind, and so on. At least, however, even if your plants never reach their potential, and even if they do, you know not to put a 5-foot sunflower in front of an 8-inch primula. By the same token, you don't have to be so rigid that all 3-foot flower plants are in a row behind all 2-foot flowers. If they're sufficiently massed, an undulating "skyline" will be both attractive and more natural (see Chapter 9).

Once your plans are on paper and your most-wanted plant list is written; once you know the shape and size of the beds you want, where to start, and the weather is right for digging, there are some ways to help you lay out and mark the beds so that you can be sure they'll be how you would like them. These suggestions will also simplify the task (see Chapter 7).

R·E·C·A·P

1. Never plan to put trees and shrubs over septic systems, water supply lines, buried electric cables, etc.

2. Determine "traffic patterns" around house, space near windows and outside walls.

3. Leave space between beds, in case of emergencies.

4. Do not plan avenue of trees too near driveway.

5. Take snapshots of each garden area, for perspective, light, existing plantings; pace areas for dimensions, shape.

6. Sketch rough plan(s), or to scale—separately for each bed or area; indicate north.

7. Determine views to hide or enhance amount of sunlight, prevailing winds.

8. Study plant heights and widths.

9. Never plan vegetable or elaborate flower bed across ancient deer path.

Compost and Fertilizers

ne recent summer day, my sister and I were lounging in her small garden in the heart of London, catching some long-overdue rays. Just then the doorbell rang. "Morning, miss," said a cheerful elderly man, doffing his cap. "Need any 'orse manure?" For a second or two, we stood there gaping. True enough, piled high on the horse-drawn cart on the street behind him were bulging plastic sacks. There was no doubt about their contents—we were downwind.

Of course we said yes, our adrenalin suddenly wide awake. After insisting on personally carrying the several sacks we bought through the ground-floor apartment and into the garden, the man promised to deliver more of the same in a few months' time. His source? The stables of London's police.

It wasn't until afterward that the irony of this scene fully struck us. Here we were, in the middle of one of the largest, most sophisticated capitals of the world, and manure was being offered to us, packaged and delivered to the door. For a pittance, my sister had acquired an invaluable soil conditioner, the nearest thing to a gardener's diamond mine.

If *you* should own, or have easy access to, a horse, cattle, sheep, pig, or chicken farm, rejoice! In that instance, you may already know that a garden treated to applications of well-rotted manure can quickly put other gardens to shame, and turn most gardeners a bilious shade of green with envy. Alas, such farms are rapidly dwindling in number, and the demand for their manure far exceeds the supply. And there simply aren't enough police stables to go around to fill the need. Consequently, most of us are forced to enter that whole new creative dimension called composting.

Before I go further, perhaps I should explain *why* you should bother at all with manure, compost, or commercial fertilizers. The most immediately visible purpose of the first two is the friable and loose texture they add to your existing soil. They do this through the decomposition of vegetable matter, thereby becoming the organic component of the soil. Humus, in other words. The greater the humus content, the richer and healthier is the soil.

All soils, whether or not they are rich in humus, contain numerous different chemical elements that are used by your plants in varying degrees. But there are three elements that are more essential than the others; the fertility of most soils depends on them—and so does the healthy development of your plants. They are nitrogen, phosphorus, and potash. Of these, nitrogen is not only the most valuable but also the most quickly used up. Nitrogen stimulates a plant's green growth, its stems and foliage. Second in importance is phosphorus, which stimulates flower and vegetable development. And potash, the third major soil nutrient, is crucial in root development and in stimulating such root crops as carrots, radishes, beets, and parsnips.

Therefore, as your plants use up these and other elements in the soil, it's natural that, left untended and unreplenished by you, the soil would eventually grow weary, unable to provide the nourishment needed by your plants for their continued good health. And that's where manure and compost, as well as fertilizers, enter the picture.

You may want to know just what it is about manure that makes it so particularly desirable in a garden. Very briefly, farm animals like horses, cows, sheep, and pigs are all herbivores. Chickens, too, broadly speaking, although technically they're described as being granivorous and omnivorous—that is, they feed on grain and anything else they can scratch up. *Aged* chicken manure is among the most potent and desirable. In any case, the diet of herbivores consists entirely of vegetable matter. This food is largely broken down, combusted, and processed through the animals' digestive systems, before being evacuated. Because horses and cows especially are bedded on straw, hay, or sawdust as a rule, their excrement, which itself contains valuable nutrients, inevitably mixes with the bedding. It is this mixture that not only gives us the word "manure" but also stimulates the further decomposition of the bedding. In essence, you could say that each herbivore is, therefore, a kind of self-employed compost machine whose internal combustion and digestive processes accelerate the decay of organic matter.

Now, I know you're anxious to get on with things, but it's never a good idea to spread fresh (unrotted) manure on a home garden, because it does produce considerable heat and can seriously damage your plants, especially the roots. This is particularly true of fresh horse and sheep manure. If you're fortunate enough to obtain a truckload (or even a plastic bagful) of fresh manure, set it into piles no higher than four feet. To prevent spontaneous combustion, keep the heaps fairly wet over the next several months, and also turn them over at least twice. At the end of about six to eight months or more, you'll have what is referred to as well-rotted manure. This, when dug into your garden beds, provides a wonderful richness of humus and growth stimulants.

Mind you, one friend of mine can't be bothered with that method. The bulk of his gardening revolves around vegetable growing. His home garden also supports two steers, and these supply him with all the manure he can handle. Twice a year, at the end of the harvest and again in January or February, he spreads a generous allowance over his vegetable garden. In autumn he plows it in immediately; in spring he does so as soon as the ground thaws. By planting time, the manure is sufficiently rotted to cause no burn damage to roots. And by the next harvest time, my friend ends up with nothing short of "killer" crops. In fairness, there are no nearby neighbors living downwind.

Manure is likely to remain one of the most popular sources of crop-stimulating elements. The large proportion of humus it adds to the soil increases the soil's moisture-retention capacity, which in turn makes plant food steadily accessible to the plant roots.

Although it doesn't go through quite the same processes as animal manure, compost is the next best thing. As is suggested by its name, it is a composite mixture, made up of such ingredients as leaf mold, garden refuse, soil, etc., all thoroughly mingled and decomposed. Even if you have access to manure, I would urge you nevertheless to develop compost, for reasons that will shortly become apparent.

Sufficiently decayed, compost is a wonderful fertilizer and soil-enriching agent—and this at minimal direct cost to you. Apart from the good it does your soil, a compost heap lets you be productively tidy, because it utilizes all kinds of refuse that inevitably accumulates around your house and garden. In fact, with the exception of meat, bones, and sundry other items, a compost heap may consist of just about anything biodegradable. Just think of the masses of leaves, weeds, and lawn cuttings you've been raking up until now; the twigs and dead flowers you've gathered. Before this year is out, you will have pulled up numerous inedible vegetable stems, collected bags full of lawn cuttings. You've perhaps thrown all these into the woods (if you have one), or into a pit you dug for the purpose, or into your general household garbage. You know you'll have to repeat the above tasks endlessly through the rest of the year—and the next, and the next . . . And that doesn't even include the final, major cleanup at the end of the growing season (see Chapter 16).

Just think of the satisfaction you'd have from selecting one single shaded location in your garden where all your refuse could be allowed to decompose peacefully into rich, nutritive humus. Just think of all the plastic garbage bags you'd save. Most of all, think of how exhilarated you will be once you realize how many hidden assets you really have—assets you've been blithely chucking into the garbage. And that's only *out*doors. Think of what you can do with *in*door refuse!

I've been composting for many years, but even now it's a positive thrill when I learn of yet another object I can recycle for the garden. In part, this is undoubtedly due to the fact that I do love to get double value out of things. It's no exaggeration that the moment I began composting in earnest, I was able to halve my household garbage—that is, the garbage I set out for collection every week. It works very simply. I collect my compost garbage in two separate parts. Such dry goods as paper napkins, paper towels, and facial tissues all go into a brown paper shopping bag. So do torn-up cardboard boxes and excess brown paper bags, as well as shredded newspapers (no colored inks, as these contain poisons); irreparably worn or torn pure cotton or wool clothing, and leftover bits of string and burlap, etc. (no nylon or other synthetics).

In a plastic bag, or a small covered bucket, I gather such kitchen waste delectables as carrot tops and citrus rinds; apple cores; banana, potato, and other peelings; coffee grounds, including filters, and tea bags or tea leaves; leftover salad, hopelessly stale bread, finely crushed eggshells, and rotten fruit and vegetables. I regularly add the contents of both these bags to the compost pile, lightly covering them with soil. This helps activate the decomposition process, prevents odors from rising and paper from flying off, and discourages rabbits and suchlike from nosing around. I also keep a third receptacle—a small lidded bucket filled with water into which (dare I say it?) I empty ashtrays (see Chapter 13).

The things you should *never* add to your compost include meat, bones, fish, grease, or eggs (except dried, ground shells), as these not only tend to attract animals but may also introduce harmful parasites, not to mention vile odors. If you have fish bones, you could dry these, then grind them up, and sprinkle the powder on your compost heap: fish meal is a highly desirable addition to any garden soil. As for beef bones, unless you own a heavy-duty grinder, you're probably best off letting your dog sharpen his teeth on them. Otherwise, bone *meal* is a wonderful source of nitrogen and phosphorus. Finally, although they're bio-degradable—provided you can wait long enough—tin cans in your compost are not a terrific idea because, more than likely, you'll cut yourself long before they crumble.

When you're structuring a compost heap, it's best to select a spot in your garden which is well ventilated, receives at least partial shade, and isn't too far from your garden beds, or out of reach of your watering hose. There are two basic methods for composting: the lazy person's so-called cold-rot way and the eager beaver's so-called hot-rot way. By and large, both means serve the same end; however, the former takes longer, albeit with less work for you, whereas the latter requires more of your attention but makes usable compost much more rapidly available. It depends greatly on how much time you can or want to devote to the task of composting. Let me hasten to add that neither method is difficult, and you may well choose to combine the two.

A compost heap may be round, square, or rectangular, a freestanding mass or enclosed. There is no need to prepare the ground for it, or to dig a shallow base pit. Just pile the compost materials directly on the ground. For practical purposes, the heap's dimensions should be about 6 feet wide and 4 to 5 feet high. Of course, if you have literally tons of vegetative refuse, you should construct several piles of roughly these dimensions or else make a single heap, long and narrow. Because of the difference in the two methods, cold-rot composting lends itself more readily to being enclosed than does its hot counterpart, as you'll see below. However, it's an entirely personal choice, and many people prefer to be neat about all their compost, by keeping it within boundaries in what's usually called a bin.

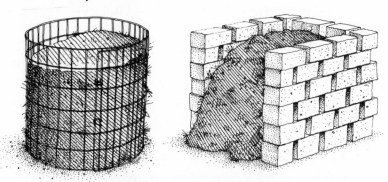

Compost bins *may be made of many materials, provided air can freely circulate.*

A bin may be made of cinder blocks or snow fencing, of wooden slats or wire mesh. Polypropylene bins are available through garden centers and catalogues. Such bins are particularly well suited to city or other small gardens. They consist of ventilated sliding panels (for easy access to finished compost) and a hinged lid. These bins are large enough to earn their keep as efficient composters, and compact enough not to be intrusive in limited spaces.

Nothing could be easier than the **cold-rot** composting method. Let me warn you at once, however, that it does require a heavy dose of patience. You see, cold-rot compost is very slow to decompose. It takes two to three years before all of it is sufficiently rotted for use in the garden. Because of its slow decay, this compost is not as rich in nitrogen as is hot-rot compost, but it provides an excellent balanced diet for all the plants that like good average soil. And precisely because of that lower nitrogen content, you can safely dig liberal amounts of it into your garden on a regular annual basis.

Whether you make one heap or several depends largely on the amount of plant and other biodegradable refuse you have. For example, friends of mine who have a fairly big garden have constructed three circular wire-mesh enclosures, roughly 5 feet in diameter and reinforced with metal stakes. The two ends of the wire mesh overlap at the front, like a little gate, and are held in place with hasps. Why three bins? Simply, these friends have opted for a rotational composting system. In the first year, they fill bin number one with all their weeds, leaves, and grass cuttings, as well as all the other household and kitchen refuse I've described. In the following year, they fill bin number two, and the year after that, it's the third bin's turn. By then, the lower portion of the first bin's contents is beautifully decayed into friable, dark soil, which they dig into their garden. In the fourth year, they begin all over again, by adding refuse on top of the undecayed plant matter remaining in bin number one. And from then on, year after year, they have a steady supply of compost, with absolutely no effort on their part, except throwing in refuse.

My own method is only slightly different. I keep up to three freestanding heaps, made of alternating layers. These consist of roughly 4 to 6 inches of vegetable matter and rubbish, covered by roughly 2 to 3 inches of soil, in ever smaller layers, to achieve a pyramidal mass. The soil I use for this purpose may be excess clumps of sod, soil-side up, from a newly dug bed, or it may be last year's window-box soil—or any other soil that's lying around idly. Soil helps decomposition and, therefore, plays an active role in composting. When I reach the top of the heap, at about 4 feet, I end with a layer of soil. This also prevents, or at least slows down, any leaching. Leaching is caused by rainwater, which can dissolve many of the chemical constituents of the soil and wash them away in solution. For example, every time you over-water your indoor potted plants, when water passes through the drainage holes at the bottom, that water takes with it a good deal of the plant food in the soil.

In any case, with the cold-rot method, you need neither to water the pile nor to turn it over. You simply let nature take its course. Naturally, if you feel ambitious, you can give nature a helping hand by turning the pile occasionally, to speed up de-composition. But it isn't necessary to do this.

Hot-rot compost *can* be ready for use in one month. As I've said, this method requires more of your attention, but wait until you see what you get for your trouble! Because of its high nitrogen content, hot-rot compost is particularly welcomed by your vegetable garden and such epicurean perennial flowers as peonies, hollyhocks, and delphiniums. Not so thrilled are the plants that prefer average soil—geraniums, carnations, and poppies among them—and so you should apply this compost sparingly to these. Many catalogues and books provide information about the soil requirements of individual plants.

An essential ingredient in hot-rot compost is manure—the real stuff, fresh from the farm. The bagged and pasteurized variety available at garden centers isn't really a valid substitute, because the pasteurizing process has radically reduced the number of bacterial microorganisms so vital in hot-rot composting. Yes, of course, there is an odor to manure, but that is soon dissipated. To be honest, I like the smell. For me it holds a promise of infinite richness, a sense of life itself bursting with vitality. And that's not far from the truth, because there is more potential power in even a shovelful of manure than there is in a stick of dynamite. And it is a positive power.

The chief source of energy for the microorganisms is the nitrogen in manure and in the vegetable matter you've added to your compost pile, and those microorganisms tear into the plant matter with unimaginable lust and greed. It's a free-for-all, a bacchanalian orgy completely out of control, as though there were no tomorrow. And for many of them there isn't. They gorge themselves, and multiply at a furious rate, with everybody fighting for a share of the loot. Inevitably, the compost pile soon begins to heat up. It's just a matter of time now. Before long, the temperature is up to 140° F., and shortly afterward, it's all over for the weaklings in the crowd of bacteria. They've been left by the wayside, and only the heat-loving (thermophilic) types remain. Now that these have the pile to themselves, they waste no time in settling the place with billions upon billions of themselves, and churning through the decomposition of the compost at a feverish pitch. In other words, this is the spontaneous combustion I mentioned earlier. Within a month or two, they've finished the job (*if you help*), the heat begins to drop, and you have a stack of compost that's unbelievably rich in plant food. There's also a bonus in this method: the high heat kills off many unwanted weed seeds.

At this point, you may be so excited about the power of manure that you're thinking although you don't have any nearby farms, you just happen to have a prime herd of cats and dogs lounging about. Why not get some use out of them? Sorry; you'd be wise to abandon that idea. Cats and dogs are carnivores. As such, no matter how lovingly you feed them, they're forever on the prowl for juicy morsels of mouse or rotten meat. The feces of cats and dogs, in brief, are likely to carry intestinal parasites that could prove harmful to humans. So it's best not to add pet excrement to your compost. Instead, don't be shy to do what I once did when I still lived in the city. Armed with two empty chicken-feed sacks I'd acquired, I drove up to a farm and asked if I could have them filled with aged manure. The farmer was too startled by the modest amount of my request to refuse it— or to accept the payment I offered. Of course, after I'd driven my precious cargo back to the city and spread it around my tiny garden, my neighbors would have gladly paid *me* to get out of town.

With hot-rot compost, although you might be tempted, it's definitely better not to have an enclosure, as this will impede your activities. Start by spreading a 4-to-6-inch layer of plant material over an area roughly 6 feet wide—the shape of your choice. Depending on how much manure you've been able to acquire, cover that first layer with perhaps 1 to 2 inches of manure (more if you have it). At this point, some gardeners like to sprinkle a dusting of bonemeal and/or lime across the top. Bonemeal is rich in nitrogen and phosphorus. Other gardeners like to scatter a handful of commercial all-purpose fertilizer. All three aid in decomposition. A word of caution, however: *never* add lime to fresh poultry manure, because of the major liming effect already inherent in this manure. The result could well lead to a soil alkalinity level above the normal range (see Chapter 3). Similarly, lime and wood ashes should not be applied together to your garden. Next, some gardeners, myself included, spread a 3-inch layer of soil. This layer is optional. Now bring on your watering hose, as it's important to moisten the heap thoroughly, but *without drenching it.*

Keep repeating the layers and water until your heap reaches a height of 4 to 5 feet. Be sure the layers become smaller, to form a slope. End with a layer of soil. If you have chosen not to use soil, then cover the completed heap with black plastic, or some straw or hay. This not only helps prevent leaching; it also helps to motivate that lecherous mob of hot-rot bacteria.

At the end of one week, it's time to turn the compost pile over. Use a digging fork or a shovel to do this. Simply lift the top layers to the ground beside the existing pile and build it up again, with sloping sides, until the original bottom layer is at the top. If the materials seem dry, moisten them with the hose, then cover the heap once more. Don't be surprised if you see steam rising as you turn the heap—that proves that your little marauders are hard at work. By turning the compost over, thereby mixing all the vegetable materials, you're giving them an essential chance to come up for air, in order to work even harder to finish the job. So it's important that you do not omit that first turning. Of course, if you really want to keep the bacteria hard at it, then a total of three weekly turnings can see their job done in as little as one month. Not bad, considering you can't even see the work force with the naked eye. If one turning is enough for you, however, then you will have to wait about three months before your compost is finished.

As you can see, both the above methods will introduce into your garden a wealth of nutrients and humus. The biggest problem—perhaps the only one—is that compost creates a vicious circle: the more joyously your plants prove its benefits to you, the more flower and other beds you'll want. And that, of course, means more compost—and so on, round and round. It's simply a fact of life that you can never have too much compost.

There is one more general point. On the principle that the

finer or less dense the vegetable composites of your compost are, the more rapidly they will decompose, I keep a separate pile for such debris as pruned or fallen tree limbs, major underbrush clearings, and the stumps of trees and shrubs. If the bulk of these becomes too enormous (although even such a heap will eventually decay), I burn it and save the ashes for the root crops (also see Chapter 13). Or you could dust the ashes either over your compost pile or directly over your vegetable bed. Similarly, if you burn wood *only* in your fireplace, you can use such ashes, too. You see, those wood ashes contain about 5 percent of the very potash your garden needs! Old hat as they may be to the experts, it's first-time encounters with little revelations like this which make gardening the joy it is.

Now it is time to speak about **commercial fertilizers**. So-called complete all-purpose fertilizer mixtures may be bought at most garden centers and nurseries. Although they can never replace manure or compost, as you will see below, there is a place for them in your garden. As you've already seen, fertilizers may be lightly used in the preparation of your compost. In fact, the key phrase in the use of all commercial fertilizers should be to use them sparingly. The reason for this is that they are, in essence, a kind of booster shot.

To compare a commercial all-purpose fertilizer's merits with those of manure or compost is a little like the proverbial comparison between apples and oranges. Their objectives are quite different. Basically, this difference lies in the fact that commercial fertilizers offer quick and surefire success with your plants, over the short term, with practically no permanent value to the soil, whereas manure and compost add permanent value to your soil, in the form of humus, as well as long-lasting benefits to your plants.

In theory, to warrant being described as "complete," a commercial fertilizer should be composed of all the varied plant foods to be found in a perfect soil. However, many of these foods are already adequately present in all soils, and not all plants require all the same nutritional elements. Therefore, it is accepted practice for commercial fertilizer mixtures to contain only the three most important and most rapidly exhausted elements—nitrogen, phosphorus, and potash. If you are buying a complete fertilizer, these three elements should *always* be clearly indicated on the front of each bag or package, in the form of three hyphenated numbers, such as 4–8–4. In the United States at least, the first digit always refers to nitrogen, the second to phosphorus, and the third to potash. Interpreted, the numbers mean that the package—whatever its weight or size—contains 4 percent nitrogen, 8 percent phosphorus, and 4 percent potash. (This particular formula, incidentally, is good for your vegetable garden.) The remainder of the package's weight—whatever its size—consists of a legally determined inert "filler," such as sand, which has been thoroughly mixed with the three fertilizing elements. The reason for this is to facilitate the even distribution on your garden beds of all three essential elements.

It is important for you to know that the prolonged and *exclusive* use of commercial fertilizers can lead to problems. Because your plants may not use up every smidgen of the fertilizer's three essential elements, a residue remains in the soil at the end of the growing season. Suppose you bought a large bag of one of the most commonly used formulas, 5–10–5 (or any other), and you distributed this regularly, even frequently, on your garden, year after year. And suppose you did so in lieu of working the soil, in lieu of green-manuring it, or composting or mulching it. Of course, it's a temptation. For one thing, it's much easier, less tiring and time-consuming. Besides, when we scatter fertilizer, we can quickly see what a single light dusting does for the growth of our plants. Just think what we could achieve with twice or thrice the amount and frequency! It staggers the imagination— a kind of Alice in Wonderland garden. And, of course, your plants *would* flourish—for a time—but bit by bit such fertilizer overdoses would alter the character of your soil. The soil would begin to cake, its humus content would grow weary, depleted. Then, too, depending on the *sources* of the nitrogen, phosphorus, and potash in your fertilizer, you might well end up with soil that is more acid, or more alkaline, than when you started out. Needless to say, some of your plants would show signs of resentment. Finally, it's never a good idea to add commercial fertilizers (or fresh manure) to the hole at planting time, as this may cause the roots to "burn."

I do use commercial fertilizers occasionally—as a rule, in early spring, preferably before the last of the snow has melted. I scatter a cautious dusting on my raspberry patch, the perennial beds, and around my fruit and flowering bushes and trees. However, I never apply fertilizers after the end of June, except around the broad-leaved evergreens I discuss in Chapter 16.

On the whole, quite frankly, I would much rather, at all times, spend my time on improving the structure and content of the soil. As I've said, this may take longer, but in the long run I think it's more rewarding. In any case, the choice is yours now, the options are before you. By all means, use a commercial, all-purpose fertilizer in your garden, but I urge you to treat its use in much the same way as most of us treat a dollop of whipped cream— as a dressing rather than as the main dessert.

R·E·C·A·P

1. Build compost heap in shaded, well-ventilated area, near watering hose and garden.

2. Heap may be freestanding or enclosed in well-ventilated bin; round, square, or rectangular.

3. Freestanding heap should be pyramidal, roughly 6 feet at base, 4 to 5 feet high, sloping sides.

4. "Hot-rot" composting requires fresh manure, frequent watering, turning over at least once. "Cold-rot" compost needs no attention; ready in ca. two years.

5. *Never* mix lime with fresh poultry manure or with wood ashes.

6. *Never* use fresh farmyard manure directly on established beds, or less than two months before planting.

7. To age fresh farmyard manure, pile as in #3, keep moist, turn occasionally, allow to age one year before using.

8. Commercial all-purpose fertilizer packages should *always* state ratios of nitrogen-phosphorus-potash.

9. Use commercial fertilizers sparingly; never add to hole at planting time.

Preparing the Beds

One of the most perplexing experiences I have ever had came with my first country garden. For years I'd lived in the city, where the garden I had behind my brownstone apartment was exactly the same size as all the others along the block, give or take a few precious inches. No matter how artfully I introduced curves and contours in order to increase the feeling of space, that space remained a stubborn 20 by 40 feet. I used to spend long hours cogitating on my miniature patio, studying the miniature flower beds around the minuscule lawn—and dream. Suppose I could have a vegetable bed as large as the whole garden. What couldn't I plant in a garden the size of three lots! If only I could have several large flower beds, or a lawn with trees and shrubs. It boggled the mind.

And then the day came when all those idle cogitations became reality—and that reality sent me into total panic. In my first country garden I actually had all that space I'd been dreaming about, enough to fit a whole neighborhood of city gardens into it. Suddenly I was attacked by a severe case of agoraphobia. Through the years, I'd become so adept at making the most of every square inch, horizontally and vertically, that now I couldn't cope with so much expanse. My driveway alone took up more land than the three city garden lots I'd fantasized about. Believe it or not, it was a terrible dilemma.

Fortunately, I'd moved to the country in late autumn, and so I spent the entire winter trying to gain a sense of perspective, making plans, pacing the grounds. To help me make the psychological adjustment, I hung large signs all around the house—on mirrors, doors, and walls—which constantly reminded me to THINK BIG! I discovered that it may be easy to think big, as in opulent, but not at all so easy, as in large. After having worked with beds that were perhaps 2 by 5 feet, it was nothing short of traumatic to contemplate beds measuring 10 by 50 feet, or a vegetable bed of 50 by 80 feet, or spacing trees 25 feet apart and still having plenty of room for more. If you find yourself in a similar crisis, I urge you to keep a sense of proportion about the size of your beds in relation to the area around them. A 3-foot circular bed may have been a showy centerpiece in your city garden, but it will be a mere pimple on an acre of land. So be generous, make it a 20-foot diameter, or group several small beds near each other. Or, if you intend to plant a grouping of trees or shrubs, rather than preparing individual holes for these, or having the later bother of mowing the grass among them, you could dramatize as well as unify them by creating a single free-form bed. If such a grouping already exists, it can be unified with a densely planted ground cover (see Chapter 15).

This is a good time for you to be introduced to "topsoil" and "subsoil." Topsoil is what you're standing on. It is the layer of soil that has been worked through cultivation and the decomposition of leaves and other organic matter. If you dig to roughly the depth of one shovel blade you'll see a distinct horizontal demarcation line running through the earth. The depth of this line can vary greatly, not only within your garden, but also in different soils. The line separates the more friable, generally darker, layer of topsoil from the lighter-colored, always more compacted subsoil underneath.

When subsoil consists largely of clay, or of compressed clay and silt, it is referred to as "hardpan." This hardpan can cause all sorts of problems. It'll resist drainage—in fact, water may even accumulate on it—and it will prevent roots, especially taproots (see Chapter 12), from penetrating deeply enough to establish a firm foothold. As a result, all but your shallow-rooted plants will be forced to form lateral root systems. And if some of these plants happen to be trees or shrubs, they may easily fall victim to gusty winds one day.

Whatever its composition, subsoil is compacted, sunk into itself, because it is deprived of all the attention and nourishment given to its upstairs neighbor, the topsoil, by nature and by humankind (see Chapters 6 and 11). But with a little help from you, and some elbow grease, as I explain below, that under-nourished subsoil will quickly become your devoted ally.

Frankly, the best time of year to do any digging is in late autumn. The soil should be slightly moist, not wet. If you dig a new bed in late autumn, the work is less arduous than in spring, because it is actually better to let the rough turned-over clumps of earth winter over without breaking up or raking them. Frost and snow and air will circulate among these clumps, loosen and mellow the soil, and by the following spring, most soils except the very clayey kinds can be simply raked and planted. And the grass you turn under in autumn digging will have time to de-compose and provide necessary humus to the new bed.

However, if you can't wait until autumn, or prefer not to, then here's a test that will let you know when the earth is ready to be worked in spring. If a shovelful crumbles when you let the soil drop off the shovel or spade, the time is right for digging. If the soil remains in a solid lump when it lands on the ground, you'd better wait and let the earth dry out a little. I know you're anxious, if not downright impatient, but take the word of one who has paid the penalty for such impetuosity—a stiff and painful back from having to do the job twice. You see, when you dig wet soil, even if you break up each turned-over clod, the earth will dry into a rocklike hardness that will make it extremely difficult for plants to develop healthy root systems. The right time for digging in spring depends entirely on how much rain and snow the earth has to absorb—what kind of winter it's been—and this varies from year to year.

Whichever time of year you choose to prepare your new beds, the work goes more smoothly if you mark the contours of the proposed planting areas, whatever size or shape these may be. To do this in my own garden, I've devised a simple method. I call it my stake-spool. Crude as this is, it has never failed me.

The stake-spool consists of two sturdy flat lath strips (I got my supply from remodeling old plaster walls), about 1½ inches wide, ½ inch thick, each about 2 feet long, with a sharp point at one end. Thick dowel sticks, leftover pieces of wood molding, or an unused cane cut in half will do as well. Over one of these lath strips I slip the empty cardboard tube of a paper-towel roll (a toilet-paper tube will do). Around the tube, I tie and wind about a 10-foot length of thick nylon string. This length is arbitrary; it lets me measure beds up to 20 feet long. Presto, stake-spool at no cost, and now I'm in business. Of course, if you prefer, so-called planting lines or row markers are commercially available for the same purpose.

Say I want a freestanding square bed, with 5-foot sides. I place the stake-spool deeply into the soil, in the center of the area where the bed is to be. Then I firmly tie the free end of the string to the second stake and reel out 2½ feet of string— half the 5 feet. So that the string holds fast at that length, I secure it with a rubber band around the spool (the cardboard tube) and, stretching the string to its full 2½ feet, I place the second stake into the ground, in what will be the center of each of the four sides. At each of these four points, I make deep cuts in the soil, using a shovel or spade or digging fork:

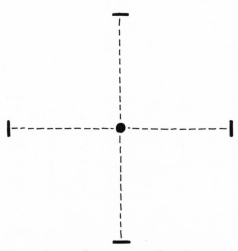

*This is the simplest way to outline dimensions
of freestanding square bed.*

Once these cuts are made, I complete the digging of each side
by "eyeballing" their straightness. However, if you do not trust
your eye, mark two intersecting center lines—with powdered
chalk available at sewing centers, with flour, or with baking soda.
Using the chalk line(s) as a guide for your stake-spool, make your
cuts on all four sides:

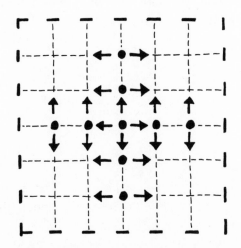

*Work from central intersecting lines to outline
freestanding square bed at regular intervals.*

Follow the same procedure for rectangular beds, except that here one center line will be longer than the other, say, 5 feet and 2 feet, respectively, for a 10-by-4-foot bed:

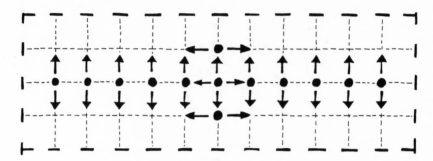

For freestanding rectangular bed, again work
from central intersecting lines to mark dimensions.

For circular beds, again the stake-spool is placed in the proposed center, the string measured to the length of the circle's radius (half the diameter). All you have to do then is walk the second stake around in a circle, making your initial marker cuts at regular intervals. Again, if you feel more at ease doing so, sprinkle chalk, flour, or baking soda around the perimeter before making your cuts. With either method, you end up with a perfectly round bed:

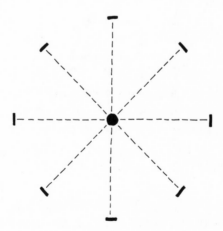

Easiest of all to outline is the perfect circle.

Simple, *n'est-ce pas?*

For large free-form beds, I use my watering hoses, all coupled together. Heavy rope will do just as well, as will old lath strips. (Oops, don't tell me you threw them out when you remodeled the old plaster bedroom walls! Didn't I tell you that gardeners are hoarders? Lath strips also make marvelous stakes for tall plants like hollyhocks and delphiniums, and for young trees.) With the watering hoses, I lay out the shape of the bed I want. Because they are flexible, I can move them about easily, adjust a curve here, elongate the bed there, until the contours are just how I'd visualized them. In between, I step back, walk around the entire shape, to see it from all perspectives. I go away altogether, back to the house, eat lunch, make telephone calls, then approach it from a distance, with a fresh eye. If the shape is pleasing and proportionate to its surroundings, no matter from which direction I come upon it, it's time to dig around the circumference, just inside the hoses, rope, or lath strips, and to remove these when I finish.

Of course, this perimeter digging is necessarily crude; there will be a few nicks here and there, slight unevennesses. These can be adjusted later. By having completely turned over each shovelful of grass (sod), exposing the soil, I now have the bed fully outlined. At this point, I usually let the bed rest overnight, to get an entirely fresh look at it the next day—my last chance to alter or amend the shape before I dig in earnest.

Make no mistake about it, digging is work. And I do hope that you've remembered not to put your proposed beds over an area in which your probing discovered a shallow rock ledge, or other obstructions, during your walkabout (see Chapter 2). If your subsoil consists of hardpan, or if your topsoil is poor, now is also the time to improve the soil through the double-digging process described below. The good news is that, in most except the poorest soils, you'll have to do double-digging only once per bed.

The point of digging at all is to loosen and aerate the soil, and to turn under the surface vegetation—nature's own compost and fertilizer. I personally also remove all large and medium-sized stones, and densely matted clumps of grass roots. If the surface grass is dense and clumped, or the soil is very compacted and clayey, I find it easier to work with a digging fork. A fork can more easily slide between and dislodge such hindrances. If the soil is fairly light, and clear of obstructions, I generally use a shovel or spade for digging. The important thing to remember is that the more you loosen your soil, the easier it will be to plant and maintain it later.

You might not think so, but there is a right way and a wrong way to dig. If you've ever watched a civic ground-breaking ceremony, you can always spot the gardener among the group of officials by the way he or she holds the shovel. While the others bend forward, skimming a bit of earth off the surface, with their shovels held at a pronounced slant, the gardener stands upright and inserts the shovel almost vertically into the ground. If you dug an entire bed bent forward and holding your shovel at the same slanted angle, as most of the officials do, you'd soon end up on the chiropractor's table. Worse still, you'd have to do the job all over again. The proper and by far most successful and least laborious way to dig is to drive the shovel (or spade, or digging fork) virtually straight down, to nearly the full depth of the blade, by providing the added push with your foot. For easier digging, I always begin by making four preliminary cuts to blade depth and width, in a square as though I were cutting a brownie. In this way, each shovelful is roughly the same size and weight as all the others. To turn each shovelful, be sure to bend your knees, so that your legs and shoulder muscles—*not your back*—do all the strenuous work.

Begin at one end of the bed, working in rows left to right (or right to left), and walk backward as you progress with the digging, without ever having to tread on the turned-up earth. If you're doing your digging in the spring, break up the soil clods in each shovelful by chopping them with the side of the blade; in fall digging, it's better to leave the clumps whole, as discussed above.

If all this sounds hopelessly complicated, it really isn't—in fact, it's by far more difficult to describe here than to do it. After a short while, you'll develop a rhythm that feels entirely comfortable. Of course, at the beginning, you'll undoubtedly discover some muscles you didn't know you had, but a hot shower or bath will quickly soothe these. Remember, you're in complete control; therefore, if you've had enough for one day, simply stop.

Whether you've dug your bed in the previous autumn or in spring, once the soil is dry enough to crumble, spring is the time to rake it smooth and to adjust the neatness of the perimeter, evening the straight lines and curves. And that's that—your bed is ready for planting. Just keep in mind that although much of the turned-under surface vegetation will decompose, some of its seeds and hardier components will start to regrow, particularly during the first summer. If you're vigilant (see Chapter 12), this will not become a problem and the newly loosened soil will readily yield most of these obstinate little fellows.

Double-digging is particularly good for soils lacking in humus content. Such soils might be very clayey, very sandy, very gravelly; they may have been recently exposed from under a concrete or flagstone covering; they may be soils where even grass growth is sparse and yellow, soils long disused or abused, or soils used for landfill. They may be soils deprived of cultivation or of the leaves from nearby trees. They may simply be soils long neglected, soils-in-waiting—waiting for your help. Some gardeners prefer double-digging their new beds, no matter what kind of soil they have, and they're unquestionably right—the resulting growth is proof of that. Alas, I have to admit that I double-dig only if I have to. There's no question that double-digging is more work, just as there is no question that it's well worth the extra effort. You could call it in-depth soil improvement.

Arm yourself with shovel (or spade) and digging fork, as well as a cart or wheelbarrow—if you don't have one of these yet, an old shower curtain will do quite well. You'll need a pile of compost, leaf mold, or well-rotted manure (see Chapters 6 and 11). As described above, start at one end of the bed and, working in a row, dig up a shovel depth of topsoil. Instead of turning this, however, place it on the cart, wheelbarrow, or shower curtain for later use. Then, with your fork, thoroughly loosen the subsoil you've exposed and add a 2-to-3-inch layer of the leaf mold, compost, or manure you've piled nearby. When you've done that, dig the next row of topsoil, and turn it upside down, on top of the improved subsoil in the first trench, breaking up the clods as you go. Loosen and improve the subsoil in the second trench, just as you did with the first, and fill it with the topsoil from the third row. Work your way to the other end of the bed in this fashion. When you've loosened and improved the subsoil in the final row, fill that trench with the topsoil you set aside from the first row.

Should you be unable to finish the task in one day and there's a threat of rain, be sure to cover the cart, wheelbarrow, or shower curtain, so that the soil you set aside won't turn to mud.

If your soil is very clayey, it's a good idea to work more of the organic matter into the topsoil as well of each completed row. Be generous. This organic matter will decay and provide invaluable humus to your soil, adding structure, body, and nourishment. To give the decaying process a chance to work, double-digging is best done in autumn. However, if yours is a spring-dug bed, wait at least a month before planting.

As I've said, double-digging is work, but you'll soon forget your aches and pains when the flowers you plant in such a bed flourish with an abandon that will say "Thank you" a thousand times.

R · E · C · A · P

1. Best time for digging new bed is late autumn.

2. Before digging in spring, let soil dry sufficiently, until shovelful breaks or crumbles when dropped.

3. Mark outline of beds with stake-spool; large beds with watering hoses, rope, or lath strips.

4. Be sure bed sizes are proportionate to surroundings.

5. Proper way to dig—for you *and* soil—is to drive shovel, spade, or fork nearly vertically into ground.

6. Dig perimeter of large bed, observe from all angles; let it rest overnight, to make sure it's right.

7. Turn over and break up each spring-dug shovelful of soil; merely turn over each autumn-dug shovelful.

8. Double-dig undernourished, compacted, and clayey soils.

Buying Your Plants

his is the big moment you've been waiting for. If you're like me, you will stretch that "moment" into at least two, possibly three, months, depending on the kind of winter it's been. Here, in the Northeast, let there be just one mild sunny day when I think I can smell the dark wet soil; let there be even one wild goose flying overhead, or the faintest hint of a blush of color in the trees, and I'm off, seized by plant fever. I begin to haunt all my favorite nurseries, long before some of these open for the season—and the moment they do, I'm there.

In theory, you have prepared your garden bed(s) and the soil is smoothly raked and waiting to be sent into action. With the help of books and catalogues and friends, you have decided more or less which plants you would like to have. You may even be so organized that you have made a list and assigned yourself a budget.

Good for you; but you may as well leave the list at home—unless you have superhuman control. As a new gardener, you are about to discover the delicious and remorseless corrupting influence of plants. Here you are, wise to the ways of the world, a responsible, mature adult, and you are about to fling yourself wantonly into the arms of the ultimate seducer, practically begging to sell your soul for a mute sea of radiant color. Oh, you may indeed buy some of the plants on your list, but the visual lure will be so overwhelming that it will drive away any last vestige of caution or reason. You will buy plants you had neither heard nor read about, plants whose names or colors had not particularly appealed to you, plants you had thought of perhaps putting in a bed that hasn't even been dug yet. In brief, you will break every sensible personal and gardening rule. You cannot help yourself: you have been seduced.

It happened annually to one of my clients. We spent the winter months studiously going through stacks of gardening books, oceans of color photographs, making endless lists, blending colors and shades, heights and widths, plotting and planning the next season's garden-bed debut. And what happened? The first chance she had, every spring (and, interestingly, always without me), she denuded some unsuspecting nursery's stock, buying everything in sight, spending a fortune, having to make several trips to bring home her loot. Not only did the loot rarely include the plants we had so carefully selected during the winter, but almost invariably it consisted almost entirely of plants for which no home had even been thought of, let alone prepared. And more than once my heart was near breaking because I ended up having to throw them away, since my client's surrender to the seduction by plants had caused their premature demise.

It doesn't help that the nurseries obviously act as seasoned accomplices in this con game by massing the various plants in a way no ordinary garden can ever hope to equal, nor ordinary mortal can ever resist. Only rarely will nursery salespeople ask if you need help—unless business is slow. And if it is, you may well ask yourself what is wrong with their plants. Most of the time, nursery workers are too busy ringing the cash register. They know that their wares will sell themselves. You will quickly learn to distinguish between caring, truly plant-loving nursery people and merely commercial enterprises by the way they answer any questions or doubts you may have. *Real* gardeners love to talk about plants and share their knowledge gladly—it comes with the turf (pun intended).

One of my own favorite nurseries is owned by a sprightly and arthritic old lady and her family. I see her once or twice a year at most, at plant-buying time. Although I am certain she does not remember me, from year to year she greets me like an old friend, and for a half hour or more she rummages through her treasure chest of plants, to find the healthiest ones for me. She hands these to me like trophies. She advises me on their care and color, urges me to inspect the latest shipments, and gives me a discount if I happen to select something she deems less than perfect. She exudes a joy, a love and devotion so pure that it borders on the mystical. When she speaks, the years and pain slip almost visibly from her face, from her gnarled and work-worn hands and body. I always go there in mid-week, just so I can meet her. It takes perhaps a little longer to get the plants I want, but to see that radiant, wrinkled face makes me feel as though I had just been handed a sampling of Eden's own riches.

As I myself am guilty (without ever *feeling* guilty) of falling prey every spring to the artless blandishments of plantdom's bounty, I will pass no judgment on your greed. However, there are some basic points to remember when you buy your plants, if for no other reason than to justify your behavior.

Once you have made your snap decision about which un-scheduled plants you want—and the same applies to those on your list—it is wise to follow certain criteria. More than likely, you will not do this the first time—you'll be far too exhilarated—but my conscience and experience dictate that I make you at least aware of these plant-buying tips. And they apply to *all* the plants you may buy, or even those you are given.

First, check the name/color tab of the plants you want. Because individual flower pots or packs in trays are closely massed, search for a plant of the desired color which has only buds, or the fewest open blossoms. The reason for this is that you want plants that do their blooming in *your garden,* not in the nursery. In addition to that, very often the process of planting, together with possible delays before then, will age the open blossoms and help to knock them off, either immediately or soon thereafter. If there are no more buds, you must wait until the following year to see blooms in some instances, or certainly a few weeks in other cases. So do not torture yourself unnecessarily. Buy plants in *bud.*

Say you are buying petunias. These are usually massed according to color—whites, pinks, purples, etc. Carefully lift out a pack or pot from the tray so that you do not damage neighboring plants. Your first surprise will come when you see how relatively small each plant is once it is removed from the rest. Not to worry, it will soon flourish in your garden. Next, check it closely for more buds under the foliage, and for signs of young growth at the base. This is usually a paler green. If there are only a few buds at the top and no pale-green new growth at the base, look for another prospect. Do the same if the plant is too long and spindly-looking. Yes, you could pinch off the top, thereby stimulating new growth at the base, but if it is early in the season, why should you pay full price for something you first have to nurture into robust life? Of course, if it's July and you suddenly remember to buy your plants, you may have to be satisfied with the meager leftovers at the nursery and do a little work to revive the poor Cinderellas.

If you are buying shrubs or trees, or vegetables, separate them, too, from the mass, and inspect them every bit as carefully.

It is very important that you check the underside of all the plants' leaves, as well as their stems and, where applicable, twigs and branches, to see if there are any stowaways—tiny insects, or dark spots, or little "cotton balls"—anything unusual lodging on or under the leaves, in the crotch of twigs and branches, anything at all that appears to be excess baggage. All these things spell trouble. If any of them are present, no matter how perfect the plant may be otherwise, do not buy it. You do not want to import disease or pests into your garden. These may come soon enough, without your help (see Chapter 13).

From personal experience, I know too well that your impulse will be simply to seize as many of the plants as you want and get them home, to gloat. But it really is well worth taking a little time over your selections. It will save a lot more time later on. For instance, make sure that each of your selected plants has an identifying tab and, if it does, stick it as deeply into the pot as possible, so that it does not somehow fall out or slide into another plant during the trip home. If it does not have a tab, select a plant that does. Or if you are *absolutely certain* of what it is, copy the name and color from another tab in the tray and *securely* affix the slip of paper to your chosen plant. This becomes particularly important if you buy, let's say, three each of red, white, and pink geraniums. Supposing two of them lack tabs and you actually followed my suggestion by buying the plants in bud only. If you planned to group each of the three colors separately, you may have a dilemma. Even if the buds have a faint blush of color, you cannot be entirely sure whether it is a pink or a red, or even a white one. Similarly, if you are buying two different kinds of marigold—tall ones and short ones—you would be unable to distinguish which is which at planting time because the foliage looks the same. In the case of certain vegetables, the absence of identifying tabs could actually make a difference to your harvest: it is virtually impossible to distinguish between young onions, leeks, and garlic; cabbage, Brussels sprouts, and broccoli; large and small tomatoes.

Incidentally, if you do lift several plants out of the massed displays, please always return those you do not want to the places from which you took them. Think of the buyer who comes after you. If you put, say, an untabbed pink petunia back among the purple, or a broccoli among the cabbages, the next person will be, at the very least, greatly inconvenienced—especially if that person has not read this book on how to buy plants!

I say this because it happened to me quite recently. I bought a large selection of plants at various nurseries. When I unloaded the car, whoops, there was one I had not chosen. It was a sweet little thing, quite inconspicuous, but I had no idea what it was. There was no tab. I had bought a large mixture of annuals, perennials, and vegetables, by the tray, and I had failed to notice it. Nothing about it was in the least familiar, but as I had inadvertently bought it, I planted it in my "hospital bed" (see Chapter 9), where I normally put unhappy foundlings and strays, or newly made stem cuttings (see Chapter 14). I could not even be sure that it *was* a garden plant. After all, weedy squatters occasionally appear among "good" plants, and sometimes these weeds choke out their hosts (see Chapter 12). As the weeks passed, I forgot about my little foundling. Then, at the end of the summer, when I was cleaning up the garden, suddenly there was this dear creature, in full bloom. Now I had something to work with—color, shape, number of petals. Within minutes, it was identified, a trailing leadwort (*Plumbago capensis*), and the little stranger became a member of the family, in its own home.

It also happens quite frequently, especially when you buy so-called field-grown plants, that there is an entirely different leaf shape lurking under a particular plant's foliage. (Field-grown, incidentally, means just that—plants raised outdoors, not in a greenhouse—and usually applies to perennials and biennials.) Nine times out of ten, that different leaf shape belongs to a weed that got into the pot accidentally. If that happens to you, simply remove it and its roots at planting time by untangling the two sets of roots, host and weed. If you do not do this, the weed may eventually dominate, and you will lose what may have been an expensive garden plant. But once out of ten times, that "weed" will, in fact, be—joy of a gardener's joys—another garden plant, an equally accidental bonus, two for the price of one. Even so, separate it just as carefully as the weed and plant it in its own space. Until you are sufficiently confident, however, that it *is* a garden plant, I suggest you treat this bonus as a weed and discard it. Still, if you're like me and can't bear to throw anything away, create your own hospital bed, somewhere away from your real garden, perhaps by the shed or near your compost heap, in a spot that gets rain and some sun but is also reasonably well protected—just in case the foundling turns out to be a treasure.

If your buying spree runs the full gamut from flowers and vegetables to trees and shrubs, I highly recommend that you extend it to at least two entirely separate excursions. The reason for this is that the planting of the latter takes considerably more time than does the planting of flowers and vegetables. I myself would recommend a further separation still in the case of vegetables and flowers. If you fear that a particular kind of plant might no longer be available by the time you return a week or two later, then make your selections and ask the nursery to tag and set them aside for you. Unless they lack space (or goodwill), most nurseries will do that. This applies particularly to those of you who can visit your country retreat only on weekends.

No matter how small a vegetable garden you plan to have, you will buy an average of six of each kind of vegetable, even if you neither want nor plant them all. The reason for this is that most vegetable seedlings come packaged in quantities of from four to a dozen. Then, too, some vegetables are not available as plants at all but must be grown from seed, such as beans, corn, carrots, peas, zucchini, beets, radishes, turnips, chard. Because vegetables are annuals, and because the sooner you get them into the ground—once it's safe to do so—the sooner you may expect your harvest, it would be wise to treat vegetables as a separate buying trip (see Chapter 9). In this way, you won't be torn between flowers and next winter's food, or be forced to rush the planting.

In any case, I urge you to buy vegetable seedlings as soon as they come into the nurseries. They are quickly snapped up, and in the blink of an eye they are gone for the season.

If you are unable to plant your purchases at once for any reason, place them closely together, in an area where they will not get full sun all day and where they are sheltered from high winds. Unless there are torrential rains before you can plant them, they should be watered daily, because their tightly entwined roots (especially in the packs) will otherwise dry out rapidly and retard the plants' recovery and growth. The reason for setting the pots and flats close together is that this will help maintain a degree of evenness in both moisture and temperature among them. More than once, I have failed to take my own advice and discovered the poor little seedlings hanging pitifully over the edge of the pots, dying of thirst. If they are not left in this state for a whole week, however, a thorough watering will usually perk them up in a few hours or overnight. But if they have to live through this sort of neglect several times before planting, there's a good chance you will lose them altogether. The best thing is to plant them as soon as possible.

If, as happens quite often in a Northeastern spring, the night temperature is expected to slip near or below the freezing point, you are well advised to move all the pots and flats either indoors— depending on how many there are—or into a garage or other shelter. Another alternative is to upend a garden cart over them. I usually rig a kind of makeshift tent, *well supported,* and gently place a sheet or a blanket over this. The supports may be a stack of bricks at each corner, as well as in the middle, or, similarly placed, wooden stakes stuck into the soil, to support the cover. Then tuck the edges of the blanket or sheet under the outer pots or weight them down. Newspaper, too, acts as wonderful insulation, as long as it is firmly secured so that it cannot blow away. The important thing is not to let the weight of a fabric tent rest directly on the plants, because the moisture of a frost will make the cover heavy enough to break or damage your tender seedlings. Most potted trees and shrubs should be able to withstand a light frost, but if you have any doubts, simply set them in a sheltered area.

In any case, you have now spent considerably more money on plants than you had budgeted—never mind, you and your family *love* tuna casserole! You *had* planned to do spring cleaning, paint the kitchen, empty out the garage—never mind, none of it is urgent. Friends want to visit for the weekend? Unless they intend to help with the planting, you're terribly sorry, but . . . In short, the seduction is working. You are beginning to rearrange your priorities. The plants come first. You are becoming a member of that growing segment of the human race called gardeners. Against your better judgment, you have become addicted to and corrupted by, of all things, plants—and you don't feel even a smidgen of guilt or shame!

You may have noticed that I have not said a single word about buying plants from catalogues, until now. I have done this deliberately, because my own earlier experience has shown that mail-order plant buying can be tricky for a new gardener, and the quality of plants received by this method can vary greatly. Besides, very few shippers fully guarantee their plants. But more to the point are several other factors. For instance, a shipment might be in transit longer than expected, or during unusually hot (or cold) weather. You might not be at home when it is delivered, or not open it immediately if you are. The plants sent to you may not have been top quality to start with, depending on the source, and in any case, as they are only seedlings, their stamina is not what it would be as full-grown plants. Then, too, even if they were only wilted upon arrival, you might consider them beyond saving.

Let me quickly add that I am not suggesting that you *don't* buy plants from catalogues—I do it every year; I merely suggest that you wait a year, until you have worked with a variety of plants in various stages of development and feel comfortable with them. Also, as a new gardener, once a wide selection of catalogues begins to arrive in the mail, you will have no way of knowing which ones to choose. A helpful way to get some ideas is to ask among your gardening friends, find out what their preferred mail-order nurseries are—and *why* they are preferred. Mind you, as likely as not, you'll find that each friend swears by one or another—and no two of these are alike. It gets confusing, I know, but if one or two names crop up more often than others, then give them a try; send a small order and see for yourself. One day you, too, will have your "swears by" preferences!

Much the same principle applies to bulbs and seeds shipped

by mail. Inexpensive seeds do not necessarily mean poor quality, but neither is the opposite necessarily true. Good-quality seeds are those in packets marked PACKED FOR 19— (the coming spring). That means the seeds are fresh and most of them will germinate when planted. There are seed houses that sell packets of seeds without a date, so that the seeds might well be three years old, for all you know, and will produce relatively fewer plants if they are that old. Needless to say, these seeds are also cheaper to buy. I have regular annual debates with a gardening friend over this issue, specifically with regard to vegetables. He likes to experiment with new or unusual or hybrid varieties that are offered as specialties rather than as standard fare. "It's worth a buck to find out what it [some novel vegetable] will look like," he argues, when I remind him how annoyed he was last year by the same company's unmarked seed packets and the poor germinating results. "That's different," he says blithely. "You bet I got mad. Last year, it was just regular carrots." And I say, "But wouldn't you rather start out with fresh seeds, so that they'd age in *your* control, while you continued your experiments?" And *he* says, "But not every seed catalogue sells the uncommon seeds." And we're off on another round. We never really agree, but it doesn't matter; the important thing is that the debate is about gardening, a subject about which we feel equally fervent. There is no such thing as being right or wrong, winning or losing an argument. It's the discussion itself that is important. And somehow, by the following year and the next round of debates, we've both learned a little something from one another, and both remained just as adamant about certain things. That's gardeners for you.

But I digress. I merely wanted to illustrate the point that every gardener has his or her own ideas about catalogue houses— as well as every other aspect of gardening. Over the years, I have tried countless mail-order nurseries and arrived at my own preferences, based on my own rules of thumb:

1. I buy my roses from a reputable rose grower, who specializes in roses; if he also offers tulip and daffodil bulbs, I may try an uncommon color, but nothing more, because

2. I buy all my bulbs from a reputable source that specializes in bulbs; I do not buy that grower's strawberry plants, because

3. I buy all my fruit plants, trees, and shrubs from a grower who specializes in these; I ignore his catalogue offer of asparagus, because

4. I buy my vegetable seeds and plants from a catalogue nursery that specializes in top-quality stock of that kind.

And so on. In any case, however, I make the bulk of my purchases at nearby nurseries, where I can see what I'm getting. Also, local nurseries are most likely to concentrate the bulk of their stock on compatibility with the local climate. On the whole, I restrict catalogue buying to things that are otherwise not easily available. As with everything else in gardening, there are no hard-and-fast rules.

One final point worth noting is that, lovely as most catalogues are to look at, you should check their return addresses before placing an order. If a catalogue originates, say, from three hardiness zones south of yours, many of its plant offerings may not be able to survive in your climate. For example, I live in a pocket of USDA Zone 5, not far from USDA Zone 4 farther north. Anything listed as hardy in Zone 4 and colder will, of course, grow in my garden. However, things get a bit iffy the moment I want a plant described as "hardy [up] to Zone 5." I have to assume that "up to" is already stretching the point, because there is a good chance that it means under ideal and well-protected conditions. We cannot always provide these, especially if winter temperatures drop to, say, $-30°$ F. Although this does not happen often, once is quite enough if you've nurtured and loved a thriving plant for perhaps three years, only to watch it succumb to that one $-30°$ F night, even if you've protected it. Some plants are more flexible and adaptable than others, of course, but at the start of your gardening career you may prefer not to play Russian roulette. To play it safe at the beginning, it may be wiser to choose plants that definitely fall within your own hardiness zone and local climatic conditions, or the next colder one (see Chapter 2).

R·E·C·A·P

1. Look for healthy, sturdy plants, preferably bearing only buds.

2. Check for new growth at base or at tips of branches.

3. Make sure that name/color tabs are in pots you select.

4. Check for possible unwanted residents and fungi in selected plants.

5. If you are buying flowers, vegetables, *and* trees and shrubs, make *at least* two buying trips.

6. If you cannot plant immediately, water plants daily until you can.

7. If there is slightest danger of frost, protect plants.

8. Check plant-catalogue origins before placing order.

9. Research reputation of catalogue nurseries among gardening friends.

10. Plant catalogue shipments immediately, to compensate for handling in transit.

Planting

Planting is the first of the three activities which most people think make up gardening. The other two are weeding and harvesting.

Of course, you bought more and different flowers than you had intended. Of course, the forsythias somehow became rhododendrons, and the maple turned into a mountain ash, and the verbena wasn't even on your shopping list. On top of that, now that you look at them all, that huge carload of plants you could hardly get home seems like a pathetically insignificant collection. Take heart. If you truly don't have enough plants, the nurseries will continue to stock up on goodies. The chances are, however, that what you've bought will be ample for a start. They may not look like it at the moment, but your plants *will* get much larger— and sooner than you suspect.

No matter how disagreeable you may find it at the start, this is the time to get your fingernails dirty. So much of your plants' healthy development hinges on proper planting that there's simply no way of avoiding grubby hands and nails. As I describe the planting process, you'll see for yourself that only your fingertips can sense when you've done it right. Gloves may keep you clean, but they also dull your sense of touch, apart from the fact that they get in the way. I never wear gloves, except to haul away brush or to prune roses. So grit your teeth, think positive, think soap and water, and dive in. Besides, there's something truly magical about the "feel" of soil, of delicate roots, of the fragile strength of life in your hands. There is such a profound happiness in being close to these, how can a bit of dirt compare with them?

Proper planting is a major element in the survival of your plants. In a short time, when you feel more comfortable with them, you'll have them securely in the ground in half the time it takes you to read this chapter. However, no matter how nimble-fingered you become, taking time to do it right is of the utmost importance. I've known people who have been so anxious that they dug a shallow hole and stuck the plant in it, pot and all— *plastic* pot, that is!—sprinkled a cupful of water in the plant's general vicinity, and walked away, expecting a miracle the next day. Alas, it doesn't work that way.

On the fairly safe assumption that you didn't heed me and bought a little bit of everything, all at once—flowers, shrubs and trees, vegetables, and seeds—I am dividing this chapter into separate sections for each group, because each needs slightly different kinds of attention. (I discuss the planting of bulbs in Chapter 16.) On the principle that the smaller the plant, the sooner it should be planted, seedlings come first, trees last. Ideally, all the plants you bought should be set into the ground within twenty-four hours, but at the beginning, that might be asking a bit much. Within two days you're still on safe ground, unless the weather is very hot and you forget to water the plants. If you neglect them for a week, you could be in trouble, certainly with the young, more delicate plants. That is why it's a good idea to make several shopping trips.

In real life, some seeds must be planted before most nursery stock is available; other seeds go in later. Exactly because their planting times are so variable, I'll deal with seeds last. Besides, seeds don't die if you delay getting them into the earth; plants do.

Certain considerations apply to all plantings. I personally believe that all plants should be removed from their containers, although I'm aware that some of these are biodegradable. On rare occasions I've compromised by carefully and thoroughly slitting such containers at planting time, to help their decomposition along. Trees and shrubs are usually wrapped and tied in burlap. With these, be sure to *remove the string at all times,* before planting, or it can literally strangulate your plants. And if it truly *is* burlap, which is biodegradable, I still slit and fold it under at planting time. Too often, however, I've found that the "burlap" was made of a synthetic material that does not—and never will—disintegrate. As an illustration, I once had to move some rhododendrons for a client. These shrubs were looking uncommonly wan and lethargic, and I thought the explanation lay in the fact that they'd been planted in an unsuitable location. That was only part of it, as things turned out. Although a local nurseryman had put them in the ground two or three years earlier, he'd left the shrubs still tightly wrapped in non-burlap burlap *and* tied with nylon cord. No wonder the poor things were at death's door! So beware.

At the start of your gardening career, you might do best to remove all the containers and wrappings, just to play it safe. Another factor that is applicable to all plants concerns the diameter of the hole you dig for them. This should always be roughly double the diameter of the plant root ball. The soil around your newly bedded plants should always be firmly tamped down and thoroughly watered. For even more favorable growing conditions, add mulch (see Chapters 10 and 11).

Finally, among these overall guidelines, I never plant anything during the heat of the day. Instead, I do so in the late afternoon, or at the first light of dawn. In this way, the plants suffer minimally from the shock of transplanting, and benefit most from the watering in and the coolness of the air. By the following day, no matter how listless they may have been while you worked with them, most of your plants will have begun to recover. Believe it or not, there is also, for many gardeners, an ideal planting time of the month, just before full moon. Granted, some people are a little fanatical about it. I've never studied this aspect too closely, but I've certainly tried it, and there may well be validity to this belief in relation to the "pull" of the moon. I mention it here because, although there's nothing mystical about gardening as such, there certainly is about gardeners. Therefore, you may want to try a "waxing moon/waning moon" experiment of your own, to see how it works.

· FLOWERS AND SEEDLINGS ·
(ANNUALS, PERENNIALS)

As I say elsewhere, plants are generally most resilient. They forgive a *little* neglect, a *little* abuse, but obviously, if you were to play touch football with them, they'd probably resent it. I mention this only because I've found that most beginning gardeners are almost reverential in handling young plants, for fear of damaging them, and so do not plant them properly.

The very first thing to do with your flowers is to make sure they all have name tabs. Next, group them according to whether they'll live in the sunny or the shady bed you prepared for them. Now group them according to their eventual height. This information is usually included on the tabs. If not, you should find it on the plant list you made when you designed the bed. My own next step is to set the potted plants *on* the bed, in attractive groupings, to approximate the eventual undulations, colors, textures, patterns. The tall plants are in the background, the shorter ones toward the front. Start with the potted flowers; these are usually perennials or biennials. Annuals are more often in flats, six or more seedlings per flat. (Some clumps of perennials, such as creeping phlox or yellow alyssum, come in flats but consist of only one plant.) Since most identifying tabs also indicate how far apart the plants of a particular kind should be set, place the individual pots accordingly. If for any reason you do not have this information on spacing or can't find it, then a fairly adequate rule of thumb is a 12-inch distance apart.

Personally, I do not like rows of anything, unless it's meant to be a border, hedge, or edging; even then, I try to break it up by having different heights or textures. So generally, I would suggest that you avoid lining up your plants in a row, like little soldiers. This sort of planting quickly becomes boring. An exception to this would be if you had a passion for, say, delphiniums or snapdragons and you wanted only a wide border of either, all massed together; the same would apply if yours were to be a formal garden design of, say, intertwining red, pink, and white begonias surrounded by an edging of boxwood. On the whole, though, I believe a garden looks more natural if the flowers appear in "spontaneous" groupings, even if that so-called spontaneity is painstakingly achieved.

To make different varieties produce a satisfactory show, groups of three work well. For smaller plants, you might do better with groups of five. This is also true if yours is a very large bed. Incidentally, odd numbers minimize symmetry, on the principle that nature itself never bothers about symmetry. Of course, if you're planning to have one hundred Shasta daisies, don't waste your time counting out ninety-nine. By then, it won't matter any more.

In any case, it's important to create a sense of flow and continuity by repeating colors and groupings, and complementing others, throughout the bed. At the same time, some plants are *so* showy that only one of them here and there acts like a whole clump. Such a plant might be *Achillea* "Coronation Gold"; another is *Asclepias tuberosa,* the Butterfly Weed. It's really essential that, in placing the pots, you keep in mind the colors of each plant, so that you don't end up with all the blues at one end, all the pinks somewhere else.

As the tabs also usually provide information about blooming times, adjust your groupings so that you'll have a spread of colors over the entire bed all through the summer months, instead of a spring patch here and an autumn patch there. Do take your time over this arrangement of the pots. It may spare you later irritation or the need to transplant. Once you're satisfied with your layout, the planting itself will be fairly straightforward.

During all this, don't forget about the annuals in the seedling flats. Leave space for the ultimately taller ones. The same applies if you intend to try your hand at raising some annuals from seed.

Only after all the potted plants are arranged the way you'd like them is it a good idea to tackle the seedling flats for this practice run. Say you bought six flats, two each of three different kinds of flowers. In order to get an idea of how their colors and textures will augment your bed, you'll have to remove them from the flats and separate them from their mates.

To dislodge the seedlings, lace your fingers among their stems, then tip the flat onto the palm of that hand. If you can't simply pull off the container—sometimes the roots have already grown through its slits or holes—then give the container a sharp tap or two. That usually frees the plants. If not, you may have to

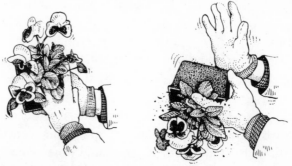

If sharp tap does not dislodge seedlings from container, then cut them free.

cut the container free. Inevitably, a few of the young roots will break. Don't worry. Once freed, turn the seedlings right side up and separate them with your thumbs—gently, steadily. Again, some roots will break. Again, don't worry. I find separation easiest if I divide the root mass into halves and quarters. I also know at least one gardener who performs this surgery with the help of a sharp knife. Just remember, because these plants have been born and raised in their flats, they've outgrown their playpen. They've used up most of the nutrients and moisture in the soil, and their roots have become thickly enmeshed. As a result, the moment they are pried apart and exposed to sun and air, they'll begin to dry and wilt. That means that they have to be planted as soon as possible.

When all the plants are in place, stand back a moment and try to imagine them fully grown. Are their eventual heights, colors, textures evenly and attractively distributed? Did you leave enough space between groupings, so that they'll be defined at maturity and not have to suffer an identity crisis by crawling into each other's roots? If you're reasonably sure that the answer is yes, then it's time to arm yourself with trowel and shovel. Use the former for seedlings and small potted plants, the latter for anything in pots whose tops have a larger than 6-inch diameter.

Seedlings come first. No matter how tall or strong these may look, I like to plant them to a depth of at least half their stems. I know you're thinking, By then, there'll be nothing left to show. It'll be next winter before they ever make it. But try to see it from the seedlings' viewpoint. Since seedhood, they've lived in the same flat, raised under ideal conditions of temperature and moisture at the nursery. Now suddenly they're uprooted and separated from their companions, at a tender stage in their lives. Therefore, if they are planted deeply, the earth will keep them warm and snug, they'll be assured of having wet feet, they won't have to fight against alternating daytime heat and nighttime coolness, and they'll recover more rapidly from the mauling they've inevitably suffered during the transplanting. As I've indicated earlier, plants are like people: the less they have to struggle for the essentials of life, the more they can thrive.

Once you've dug the hole to roughly twice the diameter of the root ball and to the appropriate depth—in the case of potted flowers, the depth should be about the same as the pot's—gently loosen the roots and spread them around the bottom of the hole. Add soil evenly around the base and tamp it down, until the plant is supported upright. Add more soil, tamping it, until the hole is filled. There should always be a saucer-like indentation in the soil immediately around the plant. When you water the plant in, the "saucer" will both hold the water and direct it to the roots, instead of letting it run all over the neighborhood (see Chapter 10).

In the case of seedlings, should your planting of these be interrupted for more than, say, an hour, you should find some means of keeping their roots from drying out. You could set them in water or cover them with a wet cloth—*never* plastic, as the buildup of heat will roast them—or completely cover the roots with soil. Remember, the longer a seedling's roots are exposed, the greater is the shock and the longer it will take the plant to recover. Left too long, some seedlings never do recover.

For larger, more fully developed flowers, follow exactly the same procedure, except that these plants need not be buried as deeply as seedlings. However, as their roots are likely to be more densely packed, it's essential that you give care to loosen and spread them at planting. Sometimes it happens that a few roots are wrapped several times around the top of the rootball. They'll be more difficult to unwrap, but please take the time; your plants will shortly reward you. When the roots appear like this, a plant is described as being "pot-bound." It just means that it has outgrown its vessel.

· VINES ·

Although the planting of vines does not differ from flowering plants, clearly they'll require some means of support to climb on. Much as I love the look, I do not like any plant to climb up on the walls of my home—for several reasons. Yes, I realize how charming a cottage can look covered in ivy, rambling roses, clematis, or wisteria. It *is* a temptation, I know, and a part of me longs for that appearance of warmth and coziness.

However, consider the following: vines cling and attach themselves to any surface that promises a firm hold. This means they'll dig into the siding of a house, or into the mortar between the bricks. As for stucco, that makes them feel right at home. Even if, by chance, you don't mind all that, when the vines reach the eaves, they'll also become repositories for all kinds of wildlife—insects, squirrels, and chipmunks—not to mention desirable real estate for bird's nests. And if even that doesn't cause you to have second thoughts, there's the matter of what to do once the house needs to be painted. Mind you, in defense of house climbers, it may be said that it takes them a few years to reach their peak of destructiveness; screen windows will keep undesired guests from creeping or leaping inside; it's a delight to watch nesting birds up close; and the house is unlikely to be painted too often.

Friends of mine constructed a wide lattice up one side of their house and trained a vine on this by stapling the tendrils to the outside of the lattice. When the time came, a few years later, to paint the house, they removed the staples and carefully lowered the vine. When the painting was finished, they again "hung" their vine.

Personally, I still would rather train climbing plants on a trellis or a sturdy fence—away from the house. But it's an entirely personal matter.

· SHRUBS AND TREES ·

These are sometimes more difficult to remove from their containers, if for no other reason than that they're larger, heavier, and more unwieldly than flowers. If a few sharp raps with the heel of your hand around the sides and base of the container don't dislodge the plant, you'll have to cut it free. Although it does make trees and shrubs that much heavier, I like to water them thoroughly about an hour or two before planting time, as this helps to hold the soil around the root ball. Left dry, a good deal of soil might spill on the lawn during the unpotting.

As is true of all plants, the nursery which raised your shrubs and trees will have them in a medium (soil mixture) best suited to each variety. Therefore, it's always best to mix as much as possible of the plants' familiar medium with your own soil at planting. If you have children, you already know that one of the most important items to be taken along on any trip is a favorite toy. That toy represents an anchor, a link to familiar home ground. With plants it's literally a bit of home ground they like to take along when they move.

Dig the hole to at least double the diameter of the root ball, and 2 or 3 inches deeper. Be sure that the sides of the hole are straight up and down. Make two piles as you dig—one for the pieces of sod and the grassy clumps and one for just soil. As you'll shortly need the sod, shake out all the loose soil and stack the pieces *upside down,* grass roots up.

To gauge the proper depth, I keep an old broom handle close by, to act as a level (a cane or narrow board will do). When you think the hole is deep enough, set the root ball in it and loosen the roots. You'll undoubtedly have to dig your fingertips into the

An old broom handle can help ascertain the proper depth of hole for planting a tree.

base of the root ball to untangle the mass. This isn't always easy to do, and your nails will get dirty, but believe me, the effort is worth it. The freer the roots, the sooner they can establish themselves in your garden. As I usually work alone, I've found it practical to lean the plant against one shoulder, with my arms in a kind of loose embrace around it, while I work on the roots. The plant's soil will fall directly into the hole. Mix it with a little of your own soil, add some compost, and shape the mixture into a low mound.

With your plant standing centered on the mound, spread the roots over the downward slopes. Hold the plant upright with one hand, and with the other evenly cover the roots with a layer of sod, in much the same way you would arrange mosaic tiles.

Once decomposed, the sod is transformed into valuable humus. Now at last you may get off your knees. Still holding the plant upright, firmly tamp down the sod with your feet. The plant should be able to stand alone, provided you don't bump into it. Next, lay your level across the hole, against the plant stem, and step back a little. What this exercise shows you is whether the "soil line," or the "bud union" on your plant will be properly bedded. The soil line is the point at which the shrub or tree emerges from the soil in the pot—a dark brown below, lighter above. That's the line to which you must plant it in your garden.

And what is this thing called "bud union"? On some trees and shrubs you'll notice a knob or bulge above the roots. Such a bulge indicates a graft. It can be easily recognized in hybrid roses, for example. A short, thick stump emerges from the roots. From the side of the stump, near its top, appear two or three branches. This is where a hybrid variety has been "budded" (grafted) to a basic rootstock. ("Rootstock" describes a plant's root system and a small part of the stem.) The resulting bud union is essential to the healthy development and growth of the hybrid. In the planting it should, therefore, remain *above* the soil level. If a bud union is planted below the soil level, the original rootstock will reassert itself; the hybrid will fail to develop. Instead, "suckers" will appear and rapidly outgrow the rest of the plant.

Suckers are shoots that appear from the base of a shrub or tree, either at ground level, below the bud union, or from below ground. In the case of trees, these shoots should *always* be removed. The same applies to *grafted* (hybridized) shrubs, such as lilacs, roses, rhododendrons, and viburnums. The common name "suckers" probably derives from the fact that they drain off a plant's energy, weakening the new hybrid stock, so that the original stock comes to dominate. The best way to remove this unwanted growth is to trace it to its source and either to twist it or to cut it off at that point. *Never* cut below-ground suckers above the ground. All *that* accomplishes is to encourage their growth.

Of course, as you might guess, there are also the good-guy

suckers. Known as "true" suckers, these are among the easiest sources for increasing many of your favorite shrubs. But we'll get to that later (see Chapter 14).

Back to planting. If the broom handle test shows that your plant is set at the proper depth, and the sod on the roots is sufficiently tamped down to hold the plant upright, unsupported, it's time to pour the first of three buckets of water into the hole. Do this *slowly;* a gush of water will quickly topple the plant. Depending on the density of your soil, the water may disappear slowly or quickly. In either case, I suggest you watch closely. As the water settles under and around the roots, you will more than likely notice a number of bubbles on top of the water. Take careful note of where these are, as they indicate air pockets. When the water's completely soaked in, be sure to add and tamp more soil around the roots where the bubbles appeared. It's best to do this by hand, not with a shovel. Once again you find yourself on your knees. I promise you, gardening provides a wonderful physical workout—among its other virtues!

If you think you've eliminated the air pocket(s), add more soil, spreading it evenly all around, until the hole is two-thirds full. Make sure the plant remains upright. Holding the top of the plant, tamp the soil firmly with your feet until you've pressed down the entire surface. Because the soil underneath is wet and squishy, it will "give" a little under your tread. That's why holding the plant while you tamp will help to keep it vertical. Now, at a distance of a few yards, walk slowly all around it, to make sure the plant stands erect from all angles. If it does, pour water bucket number two into the hole. A few tiny bubbles may appear around the outer edge. These you need not worry about, but if they're in the center, you'd better tamp some more. Add a little more water, so that you can be sure the bubbles are gone. At that point, you may fill the rest of the hole. Tamp the soil one last time. As you will see, this creates a basin all around the plant, and that's how it should be, so that water will seep straight to the roots. Now empty the third bucket of water into the basin. When that's sunk in, cover the basin with mulch (see Chapters 10 and 11).

Properly planting trees and shrubs may take as long as three or four hours *each,* certainly at the beginning, depending on their size, on digging conditions, and on whether or not you were able to persuade a kind soul to lend you a hand. Please do remember, however, never to rush plantings; those underground air pockets could invite disease and harmful beasties to attack the plants' roots.

A MOST IMPORTANT ADJUNCT to planting is to mark all plants with appropriate tabs, as it will be a while before you can memorize all their names—or locations. Mark even the annuals. Although most of these won't return next spring, except possibly where the wind carried their seeds (in which case they're called "hardy annuals"), you'll need to know where to plant next year's crop. Tabs also help when you're weeding, so that you're less likely to pull a good plant.

If your house has no rain gutters, there is bound to be a "drip line" directly below the eaves. This is easily recognized by the fact that all the soil's been washed away, in a line, exposing pebbles. Never set your plants directly under such a drip line, as they could be seriously damaged or misshapen by the waterfalls from above.

It is quite possible that once your garden begins to grow, you will look out one day and decide that one or another plant does not please you in a particular spot. It may be too dominant or too obscured; its height or color may interrupt the overall flow; it really should be a few feet farther along and set back a bit. But, you think, it's too late now, you're stuck with it. Not at all.

Provided they're handled with reasonable care, plants are most forgiving of human whims and lapses in good judgment. All they require is a little respect. That means digging them up with minimal disturbance of the roots, and leaving their root ball intact. It also means making the new hole large enough to accommodate the root ball comfortably. In this kind of transplanting, you merely loosen the outer roots, then plant as described above. Be sure to water transplants thoroughly for two or three days (trees and shrubs for a week), to help them settle down. Mind you, I do not recommend playing musical chairs with your plants, uprooting them once a month, nor would I do any transplanting at peak blossom or fruiting time (see Chapter 15).

· VEGETABLES ·

In preparing a vegetable garden, it's important for you to bear in mind that tomatoes, squash, and cucumbers, for instance, have a much wider spread than the radishes, carrots, and lettuce, so you should prepare their beds to the appropriate widths.

Although it's easy to be carried away when you see the lush vegetables illustrated in catalogues and on seed packets, you'll do best to ease into vegetable gardening. Vegetables require considerably more regular attention than do flower beds, because you may expect to start harvesting in a matter of weeks. So that the veggies can do *their* best, you'll have to do *yours,* by keeping them free of weeds, loosening the soil around them, watering them during hot weather, or covering some of them up if there's an unexpectedly late spring frost. Believe me, however, it's all worth it. There is absolutely no food on earth which tastes as good as the food you pick from your own garden.

A sensible way to start is to make a list of your most wanted vegetables. Keep in mind, though, that you may adore broccoli but your family says "yuk." Or they may love carrots; you could live without them. So you may want only half a row of each. In any case, let's suppose you want string beans, lettuce, green squash (zucchini), tomatoes, green peppers, carrots, peas, and broccoli. I list these because they're among the easiest to raise. Divide this list according to which vegetables are available as plants (tomatoes, peppers, broccoli) and which must be raised from seed (peas, beans, squash, lettuce, carrots).

Plant your seeds when the weather is mild enough to do so. Guidelines for suitable temperatures, as well as for seed spacings, are printed on all seed packets. When these say "Plant after all danger of frost," in the Northeast that means after mid-May. However, it all depends on the kind of winter it's been. Sometimes all danger of frost may not be passed until early June; in other years, it has been early May. Vegetable seedlings can be planted once your local nurseries have them for sale—especially if you see trays of them displayed *outdoors.*

Although it would look neater to have your vegetables descend evenly, from the tallest to the shortest, in practical terms this isn't quite possible. That is because many vegetables, if they're planted right next to each other, actively inhibit each other's growth, while others are the best of friends. As among people, it's therefore best to keep enemies apart and friends together. In gardening, this is known as "companion planting." Here I will include only a few of the compatibility ratings. However, it's a subject well worth looking into, particularly as it can influence the harmful insect populations and diseases in your garden (see Chapter 13). An added bonus is that companion planting includes various aromatic kitchen herbs and showy flowers.

For the **peas,** which are vines and which should be planted as soon as the ground can be worked in early spring, you will need something they can climb on. This may be strong nylon netting or chicken-wire fencing firmly attached to several sturdy poles; or, for a more natural look, it may be dead tree branches pushed deeply into the ground and crisscrossed. Put peas at the northern end of the bed, as they'll reach maturity well before the other vegetables. Press the seeds a good 1 inch into the soil, 2 to 4 inches apart, and thoroughly tamp the soil so that they will not be washed away by rain; of equal importance, so that birds don't think you intend them to be the sole beneficiaries of this largesse. If you have wood ashes, spread them around the base of your peas, once they come up, to help control aphids (see Chapter 13). Peas are among the friendliest plants, although they do not like onions and garlic.

There are so many kinds of **beans** that only you can decide which you would like. My own favorite is one of the bush variety of green snap beans. All beans are good-natured, but the onion family seriously inhibits their growth. An occasional celery plant is all right, but definitely no fennel. On the other hand, beans are really happy near cucumbers, strawberries, and especially carrots. Bean seeds (kernels) must also be protected from thieving magpies and other feathered friends.

To keep destructive insects off your **squash** (or cucumbers), plant a few icicle radish seeds in the same hill with the squash and let the radish go to seed. Be sure to keep these squash hills 5 to 6 feet apart, and at least 2 to 3 feet away from neighboring rows on either side. Tobacco ash or other tobacco residue (no filters) added to the seed hills is another insect repellent. If you have no radish seeds and aren't a smoker, then plant nasturtiums close by.

The different squashes are very confusing, because there are so many of them, all under different names. Among the most popular ones are the so-called summer squashes (crookneck, Pattypan, zucchini, etc.) and winter squashes (acorn, butternut, Hubbard, etc.) Marrows fall into the latter group as well. And just to keep you on your toes, young zucchini, when these are served in fine restaurants, are often called "courgettes." Got that?

Onions are restored to favor when it comes to **lettuce.** Like Mutt & Jeff, onions and lettuce like to stay close to each other in order to give their best. Lettuce also goes well with radishes and carrots. To prolong your lettuce harvest, start your seeds in a cold frame (see *Seeds* below). In open ground, stagger seed sowings over several weeks in spring. Keep the sowings small, because lettuce grows quickly in cool weather with plenty of moisture. Once the weather turns hot, lettuce will soon "bolt"— go to seed—before you can eat it. An autumn sowing will provide a late harvest.

Carrot seed, like lettuce, is extremely tiny. As a result, it's often very tempting to compensate by planting it too thickly. But this will only mean later thinning, once the green tops come up. And *that* means that you'll lose quite a bit of your crop (carrots do not like to be transplanted). If you don't thin, you will end up with a lot of teeny-weeny gnarled and knotted dollhouse veggies. So it's best to sow carrots thinly. A decided advantage of carrots is that you may leave them in the garden through most winters, especially if there is a good snow cover; in any case, frost sweetens their flavor. Carrots may really be described as the boon companions of the vegetable garden; they get on with everybody. Only dill rouses a carrot's negative vibes—but then, nobody's perfect.

Among the seedling vegetables (actually this one counts as a fruit) **tomatoes** tend to be the most undecided. Neat and erect as seedlings, they soon begin to flop and sprawl on the ground if they're not supported. Y-shaped wire baskets and other supports are available for this purpose, but must be pressed deeply into the ground while the young tomatoes can still be trained into them. Once they outgrow the height of these baskets, they must be regularly pruned; even so, repeatedly in my garden, full-sized tomato plants, top-heavy with masses of fruit, have keeled over, yanking the baskets out of the ground. Since then, I let them have their way, giving them plenty of room to crawl on a thick bedding of mulch. However, I know several gardeners who train their tomatoes on sturdy poles, tying them at regular intervals. Whether they grow horizontally or vertically, tomatoes are gluttons for the nutrients in soil and need lots of compost. As long as this is available to them, unlike other vegetables tomatoes don't mind being planted in the same place year after year. To make sure that they always have a plentiful supply of compost, I add it to the soil at planting time, and also plant them so deep that only the top one or two pairs of leaves are exposed. I've found that this immeasurably increases the plants' strength and productivity. One thing is important to remember—tomatoes and the *Brassica* family (broccoli, cabbage, Brussels sprouts, cauliflower) have a feud even more unmitigating than that of Montagues and Capulets. Never plant them near each other.

Instead, plant your sweet **peppers** in the row beside tomatoes, as they will protect them against insects and disease. Peppers, too, benefit greatly from being set deep in the earth. Sweet as they are to the taste buds, peppers will give you a bumper crop if you provide them with sour soil. To do this, simply place half a dozen book matches and a large helping of compost into their hole at planting time. It's the sulphur in the matches which provides that special ingredient. Peppers do well if they're planted alternately in a double row, about one foot apart from each other.

Your **broccoli** plants (and the other *Brassica* family members) will positively rejoice if you put dill among them. Just as this wonderfully aromatic herb is repugnant to carrots, so it is pure elixir, the fountain of youth, health, and strength, to broccoli. This vegetable is particularly satisfying because, even after you've eaten the first bouquet of tight green florets, other bouquets continue to appear well into autumn. It is a hardy plant that may be left in the garden until after the first frost; in fact, broccoli's sister, Brussels sprouts, tastes best after a hard frost.

If you decide to plant vegetables other than those I've suggested, the distance between them, as a rule of thumb, should roughly equal the plants' height at maturity. Treat cucumbers the same as squash, and eggplants like peppers, except that eggplants actively benefit from growing near beans. Beets and kohlrabi may be planted alternately in the same row, one of them fruiting above ground, the other below. Both are on friendly terms with the *Brassica* family. Kale is another tasty vegetable, although it isn't grown nearly as often in the home garden as it deserves to be. Easy of care, rich in vitamins, and hardy well into most average winters, kale is as "friendly" a vegetable as you could wish for. Spinach, like lettuce, does best in early spring, and again in the autumn. Then there's Swiss chard, a delicious vegetable that doesn't mind a frost or a cover of snow. And, of course, corn, sweet, juicy corn, for a special treat. And numerous others.

· SEEDS ·

There are many advantages to raising plants from seed. Chief of these, for me, are the sheer pleasure, drama, and wonder of watching life emerge from seeds that are often no larger than specks of dust. Then, too, seeds are considerably cheaper to buy than plants. They'll also keep until next year if you don't have time or space for them right now (although a certain percentage of them will lose growing power). By being available sooner, seeds also let you extend the growing season by at least two months.

Some seeds prefer to be sown directly into the garden, after all danger of frost is past; some plants are unavailable at most nurseries and *must* be raised from seed; others *are* available as plants but can be grown from seed at home at a fraction of the cost. "Oh, but I don't have a greenhouse," you may say. As it happens, you don't need a greenhouse—only a greenhouse atmosphere, and that's easy to create. At this moment, I have three juicy green peppers ripening in my bathroom window. The plant emerged three years ago from among some geraniums in that pot. I can only think that a "live" pepper seed must have rested in the compost I'd added to the geraniums' soil. Within a few months of making its appearance, the pepper had bumped off the geraniums and taken possession of the pot. Simply because I was curious, I nurtured it throughout that first winter. In spring, I set the pot outdoors, to see what would happen. By this time, the plant was about two feet tall and equally wide. It bloomed and formed a few peppers, but these dropped off. Because it was a lovely plant, its leaves dark and shiny, I brought it back into the house the following winter. Sometime around that Christmas, I harvested three small peppers. Now I began to pay more attention. I fed and watered it more regularly, and during its second summer, this pepper plant became a major conversation piece: there were thirty-four peppers ripening on it! That was more than I've often had from an entire row. This is its third winter and it's still going strong. Why is it in the bathroom? Because that's the nearest to a summer atmosphere I can provide—as long as I take lots of showers, to create enough moisture.

This pepper, of course, was a seed I planted involuntarily; nevertheless, it proves the point about how easy it is to raise plants indoors. As long as you have windows or electrical outlets, or a handy carpenter in the family or among your friends, you will be able to create a suitable atmosphere. My own earliest attempts with seeds began with a plant-light stand which somebody gave me eons ago to cheer up a dark corner of my dining room. It consisted of two metal uprights that supported two neon "grow lights" attached to a narrow reflector, which shone down on a plastic tray. The whole unit fitted comfortably on a small table or stool. As I owned no seed flats at that time, I filled cardboard egg cartons with potting soil and planted my first seeds, keeping the soil moist and lowering the lights over the egg cartons, without switching them on, however. Covering the entire assembly with clear plastic, I placed it in that dark corner. Presto, instant greenhouse. And it worked. Before long, the first hints of minuscule green appeared, and nothing can convince me that my sense of exhilaration was any less than Sir Edmund Hillary's when he stood on top of Mount Everest. Then I turned on the grow lights.

From that moment on, virtually my entire home was converted into a series of "greenhouses." There were glass shelves (glass to let the light through) across a large window, the shelves covered with an assortment of earth-and-seed-filled containers, and a huge sheet of clear plastic over the whole, instead of curtains. Individual containers became mini-greenhouses inside plastic bags blown full of air, tied and taped shut, and lined up on all windowsills. Nothing and nowhere was safe. As soon as green began to sprout, I turned on the lights directly over the containers in dark corners and moved the minis into the sunny places. I made sure that the temperature in the rooms did not drop below 50° F. at any time, and when the soil began to dry out, I misted it from a discarded plastic pump bottle that had been thoroughly cleaned. As the window seedlings began to lean toward the sun, I turned the containers. For the seedlings on the plant stand, I raised the lights only enough so that the tips of the seedlings did not touch them. With the lights too low, the seedlings might get burned; with the lights too high, the seedlings would become too straggly from reaching for the light.

Of course, there were some failures. Some seeds never sprouted at all; others were aborted when the room temperature fluctuated; still others succumbed to too much, or not enough, moisture inside their plastic bubbles. I learned from the failures and was spurred on by the successes. I still do not have a greenhouse, and I still raise many of my plants from seed. The means and methods have become a little more sophisticated, but not very much, because I still do it mostly for the pure thrill of advancing spring to late February. One gardening friend raises all his seeds on an easel-like structure of his own invention, which works so well that the increase in "easels" around the house in late winter sometimes appears to threaten the continued health of his wife and horse-sized puppies. Another gardening friend regularly commandeers the entire south-facing enclosed porch and all the downstairs windows, tables, chairs, and stools for *his* late-winter indoor nursery. Even as we shiver with cold and watch the snow pile up outside, all we talk about is how soon we can start planting our seeds. And, of course, there *is* a way for us early birds.

It's called a cold frame. Strictly speaking, cold frames are just that—cold, unheated, except by the sun. A cold frame is basically nothing more than an unheated bottomless box of perhaps 3 feet by 6 feet, with a removable glass top called a sash. The back of the box, set along the south wall of your choice and directly on the ground, should be higher than the front. Hinged to the back

Large or small, with one sash (shown)
or more, cold frames should
always face south.

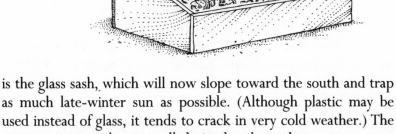

is the glass sash, which will now slope toward the south and trap as much late-winter sun as possible. (Although plastic may be used instead of glass, it tends to crack in very cold weather.) The entire unit must be on well-drained soil, so that water cannot collect under it. Into the frame place a layer of at least 6 inches of friable, compost-enriched soil mixed with *well-rotted* manure.

And that's all there is to it, except for the thermometer you should keep in the cold frame.

Although various types of frames are available on the market, large and small, heated and unheated, glass and plastic, expensive and less expensive, a cold frame is really very easy to construct at home. It can literally be made up of odds and ends you might have considered donating to the sanitation department. I can't say it often enough: gardeners are hoarders.

Some pieces of board, left over from building the bookshelves, will do for a start. Perhaps you have an old window or a glass door you replaced. You probably even have a couple of hinges lying around, because they were the wrong size for the cabinet door you rehung and you forgot to return them for a refund. You see, you didn't know you had a cold frame scattered all over the house! And you're bound to have southern exposure some-where, well protected from winds, by the house, garage, barn, shed, fence, or hedge. So why not give it a try?

Long before you can do most other outdoor sowing, you can start your lettuce, radishes, onions, and spinach in the frame. But you do have to be vigilant. Although the days may be sunny and mild, the nights might yet become bitter cold. It's best not to sow anything until daytime temperatures are at 32° F. or above. Inevitably—in my region, at least—there will still be some night-time frosts. To protect your seeds and seedlings against these, keep a blanket or two nearby, to cover the cold frame. The manure in the frame's bedding will help to keep the soil warm. Next day, when the sun shines, the temperature inside the cold frame may climb to 90° F. or more. If it does—in fact, whenever it goes above 80° F.—raise the sash about an inch or two so that air can circulate inside. Just be sure to remember to close the sash again in the evening. As the plants get stronger and daytime temperatures rise, you can open the sash more and more, eventually altogether, closing it only at night.

If you've raised some vegetable seeds in the house, the cold frame is also good for "hardening off" the seedlings once daytime temperatures are above 32° F. Simply set the seedling flats of such veggies as broccoli, tomatoes, and peppers into the soil of the frame. "Hardening off" denotes a necessary transition between indoor and outdoor life. In fact, all seedlings you raise indoors should be allowed to harden off before going into the garden. With most of them, this is simply a matter of setting them outdoors during the day, at first sheltered from direct sun, and returning them indoors at night. Do this for about a week, in roughly two-hour increments of partial sunlight per day, before planting the seedlings outdoors. Without a hardening-off period, the dramatic change of temperatures and environmental conditions will shock the plants to death.

Most seeds to be planted directly into your garden should wait until all danger of frost is past. This becomes one of the most frustrating, tantalizing periods for gardeners every year, especially when the daytime temperature rises to the 50s and 60s. The buds swell on shrubs and trees, the grass begins to turn green in patches, and here you are, soaking up the spring warmth, supposed to *wait*. If I haven't said this before, gardening consists largely of what I call the four W's—weeding, watering, watching, and waiting; not always in that order.

When it is finally time to plant seeds, be sure to sow them thinly, no matter how tiny they are, as I've already mentioned. If you bought seeds from one of the larger reputable concerns, and the packets are stamped with PACKED FOR 19— (the current year), then most of them will sprout. Crowding the seeds will simply prevent them from developing into the best possible plants. If you plant flower seeds you may sow many of them directly into the areas you planned for them in the flower bed, or into a separate location from which they can later be transplanted. Please do remember, though, that 99 percent of the time, each little seed will become a full-sized plant.

If you don't remember that, you will have to undergo the painful task of thinning. Even if you weren't carried away in the sowing, the thinning process will be necessary, only less so. It means removing the weaklings in the crowd in order to let the strongest plants thrive. If some of the weaklings look strong enough to survive on their own, and you need or want more of that particular plant, then simply transplant them. Transplanting should not be undertaken until the seedling has at least two pairs of leaves. The method of thinning is to pinch, or cut off, the tops of the doomed seedlings; pulling them out of the ground would disturb the roots of their neighbors. In the case of vegetable bed plantings, an effective thinning method is to pull a rake *lightly* through the seedlings and to discard the unfortunates that stood in the path of the rake's teeth.

It may happen that in the spring following your first (or subsequent) crop, some unscheduled surprise vegetables turn up. These are most often tomatoes, squash, and cucumbers, and are the result of fallen, rotten, or forgotten fruit that dropped on the ground the previous year. Known often as "sports," these are best discarded. True, left undisturbed, they'll grow into full-sized plants, but they're rarely considerate enough to appear in next year's rows, nor can they be relied on to produce fruit.

Finally, be sure to mark all your seed plantings. One simple method is to tie the empty seed packet to a low stake at the end of each row. So that rain and sun don't obliterate all the useful information on the packets, cover them with a plastic sandwich bag.

R · E · C · A · P

1. Always allow plenty of time for planting; ideally, plant within twenty-four hours of purchases, as soon as unpotted; avoid planting in heat of day; never plant under roof drip line.

2. Plant nursery stock when available *locally;* if mail-order stock arrives too early for your area, hold packaged plants, except seedlings, in *cool* ventilated location, out of sun—maximum two weeks.

3. Unpack mail-order seedlings; keep moist, cool, in good light, out of direct sun—maximium two weeks.

4. Dig holes to same depth and roughly double diameter of root ball, except seedlings.

5. Plant seedlings to depth of roughly half their stems.

6. Slit and/or untie all biodegradable containers at planting time; remove from root ball all plastic and other nonbiodegradable containers.

7. Loosen and evenly spread roots when planting.

8. Group annuals and perennials according to eventual height, spread, color; except with vegetables, groupings of threes and fives are preferable.

9. With trees, check proper planting depth with aid of broom handle or board.

10. Firmly tamp soil around all new plantings; be sure plants stand upright.

11. Thoroughly water all new plantings; eliminate air pockets.

12. Mark all plants with identifying tabs.

13. In vegetable bed try companion planting as preventive pest control.

14. For raising plants from seed, or hardening off seedlings, build simple cold frame; try indoor greenhouse atmospheres.

Watering Your Plants

T here is no denying that the subject of watering is a bit tricky. Oh, I know this sounds absurd. After all, what can be tricky about turning on a faucet? Right?

Well, yes—and no.

You see, so much in a happy garden depends on weather conditions; not only local, regional, or seasonal conditions, but also the conditions in any given week or month. I know I've said repeatedly that there are no hard-and-fast rules in gardening. And I know I've then proceeded to give you one set after another of guidelines for doing things. When it comes to watering, however, most guidelines become so vague, so noncommittal, that they resemble bureaucratic doublespeak. And for good reason: there is simply no way to state unequivocally how much watering a garden needs—or how often. By the same token, watering is the most vital of my four W's (remember them? The others are weeding, waiting, and watching), although no other gardening activity so stubbornly defies definition. All the same, I'll take a stab at it.

First of all, let's look at the extremes; these could occur almost anywhere. As an illustration, I will use the month of June. This year, June may go on record as the hottest, driest, sunniest June ever. Last year, it may have been the wettest, coldest, bleakest June in fifty years. Consequently, this year many young emerging crops will be burned by the drought; last year, the crops were washed away. Yet by the end of this summer, it is more than likely that the *average* rainfall for both summers will be shown as approximately the same. That becomes a statistic. But what about your plants? They know nothing about statistics. They need water *regularly*—enough water, especially early in the growing season, because that is when they do most of their developing. And for that, June is a crucial month.

Already I've set before you one of those vague terms that tend to appear in gardening instructions—"water regularly." Perhaps the best way for you to understand—*really* understand—what your plants suffer during such extreme weather conditions is to pretend you're a plant yourself.

Suppose you had to stand barefoot for an indefinite period, on hot sand at the beach, with the sun beating down on your bare head and body, without a drop to drink. It wouldn't be long before you'd succumb to sunburn and heat exhaustion. Or suppose you were made to stand barefoot in a puddle, for days and nights on end. Before long, your skin would wrinkle, you'd sneeze a lot, feel sick all over, and need a shot of brandy. Under both circumstances, if you were properly clothed and shod, and were offered a tent and a glass of water in the first situation, a warm blanket and a hot toddy in the second, such an experiment might not send you into ecstasies but you'd remain unscathed.

It's the same for plants. Both humus-enriched soil and mulch act as protective clothing for your plants at times of stress from the elements. Please understand, humus and mulch will not entirely prevent plant losses in extreme conditions—high winds, heat and cold—but mulch and improved soil will certainly minimize losses and make it possible for even affected plants to recover more easily.

In brief, *without* enriching components in your garden beds, even "enough" water can spell trouble. That is, light and sandy soils allow water to drain away too quickly; clayey soils do not allow water to drain quickly enough, thereby forcing plant roots to remain in subsurface "puddles." In times of drought, light sandy soils become dry and hot, leaving roots without access to water and nourishment. Clayey soils, when they dry, become like cracked pottery and choke the poor roots that venture forth in search of food and water.

Before I offer my own version of doublespeak about watering, I should perhaps explain *how* water benefits your plants. The important thing to understand is that no plant can survive without moisture in some form—be it running, spuming, rain, ground, or tap water; mist, condensation, tropical steam, or melted snow. Some plants can't get enough water—they're usually water plants; some hoard the stuff, as does the teasel (*Dipsacus fullonum*), for example; still others prefer to drink sparingly. For all of them, however, water is not only a nutrient in itself but also nature's means of conveying other nutrients from the soil to the roots of each plant.

That brings us to a plant's major life-support system. You may think that a root is a root is a root. But no. You see, even plants have a kind of hierarchical structure. Therefore, if you regard the plant you bought, the aboveground visible part, as a botanical chairman of the board, the larger roots—the ones you so carefully loosened and spread out at planting time—serve as corporate management. It is their primary function to see to it that the company is securely anchored in the ground, and that they (the roots) properly transmit all necessary support to the chairperson. As long as that figurehead is satisfied, then he/she/it can win the continuing admiration and goodwill of you, the chief benefactor. Now, clearly management cannot be expected to do the menial work, can it? Consequently, all plant roots are endowed with a field staff of countless root hairs. These are the often barely visible minions, tiny knobs and nodes located along the length of the larger roots, which do all the hard work. Their entire existence revolves around gathering food. In this task they are aided by a kind of peripatetic field supervisor called water. Water not only offers its own nutritive elements to the food gatherers but also conveys to them the soil's food constituents, in solution. All of these the root hairs absorb and deliver posthaste to their bosses, the larger roots. These, in turn, as befits any self-respecting corporate management, make their presentations up the ladder, to the chairperson. At this stage, that admired individual is prepared to sing the company's praises to the public. Looking healthy and groomed, the figurehead assumes its role in the cycle by exuding an air of well-being—moisture transpired through the surface of its green tissues, the leaves and stems. Inevitably, this stimulates the root hairs to continue working hard, in order to keep a constant supply of food entering the corporate body—the plant.

It stands to reason, however, that if there's a prolonged drought the poor little minions can't do their job. As a result, management shrinks quietly into itself, idle; and before long, the chairperson also feels the pinch. Left holding the fort alone, deprived of vital supplies, with production at a complete standstill, sooner or later the chairperson has to face the truth. Without a revitalization program, all is lost. And so, there's only one recourse—to appeal to you for help, by developing curled-up, yellowed leaves and drooping flower heads. With luck, you'll notice the urgency of the situation and provide a generous infusion of new resources—water.

Of course, obverse conditions, when there is prolonged, incessant, or heavy rain, cause plant cells to become so distended that the plant eventually "drowns." That is, unless the plant stands in well-drained soil. On the whole, drowning is more often a problem faced by well-intentioned indoor gardeners who overwater.

In addition to the moisture provided by rainfall, dew, and your watering can, there is also another source, one that few of us ever think about. Somewhere under all of us there is a water table of permanent groundwater. You're not likely to find it when you do your planting, nor even when you dig for the foundations of your house. But it's there. Moisture rises constantly from this source, transmitted by each individual soil particle, around each of which it forms a film. On its way up, this moisture either serves the needs of plants, helping to keep full employment among the root-hair labor force, or else it evaporates. Clearly, if your soil is rich in humus content, a great deal of this moisture is conserved, because the heat and drying effect of sun, air, and wind can't penetrate the surface too readily to cause evaporation. If, in addition, there are regular rainfalls, it is conceivable that your perennial beds need no particular attention from you, as regards watering.

On the other hand, if you thought you could get away without enriching or, at least, mulching the beds, then a heavy drought will likely do your plants in—the soil will heat up and aid the above-ground heat in the evaporation process of the rising groundwater moisture.

It all comes down to moderation. Much as *we* may complain about the debilitating effects of high humidity, most average garden plants thrive on it; it's the heat (or cold) that gets many of them. If most plants had their druthers, they would choose frequent *moderate* rainfalls, alternating with *moderately* hot, sunny, or *moderately* cold weather. Such temperate conditions are a major reason why we admire the lush gardens of England so much. Those same endlessly overcast skies, "summer" days at 68°–72° F., and frequent, albeit largely gentle, showers, can drive *us* around the bend (especially if we're on a hard-earned, two-week vacation), but the plants are in seventh heaven. Such a moisture-laden atmosphere enables them to do their growing without having to expend too much energy on foraging for nourishment. Therefore, the next best thing that we can do is to work toward creating as nearly similar conditions, or at least compensating, to some degree, for the conditions we're stuck with. And that is where enriched soil and mulch come in.

Now that you have a general understanding of how water benefits your plants, it's almost time to turn on the tap. First, however, let's deal with the meaning of "water regularly." You've undoubtedly read it on seed packets, in gardening books, even catalogues. But what does it mean? I always think it's a little like telling a small child to *wash* regularly. My son, in his early years, used to consider it more than ample ablution to splash a little water on his nose once a week—*if* I reminded him. By contrast, a little girl I used to know was positively obsessive about washing her hands all day long. (Incidentally, this is not intended to provoke a gender war.) In their own terms, both these children washed regularly. The amount and frequency satisfied *their* personal needs. And so it is with plants.

As I've said, the subject of watering is tricky. It literally becomes a matter of feel, of trial and error, of close observation and practice. Only *you* can know when *your* plants need watering. Even your next-door neighbor can't be much help to you. His or her soil may have been worked, enriched, and mulched for the past twenty years, or simply be a different composition from yours; there may be more/less shade, larger/smaller/different types of plants, etc. Any number of factors. There are, of course, some general guidelines.

First of all, whether you use a watering can or a sprinkler system, watering your garden in the early-morning hours is generally preferable to doing so in the evening, so that the foliage can dry off in the course of the day. This is especially important in cool, moist climates, or in spring, when nighttime temperatures can drop sharply. If they are watered in the evening in these circumstances, your plants will remain wet overnight, and this in turn could invite fungal and bacterial attacks. On the other hand, in areas like mine, where midsummer heat varies little between day and night, I prefer to water my plants in the evening, so that they can sip leisurely and still dry off. The only time it's never wise to water is during the heat of the day, when the sun beats down and your plants are forced into a race against evaporation. Of course, if you live in an arid region, you may prefer to let a soaker system do the watering for you. Placed on or under the surface of your garden beds, winding among your plants, or laid between rows, the perforated hoses of such a system slowly, steadily leak water directly to the roots, without wetting the plants' foliage.

Following are some other considerations about judging the right time to water the garden. If it's been raining steadily for a week, your garden has been evenly saturated and will not require watering for a few days. A thunder shower that may leave your driveway flooded and your flowers flattened out may not, in fact, have achieved more than to wet the top half inch of your soil— if that. A gentle drizzle, especially if it follows a dry spell, will barely moisten the surface of your soil. And one of those mischievous cloudbursts, even though it scatters your picnic party to the nearest shelter, rarely does more than dampen your spirits.

Other points to bear in mind, when you ponder whether or not to activate your bucket brigade, include the following: If the atmosphere is dry, sunny, and windy, your plants will dry out and need watering sooner than when the atmosphere is equally rainless but overcast and moist. Even *with* sufficient rain, some of your plants will wilt from the sheer shock of a sudden burst of steamy hot sunshine following an overcast period. In such a case, you can restore the plants' sense of equilibrium by gently spraying their leaves with water. And, of course, you already know what happens to plants whose roots can no longer provide the necesssary water supplies from the soil—in which case, definitely summon the rescue squad—just as you know how despondent your plants become if they're forced to stand around too long with wet feet. (I promise not even to hint at mulch again in this chapter!) Because plants do their most energetic growing early in the season, that's when regular watering is of utmost importance. Past the peak of summer, watering becomes less crucial, except if there is an unusually long dry period. In that instance, tender annuals, such as impatiens and nasturtiums, for example, and vegetables like beans will continue to be thirsty, and your perennials certainly won't reject a little quaff.

Of course, it's nice if a rainfall now and then does your watering work for you. And it *can* happen. Needless to say, I've done the same thing as you probably do, which is to hope for such a reprieve from above. Alas, it's rare—and you should *never* rely on it.

To learn what "water regularly" means for *your* garden, here is a test that's never failed me. It tells me both when the garden needs water and also how much. Either with my finger, or with a trowel or a twig, I dig into the soil. If this is moist from the top down, I can relax. If the soil is dry to about 1½ inches, I apply a thorough watering, either with the watering can, around each plant, or else with a steady, medium-strength spray from the hand-held spray-gun nozzle or sprinkler, until I'm confident that the soil is thoroughly moistened again. And if the soil is dry to below 1½ inches, watering assumes top priority over all other tasks I might have set myself that day.

The finger or trowel test may be primitive, but it does provide you with a personalized gauge of when *your* garden needs water. And to this day, I do it quite routinely during warm, dry weather. The objective is to ensure that the garden remains as evenly moist, *but not saturated,* as possible. The less your plants are forced to alternate between drowning in a deluge and gasping for air in desert-like aridity, the better they can give you the joy and beauty for which you bought them in the first place.

And now, lastly, although other gardening books avoid doing so—and for good reason, as I've explained—I will tremblingly crawl out on a limb and suggest some specific amounts of water to apply at planting time. Notwithstanding fools rushing in where angels fear to tread, this will at least give you an idea of how to assess the need for subsequent waterings. Even so, I hasten to add a caveat here: The amounts and frequencies of watering I suggest below can at best be regarded as only generalized esti-mates; so much depends on *your* soil's composition, *your* climate, and *your* weather conditions. Only you can know these, and so the entire business of watering comes down to feel. There! I hope this will prevent a blizzard of blasphemies being cast in my direction. So now turn on the tap.

As I already mentioned in Chapter 9—and it's vital enough to bear repetition here—the younger new plants are, the less they should be made to wait before being bedded in your garden. Such transplanting from containers is in itself stressful. If, in addition to that, young plants are also expected immediately to search for food and water, as well as to adapt to their new neighborhood, they're likely to despair. Therefore, at planting time be sure to water each bedded plant as you go along.

Suppose your seedling is a marigold, or zinnia, or snapdragon (all of them annuals in this instance), and suppose it stands about 7 inches tall. By the time you've planted it, perhaps 4 or 5 inches are showing above the ground. Into the saucer-like indentation you left in the soil around the base, you should now pour about one pint of water, pouring it slowly and evenly all around. To give the seedling a good start in life, ideally you'll repeat this watering every day for a week.

If your new plant is, say, a young delphinium, peony, or lupine (all of them perennials in this instance), and it stands about one foot tall after planting, I'd suggest starting it off with perhaps two quarts of water, followed by a quart per day, also for a week.

For a young shrub, perhaps a rhododendron, or forsythia, or weigela, I generally apply at least one gallon of water at planting time, with another gallon, or slightly under, for about ten days.

In the case of a young tree, some five feet tall after planting, or a full-sized shrub, perhaps four feet tall, I wouldn't consider using less than about five gallons at planting time. I follow this with at least two to four gallons daily, for about ten days.

For newly planted trees that are taller than that, I estimate roughly one additional gallon per two feet above the five-foot height at planting time, with approximately four to six gallons applied daily thereafter, for two to three weeks, depending on how hot and dry the weather conditions are.

During each "watering-in" period, I use only a bucket or watering can, *never* a hose, because this ensures that the plant receives the proper amount of water at the roots. It is essential, however, to pour the water *slowly,* in a steady stream, all around the base. The objective is to saturate the soil, as near as possible, in and around the immediate vicinity of the root-ball area. This allows your plants, large and small, to obtain optimal benefit for minimal work in the food-gathering business, until they're established. If the water stream is too forceful, and all in one location, it will create a hole in the soil, which could damage or expose the roots, cause the plant to tilt, or become an open invitation to undesirables.

Obviously, if it should rain heavily for several days during the initial watering period, you may skip the task for the duration—provided the rain is of the truly saturating kind! If it isn't, you'll have to gnash your teeth and keep at it.

At the end of the initial watering period, you'll notice that your plants show definite signs of well-being and growth. This is particularly evident among the garden flowers and vegetables. Generally speaking, from then on it's up to you to keep an eye on the weather and on your soil. If a whole week goes by without rainfall, but with fairly cool temperatures, there's no great danger that your annuals or perennials will die. If, on the other hand, the temperature leaps from 57° F. one day to 94° F. the next, then I'd recommend you water your young plants at least every other day. In any case, I personally believe in applying periodic waterings to all newly planted shrubs and trees throughout their first growing season in my garden.

Finally, it does happen—quite often, in fact, where I live—that there is a sudden heat wave during the "settling-in" period. In such circumstances, I *gently* spray the leaves of shrubs and trees in the early morning, giving them a hosing down. This not only helps them withstand the shock of the temperature change but also helps to regulate their transpiration process, by providing a sort of localized temperate environment. Of course, it also washes dust off the leaves and acts as a refresher—not unlike a dip in the pool for thee and me.

R · E · C · A · P

1. Study your local, seasonal weather conditions.

2. Be sure soil is humus-rich, mulched, water-retentive.

3. Discover what "water regularly" means in *your* garden; test soil for moisture at least twice weekly.

4. Water new plantings daily for at least one week (except in heavy, steady rain).

5. Water new perennial plantings frequently during first season.

6. Annuals require more frequent watering than herbaceous perennials.

7. During prolonged drought, gently spray foliage to help regulate transpiration.

Mulching

Your flowers, trees, and shrubs are now planted—the vegetables, too. All of them are thoroughly watered in. You have lovingly raked away your footprints. The plants look wonderful—surprisingly small, but wonderful. Because you still feel a bit foolish saying it aloud, you gaze at the perfection of your handiwork and *think* something like, Okay, I've done *my* bit, so now it's *your* turn—grow! With one more loving glance, you turn away, ready for a hot shower and a cold martini.

But wait. There's just one more step, one more thing to do for your plantings. It is called mulching. You grimace. "And what exactly," you may well ask a little irritably, as you stretch your aching back, "is mulching? And why do I have to do it?" They are familiar and all-too-understandable mutters. Trust me, however; you will be rewarded, I assure you. "All I wanted was a garden," I hear you moan, "no fuss, no muss." I know, I know, but we may as well get on with it.

In its simplest terms, mulch is a substance that protects plant roots against cold, heat, and drought. It also holds surface moisture around your plants. Mulch provides a relative evenness of surface-soil temperature as well, and prevents the dangers of topsoil being washed away during a heavy rainstorm or, alternately, becoming intolerably hot and hard-baked during a prolonged dry spell. Mulch also guards plants against being damaged by an early, late, or sudden frost. Not least, mulch is a means of visually unifying all the components of a garden bed. In doing all this, mulch allows your plants to do *their* job of thriving, instead of merely struggling to survive.

Already I can hear the wheels spinning in your mind: you live in an area that doesn't get frost, or where excessive heat isn't a problem; nor are there droughts or torrential rains. That may be so, but please read on.

In the process of decomposition, the mulch materials you apply to your garden gradually enter the soil under the collective name of humus. In this capacity, they not only loosen and enrich the soil to varying degrees, and increase its water-holding capability; even more important, their decay into humus introduces countless microorganisms into the soil, which are of immeasurable value to your plants. Of course, most immediately appealing from your viewpoint is the fact that *an application of mulch materials retards the growth of weeds and makes them easier to remove!*

Depending on their availability and your finances, mulch materials may be any of the following: straw; properly composted cow, horse, chicken, or sheep manure; salt hay; grass cuttings, before there are seeds; dried leaves; ground-up corn husks; sawdust; bark nuggets; wood and bark shavings; pine needles; and newspaper (see Chapter 6).

All of these serve the purpose of holding surface moisture and temperature. Not all of them, however, are equally desirable, depending on your soil. A woody mulch, for example, will eventually add acidity to the soil. Therefore, if your soil tests indicated a pH value of below 6.0 (acid), and you have planted an assortment of flowers or, say, fruit trees and fruit bushes, I would suggest you opt for chopped corn husks, salt hay, manure, straw, or grass cuttings. On the other hand, if you have planted rhododendrons, roses, or azaleas in your acid soil, then a woody mulch is fine. If your soil tests indicated a pH value of 6.0 to 7.5 (normal), a woody mulch need not be a great worry to you, provided you spread a little lime over the bed at the time you "winterize" your garden (see Chapter 16). And if the pH value is between 7.5 and 8.5 (alkaline), then a woody mulch is downright wholesome (see Chapter 3).

For the purpose of this book, I will assume that your soil falls into the overall range of "normal." If your pH tests show a *slight* deviation in either direction of "normal," this need not be a major concern.

Although many people apply mulch materials, particularly bark nuggets, to their garden beds, they do so mostly in a thin cover coating, very often for the sole purpose of giving their beds a neat appearance. They do save money that way, but frankly, it's a waste of money, as well as of time and effort. Unquestionably, *some* mulch is better than none, but the best results come with a layer of *at least* 2 to 3 inches. I usually apply up to 5 inches. In any case, once the mulch settles down, has been rained on a few times, and has lived through a winter, the thickness will be reduced. Add to this the fact that the lowest layer will begin to decompose during the first summer, and what sounded like an awful lot of mulch very soon isn't. By the third summer, your garden will be ready for another helping. The more you spoil your garden with such humus treats, the more eagerly will the soil invite them in, absorb them, become more and more friable, easier for you to work. And in the process, you will have discovered the wonderful pleasure it is to weed these mulched areas, as compared with those you may have decided to leave to their own devices.

This happened to me not long ago, accidentally. Halfway through mulching a huge flower bed, I was interrupted. Through a series of circumstances, I was unable to continue the task for about two weeks. I had distributed the various types of plants throughout the entire bed, so that, for example, some delphiniums were now mulched, while others which I had bought and planted at the same time were still waiting. If ever I needed proof of the value of mulch, here it was—a classic case of "before and after." The plants in the mulched half had shot up, spread out, developed lush new growth, while the same types of plants in the unmulched half looked almost exactly as they had two weeks earlier. In that time, some heavy rains had been followed by scorching hot days, and the unmulched darlings had been forced first to use up all their energy to stop being washed away, and then to squeeze through the dusty, packed-down soil. By contrast, the mulched plants looked down serenely at their frazzled siblings. They had been protected against the impact of driving rains; the mulch had absorbed much of the water and was now doling it out evenly, despite the relentless sun.

So, although mulching is not absolutely essential, and indeed your garden can manage without it, why should you settle for "manage" when you can have "thrive"? I guarantee, once you have tried it, you will never again consider *not* mulching.

The long list of possible mulch materials notwithstanding, I have whittled my own preferred options down to the few listed below, for the reasons I give. Of course, this does not stop me from using others if they should be offered to me at a reasonable price, or altogether free of charge. That sort of thing does happen sometimes. Your own choice is strictly a personal matter. The important thing is that all of them work.

· BARK SHAVINGS ·

These are the castoffs at all lumberyards, where huge piles of such "debris" can be found in various stages of decomposition. Although there was a time when such shavings were available for little more than the proverbial song, that time is past. Even so, however, a large truckload of shavings sufficiently mulches an average-size garden—at a fraction of the cost of bark nuggets. Moreover, shavings decay more quickly, thereby adding valuable humus the sooner to your soil. Of course, one might argue that this means more frequent mulch applications, although this would be only marginally valid. On the negative side, shavings turn a brownish-gray more quickly than do nuggets. On the positive side, should you want to add plants to a bed already mulched . with shavings, it is much easier to work the soil than among a thick layer of nuggets.

· GRASS CUTTINGS ·

These are best used in small areas, or in the vegetable bed, because rarely are there enough grass cuttings all at once to mulch a large bed. I use them instead around stalky vegetable plants, such as peppers, broccoli, eggplants, or tomatoes. Ideally, they are the cuttings of a *regularly* mowed lawn, to keep to a minimum any grass seeds from entering your vegetable bed. Always be sure that the lawn from which you've obtained your cuttings has not been treated with weed killers! These could prove harmful to you and your plants. Also, it's best to bag the cuttings in a plastic sack for about a week, so that the grass can wilt and begin to rot. This may sound like a bother, but you will quickly find that you seldom have time to undertake mowing *and* mulching on the same day anyway. If you do not have enough grass cuttings yourself, and yet you like them, ask your neighbors for theirs— especially those neighbors who mow every week. That's how I augmented my own supply. My neighbor neatly bagged his grass clippings every weekend. I often wondered what he did with them, and was finally unable to retain my curiosity any longer. "I throw them in the garbage," he said, and from that day on, I received regular supplies of mulch; he saved on the cost of plastic bags, because I returned them, and everybody was happy. One final word—because grass clippings often mildew, it's wise to incorporate them in the soil; in short, to dig them in.

· CHOPPED/ROTTED LEAVES ·

This mulch is one of my favorites. It blends naturally into the garden—after all, nature itself invented this mulch millennia ago—and it is, by far, the cheapest mulch available. In fact, it is altogether free of charge. Nature produces an abundance of leaves every spring; in autumn the leaves dry and drop. Next, depending on whether they live in a rural, a suburban, or an urban setting, many people rake, pile, and bag the leaves, to be removed with the garbage; others use the bagged leaves as insulating buffer zones around their basement windows in winter, and *then* throw them into the garbage; still others pile their leaves along the roadside, with the help of a rake or a motorized leaf blower, and let their local community pick up the piles. Of course, not all communities offer this service, but if yours does, a huge lumbering kind of vacuum cleaner trundles along the streets in late autumn, sucks up the leaves, masticates and digests them, and then disgorges them into a truck that follows close behind. Now, even if you have already invested in a leaf-shredding machine of your own, and especially if your garden contains many planted areas, I suggest you consider what happens to this public gold-in-the-making. Unless you waylay and charm the town crew attending to this rather tedious detail, the truck will be unloaded at the local dump site. Imagine! All that gorgeous potential mulch wasted on an unsightly mess of plastic, broken glass, and rusty old refrigerators. As town dumps are often a distance away, I have found that the work crew is quite happy to donate its freight to my needy garden. Naturally, I first speak to the town superintendent. Although that worthy may think that, possibly, I'm not playing with a full deck—especially as he suspiciously eyes my acres of unraked leaves and here I am asking for more?— my arguments about saved man-hours and saved gas and oil soften his heart. Dry leaves, however crudely chopped, will decay more rapidly into leaf mold than will leaves left whole. Simply pile them to a height of perhaps three or four feet, in an out-of-the-way, semishaded area. Rain and melting snow will permeate the heap during the winter months, although some dry pockets will remain here and there. Already by the following spring, you can transfer to your garden beds the large chunks of matted wet and wonderfully aromatic black leaves you'll find directly under the top of the heap. Deployed generously on your beds, these chunks will dry in the course of the summer, then crumble as you work them into the soil as humus. By the way, I do not recommend ever applying freshly fallen leaves to your garden, because they will quickly dry out and be blown away. But as long as your trees produce leaves, you know that you will have an inexhaustible supply of mulch, by merely adding each year's fallen leaves to the top of the heap and extracting the leaf mold from underneath. Not only can you apply all that saved mulch money to next spring's plant-buying spree, but you'll also be a budget-conscious member of your community. What more could anyone ask?

· NEWSPAPERS ·

These are particularly useful for vegetable gardens, or if you have enough self-control to dig a bed and let it lie fallow, unplanted, for a whole year. In that event, cover the dug bed with thick layers of old newspapers, weight them down with soil, or even with another mulch, and the paper will act as a fine barrier against all those weed seeds your digging stimulated underneath by preventing them from doing anything more than think about popping up. In vegetable gardens, shredded newspaper soaked in water for an hour can be dug into the soil when you prepare the bed. Or, shredded and pre-soaked, newspaper can be placed in a circle around delicate seedlings, if there should be a sudden early onslaught of excessive heat. The reason why shredding the newspaper is advisable is that it then decomposes more rapidly; soaked, it also does not fly away. Newspapers also work wonders keeping weeds at bay between vegetable rows. All you have to do is save all your Sunday papers through the winter. It is essential, however, to discard all color sections from this kind of mulching material, because colored inks contain poisons. *Use black ink only.* Friends of mine taught me a most efficient way to prepare such newspaper mulch. They save all their Sunday editions of *The New York Times,* minus colored and small sections. Then, just about the time in January when the first plant catalogues arrive in the mail, and everybody's gardening adrenalin begins to pump, they set to work. One of them folds two double sheets in quarters, lengthwise; the other staples the folded sheets together, end over end, into long bands that equal the length of their vegetable rows. Then they roll up these bands—one per row—and stack them neatly in their basement, ready for use in the garden. Shortly after planting time, once the vegetable seedlings reach a height of about eight inches, and once the weeds have made their determined appearance, my friends simply unroll their prepared newspaper bands and weight them down with a little soil. During the prime weed-growing months, the paper acts as a barrier to such growth, and by autumn or the following spring, its mostly decomposed remains can be easily tilled into the soil for compost. Not only is the preparation of this mulch an enjoyable and productive way to spend a dreary cold winter's day, but it also puts to good use what would otherwise end up wasted in the garbage. Considering all the trees that have to be cut down to produce one single Sunday *Times* edition, by returning the paper to the soil as mulch, you will make up just a little for the sin of denuding our forests in the name of progress. Plus, of course, both paper and staples are biodegradable.

The only place I would recommend against using newspaper mulch is in areas where you have planted bulbs. These might be too easily stifled by the paper. Incidentally, worms eat newspaper. Judging from the speed with which mine devour it, they must be the most informed, best-read worms in the world!

One important point to bear in mind in the case of all mulch: Just as these applications greatly benefit your plants during the summer months, by keeping them cool and moist, so the mulch also retains the last of winter's frost much longer than do unmulched areas. If you have clearly marked all your plants, and want to give spring a little push, with your fingers or a trowel simply move aside the mulch from the places where your plants will emerge. A note of caution, however. Do this only after the danger of frost is past—in the Northeast, that can be as late as the end of May; it might even be in early June!

On the other hand, if it's any comfort to you at all, I myself often prefer to take the risk, rather than to delay spring even a minute longer than I absolutely have to.

R · E · C · A · P

1. Ideally, try to acquire your preferred mulch material before planting, so that it is ready when you are.

2. With shovel or digging fork, and to depth of *at least* 2 to 3 inches, carefully spread mulch throughout garden bed, being careful not to cover or damage plants.

3. With hands or trowel, make sure all plants are snugly surrounded by mulch.

4. Add more mulch material as needed—depending on initial thickness, roughly every two or three years.

Weeding

Weeding is a subject very close to my heart. In fact, I am positively compulsive about it, not to mention rhapsodic. For me, weeding is restful and intensely satisfying, a time of great peacefulness, hypnotic concentration, and boundless inspiration, of deep happiness and oneness with the universe. "Decidedly lunatic," you may well be thinking at this moment. However, whether or not you will ever share my fervor, the act of weeding is perhaps the single most immediately satisfying aspect of gardening. A day rarely passes, throughout the growing season, when I don't spend at least a few minutes pulling weeds. When I weed, the day's stresses and worries slip away, and what many people regard as a dirty, boring chore becomes a kind of friendly game of one-upmanship.

In unkindest terms, weeds are the squatters, the gate-crashers of the garden. They are regarded by some with much the same dread and loathing as Attila the Hun's marauding hordes, or the swarming army ants of South America. Some gardeners despise them with a passion bordering on paranoia, and go to all lengths to banish weeds from their domain. In short, weeds are considered by most people as absolutely useless, the enemy. And so they are, if they are allowed to take over. But so is *any* plant that runs amok at the expense of its companions.

My own attitude toward weeds tends to be a little more tolerant, even ambivalent. For one thing, they were here long before we came along, and they will be here long after we are forgotten. As with squatters and gate-crashers, we may succeed in evicting them, but it takes full-time vigilance to *keep* them evicted. To achieve this, a small army of gardeners, as well as considerable financial resources, are necessary. And plain hard work. Without these, as I have found time and again, less than one full growing season will turn even the most perfect garden into an overgrown wilderness that totally lacks beauty and charm.

Because of this, I have long made a one-sided, tenuous pact with these indigenous inhabitants of my garden: I root them out mercilessly from my flower and vegetable beds, mow them down in my lawn, but let them live peacefully everywhere else. The only exception I make to this coexistence is with poison ivy. Beautiful as it is in full leaf, especially in autumn, it is also very bad for one's health, both externally and internally. Poison ivy (*Rhus toxicodendron*) is a common American poisonous, deep-rooted vine or shrub that may appear like a ground cover under garden shrubs, trailing along the edges of woods, or clinging to trees. It seems to prefer semishaded, moist areas, but I once discovered a magnificent specimen climbing up the side of a garage in an extremely dry spot. You can easily recognize this plant by its foliage—three shiny, dark-green leaflets on a single stem. Even the slightest physical contact with this plant is to be devoutly avoided—it *can* land you in a hospital! All parts of poison ivy release a poisonous, nonvolatile oil, although not everybody is equally affected by this sap. In some people, only the portion of skin which actually touched the plant develops an inflamed, itchy

Weeds are simply nature's survivors, capable of subsisting in seemingly intolerable conditions, indifferent to abuse and all ridicule. The most you can ever hope to achieve is to keep them at bay, at least out of the areas you call *your* garden.

As this is your first garden, you are likely to find yourself in one of two situations: (1) you yourself dug and planted the flower or vegetable beds; (2) there already are established beds, left behind by the previous occupant. In the case of (1), you have identified each plant you set into the ground (see Chapter 9)—haven't you? In the case of (2), a possible solution might be to do nothing at all for one full season. That way, as things burst into bloom, you could identify each plant by looking it up in garden books and catalogues, or by asking friends and neighbors, or by taking sample blossoms and leaves to a nearby nursery. Then you could place identifying tabs beside every plant of that particular kind, and if there were sizable groupings of a plant, you could place string around each such group, together with a marker.

But . . . I do not recommend not weeding for an entire season. The results could be disastrous. Unchecked weed growth leads to a free-for-all, in which the "good guys," the garden plants, almost invariably lose, by being choked to death. Better to lose some "real" plants by pulling them up as suspected weeds than not weeding at all.

For the purpose of this chapter, I will consider a weed anything that grows in your garden which you did not plant, which seems to appear out of nowhere, which interrupts your plan and design, or which seems to be creeping in from the lawn. If a type of plant appears in neat rows, in regularly spaced or orderly groupings, or only once, it is reasonably safe to assume that it is *not* a weed. Most weeds are far too exuberant and free-spirited to multiply in an orderly fashion. Alas, the same is also true of some garden plants! Still, we must begin somewhere.

One of the most effective methods of weeding—actually, one might say "*pre*-weeding"—is to double-dig the soil when you prepare your beds (see Chapter 7). By removing all densely matted grass, weeds, and roots as you turn each shovelful of soil, and replacing the bulk thus lost with compost (see Chapter 6), you can reduce the number of weed seeds in the soil and also make the remainder easier to pull out.

In principle, if a bed has been properly dug, composted, and mulched, it should need only regular maintenance weeding during the remainder of that season, and only one major weeding every early summer thereafter, followed again by maintenance weeding. Repeated composting and mulching will, over a period of years, reduce the need for weeding to almost negligible proportions, provided you remain vigilant.

Although I cannot remember exactly how I came to love weeding quite so ardently, I suspect it grew out of desperation. That is, because peak weed growth coincides with the early summer planting season, the weeds always grew at a vastly greater speed than I could get everything planted, or weeded. As it was impossible for me to be in two places at the same time, my nerve ends soon became attuned to the silent little screams for help from the garden, and my body learned to become expert in time-motion exercises. Today, they are quite automatic. From the moment I walk out of the house, until the moment I reenter, I swipe at every weed I pass. To an unsuspecting stranger, I may appear to be suffering from some strange disease as I genuflect my way about. But years of practice have now made it possible for me to walk and weed almost without breaking stride.

Here follows a necessary observation that may not endear the subject of weeding to you, namely, that it is virtually impossible to weed effectively while wearing gloves. Gloves have a way of blunting your sense of touch and control, of causing your hand to slip off a small weed at the crucial moment, when it is about to submit to your eviction notice, or of not allowing you to seize the weed firmly enough. Yes, this does mean you will have dirty hands and dirty fingernails. But surely these are a small price to pay for valuable time spent on *successful* weeding, as opposed to valuable time wasted on largely ineffectual weeding. Therefore, to help you overcome your reluctance, I'll first share with you the method with which I protect my hands routinely throughout the gardening year. It is an easy-to-make herbal hand lotion, which I work liberally and thoroughly into my hands before I do any outdoor work. If the soil or weeds are wet, or if I weed for a prolonged period of time, I repeat the applications periodically. When my work is finished, I thoroughly rinse my hands in lukewarm water, then wash and scrub them with soap. You will be amazed at how easily all the dirt washes away. Afterward, I simply work an application of a rich lotion into my hands, while they are still damp.

Mix 6 teaspoons of kaolin (available at pharmacies), 6 teaspoons of almond oil, and 6 tablespoons of an herbal infusion in a small bottle or jar. Keep the container tightly closed and refrigerated between uses, and shake thoroughly before each use. To make the herbal infusion, pour ½ cup of boiling water over ½ cup of crushed fresh leaves of burdock, plantain, yarrow, or comfrey, or over the flowers of elder or calendula. Let this "tea" steep in a *covered* bowl until it is cool. Strain, add the proper amount of infusion to the other ingredients, and discard the remaining infusion.

I suggest you make only the quantity I've stipulated, because in the absence of preservatives, larger quantities might become rancid in time. For this reason, between uses I try to keep my herbal hand lotion refrigerated. In any case, liberal as I am with its applications, even with the above quantity I rarely have to make a second batch before the end of the gardening season. And if you're wondering where you are supposed to find the herbs I mentioned above, all except the calendula grow wild, either in your own garden or along roadsides (see Appendix II). Buy calendula for your herb garden.

Weeding must be done *slowly* and *methodically*. Merely to tear at the tops of the weeds serves no purpose whatsoever, except perhaps to vent your frustration. It's no good to dive in and grab a fistful of weeds all at once. Instead, each individual weed plant, or clump of unwanted grass, should be seized at the base, where

*Shown is the hand motion in relationship to the weed—
remember, however, in practice* always weed at soil level.

the leaves emerge from the roots. Be sure that you hold *all* the leaves, then pull—*never yank*—the plant firmly from the earth. Be defining each separate weed in this manner, and by seizing the leaves where they emerge from the roots and soil, you will have optimal success in removing the entire plant. The hand action in weeding is not unlike the theatrical mime for making something disappear behind one's back, secreting it—a sleight of hand. Or perhaps it might be compared with the slight twist required in uncorking a bottle of wine. In other words, added to the pulling action, there is also a simultaneous, but only *very slight*, twist. At first, all this will seem like a hopelessly complicated and monotonous procedure, but be assured, it's really very simple, and in no time at all you will acquire an almost mindless deftness.

Of course, not all weeds come up easily, especially if they're in uncultivated, uncomposted, unmulched soil, or if they've been allowed to grow to full size, or if there's been no rain for several weeks. Some weeds also have densely clumped root masses. In certain instances, such as with the dandelion or burdock, you will feel a decided resistance, even in well-worked soil. This is because these weeds have taproots—primary tapered roots that grow straight downward. In the case of full-grown burdock, the length of such a taproot can be more than two *feet*. However, with very young dandelions and burdock, a little encouragement from a trowel will usually free the taproot. In the case of older plants of both types, nothing less than a digging fork or a shovel will evict those rascals. Even so, very often a taproot breaks, and if you leave the lower tip, you may be certain that a new plant will emerge from it. So you must be tough and determined; let them know that you're boss.

For some reason which I have never fathomed, unless you seize *all* the leaves of a weed or clump of grass at a single go, either the roots will not be fully dislodged or the incompletely seized leaves will simply tear off. In either case, you will be forced to dig the weed out of the ground. The most consistently infuriating example of this kind of obstreperousness is the dandelion. Experiment with it and see for yourself!

I've always found that, if a bed is densely overgrown, it is a good idea to divide it mentally into sections, or quadrants, and to weed each section methodically until it is cleared of weeds. Apart from the fact that you will be less daunted or tired with this approach, the contrast between the weeded section and the remaining overgrown areas will inspire you to keep going.

Besides the aesthetic value of a weeded garden, and the fact that valuable plants are protected against strangulation and possible disease or pests, the action of pulling weeds greatly benefits your beds, in that it loosens the soil around your plants. This loosening allows air to circulate, water to penetrate freely to the roots, and the nutrients in the soil to promote your plants' growth (see Chapter 10).

In time, you may discover a positive joy in weeding, when you learn of the many weeds that make delicious vegetables, soups, or salads, as well as teas, culinary herbs, even medicines. In any case, many weeds are exquisitely beautiful and add enormous charm in their season. Ruthless as I am about their not wandering into my garden beds, I make every effort to encourage such weeds to grow in what I call wild islands. These I mow into shapes that conform harmoniously with my planted beds, to become garden accents in their own right. Thus, the wild islands help to create a flow through the garden (incidentally, at no cost and with no effort on my part), while their haphazard and spontaneous color displays punctuate the more formal, premeditated surroundings of my own creation (see Chapter 5).

Finally, a word of solace and comfort for all those times when the weeds seem to have the upper hand in your garden. Just keep in mind that those famous and weed-free gardens illustrated so lavishly in expensive coffee-table books, which you admire so enviously, were created over a period of decades, or even centuries—most often by professional gardeners and nurserymen— and are maintained by them, at considerable expense. By all means, let these gardens inspire you, give you ideas, make you strive for similar perfection. But always remember that the true joy of gardening lies in the doing—in the watching, waiting, watering—*and* weeding.

R · E · C · A · P

1. Make sure all garden plants are identified.

2. Treat as weeds anything you did not plant, anything not identified, anything not growing in some kind of pattern or plan, until you really know your garden.

3. Divide to-be-weeded beds into sections; weed each section carefully, methodically.

4. Seize individual weeds *with all leaves*, at base, and pull from soil with slight twist.

5. Use trowel, shovel, or digging fork to remove taproots.

6. Curtail spread of garden plants beyond desirable area by weeding.

7. Weed a little every day, if possible; never let it become a chore.

8. Learn about edible weeds for unusual and nutritious taste treats (see Appendix II).

Pests and Pals

$\mathbb{M}$ ake no mistake about it, the chances of your never finding any pests in your garden are nil. Most of them are insects. Broadly speaking, these are divided into the good guys and the bad guys. It works something like this: While the bad guys are frolicking about on your plants, mutilating them and breeding merrily, the more decorous good guys quietly lick their chops and move in. Blessed with insatiable appetites, they then proceed to dine splendidly on choice bad-guy meat, until none is left.

It's all a part of what we humans call ecological balance, and what nature determines as natural pest control. To have the healthiest and most pest-free garden possible, it is up to us as well to prevent infestations and to rid the garden of them, if and when they occur. Soil cultivation and enrichment, regular weeding, and general maintenance are at the top of the list, and so is our constant alertness to the first signs of trouble. This includes pruning—sometimes radically—or the complete removal of plants that are beyond help or that pose a threat to others. Mind you, not all garden pests are insects, and neither are all garden pals. The range in both is from microscopic spores, fungi, and bacteria to mammals that are larger than a bread box. In fact, quite a lot of both pests and pals are numbered among your plants themselves.

For the purpose of this book, I offer only a general introduction to the insects and other beasties you are likely to encounter in your garden, depending on where you live. Mostly, however, I cannot urge you enough to add at least one book to your gardening library about the endlessly fascinating subject of natural pest control. Such a book will not only help you to identify the various insects and other good and bad garden residents; it will also provide you with invaluable information about prevention and treatments.

If I stress *natural* pest controls, it is for good reason, especially in the home garden. True, very often chemical pesticide sprays and powders fetch speedier results, but in doing so, they can create other, often more serious problems. Some chemicals destroy beneficial insects, along with undesirables; others are capable of exterminating only certain kinds of insect pests. Once the good guys are eliminated, or forced to flee, your plants are defenseless against the next batch of pests. As likely as not, this will be an entirely different species from the last. The new pests move in, ravage your plants in their own way, and force you to unleash yet another dose of chemicals. And so on. The vicious circle is perpetuated, and your plants—and you—are the ultimate losers.

Take the honeybee as an example. These beneficial creatures are particularly sensitive to some chemicals. Yet they serve a crucial function as pollinators. Without pollination, many plants cannot fruit. Although bees are not the only means of pollination, they *are* the only honey producers. Therefore, if a bee brings contaminated pollen and nectar to its hive for further processing, it stands to reason that the honey you eventually eat may also be contaminated.

I realize that some of you can't work up too much enthusiasm for bees. Consider this, however. They, together with wasps, toads, frogs, spiders, ladybugs (ladybirds), lacewings, garter snakes, worms, and praying mantises, are your garden's best friends! Oh, I know, eeek, yuk, and *¢&@#! But please bear in mind that you need never touch any one of them unless you choose to. Most of *them* are just as anxious to have no contact with *you*, either. Even the bees and wasps. Believe it or not, they sting only when they feel threatened or trapped. If you flail or swat at them, their response is to sting in self-defense. After all, if you were out for a quiet stroll, and the equivalent of the Abominable Snowman walloped you for no good reason, wouldn't you do the same? And all spiders bite if escape is impossible. Wouldn't you under similar circumstances? There are only a few truly vicious attackers in the garden—that bloodthirsty dive bomber, the mosquito, the horsefly, and the black fly.

This may be as good a time as any to try to clarify some of the confusion between wasps and bees. First of all, both provide invaluable service to your garden. Although they are only distantly related, they have certain similarities—in approximate body length, in coloring, and in that accursed stinger. Bees, however, have *hairy* bodies, which wasps do not, and bees have rounder abdomens than wasps. Just as bees are pollinators, so wasps—even the dread yellow jackets—are pest exterminators. Some wasps are outright predators, while others employ a most ingenious method for the kill. They lay their eggs inside the larvae of various insect pests, thereby either causing their premature demise or else preventing the larvae from pupating. Either way, it's a highly efficient method of pest control.

Both insects are intensely curious, and also responsive. To dissuade them from wanting to share my food and drink outdoors, I got in the habit many years ago of setting aside for them a choice morsel of something sweet, like a piece of fruit or cake, or a dab of jam. In fact, two wasps in New York came to *expect* their treat, once they grasped the idea, and we all ate happily ever after, the wasps hovering over their saucer of goodies at one end of the table, the rest of us eating undisturbed at the other end.

As for spiders, I must admit that a long-ago reading of E. B. White's *Charlotte's Web* forever influenced my attitude toward them. How could any creature so intelligent, so industrious and artistic, also be bad? Yes, spiders do bite, but the brief discomfort is a small price to pay for the magic of watching a spider weave its iridescent web. Besides, spiders thrive on insect pests.

Ants bite, too. Although most ant species are harmless, despite their nuisance value in the house, some species are the indirect cause of considerable plant damage. Among them are the arch oppressors of the insect world. Fortunately, the victims are pests, so that I don't grieve too much. For the sole purpose of indulging their sweet tooth, these ants colonize, nurture, and defend huge numbers of aphids—on *your* plants—and "milk" them for the honeydew the aphids gather from the plants. (Honeydew is so called because it is a sweet and sticky exudation that appears on the leaves of some plants in midsummer.) If you see *early* signs of such a colonization, wipe the aphids into a paper towel and drop them into hot water. Discourage the ants from importing replacements by sprinkling bone meal or powdered charcoal around the plant. But if one of your plants is heavily infested with aphid colonies, I urge you to remove and *burn* the affected limb, or even the entire plant.

Among harmless ants are those you will see crawling over the flower buds of your peonies in spring. Folklore has it that the ants encourage the buds to open, but there is no proof of this. What they're really after is the sweet secretions of the buds, and this indulgence does no damage to the peonies.

Although being subjected to insect bites and stings isn't restricted to your garden, there are some home remedies with which you can combat the uncomfortable after-effects. For this reason, it is well worth becoming familiar with, or planting in your garden, any or all of the following wild and domestic herbs: *for stings*—feverfew, hyssop, plantain; *for bites*—burdock, parsley, witch hazel. Simply press the crushed fresh leaves on the affected spot. Within minutes, the expressed juices of the herbs will relieve the itch, pain, and swelling of your wound.

Of course, more to the point might be to prevent being stung or bitten in the first place. I have found that rubbing a handful of the leaves of certain herbs on my skin keeps insects at bay: tansy (*Tanacetum vulgare*), for example, as well as American pennyroyal (*Hedeoma pulegioides*), spearmint (*Mentha spicata*), southernwood (*Artemisia abrotanum*), and wormwood (*Artemisia absinthium*). Or, if you have a lush planting of nasturtiums, as I always do, you can also make a "tea" out of any part of the plant and spray it on your exposed skin. (Incidentally, nasturtium leaves in your green salads add a delightfully tangy, peppery flavor; decorate potato and pasta salads with the flowers—they're edible, too; and pickle the buds and seed pods. They outcaper capers!) The best insect repellent, of course, is garlic rubbed on your skin, but you would probably lead a very lonely life.

Some other pals masquerade as possible pests in your garden, such as garter snakes, toads, and frogs. Let me say at once that I would never voluntarily touch a garter (or any other) snake—but neither would I harm one or chase it away. It is worth remembering that when garter snakes aren't basking in a sunny spot in your garden, or slithering away from you posthaste, they help control the garden snail, slug, and insect populations. Toads and frogs, for their part, positively thrive on a diet of crickets, ants, mosquitoes, caterpillars, flies and moths, assorted beetles, and even moles. But the *pièce de résistance* of their diet is the cutworm, that diabolical miniature automated chain saw traveling around your garden and felling choice plants. In a single day, our ugly, unkissed garden princes can consume more than a hundred of these varied pests—except perhaps the moles.

Apart from the songs and beauty they give us, birds also feed on many insect pests. Therefore, we must forgive them for munching on worms now and then, even though worms are among the best good guys in the garden.

Ladybugs are essentially the nemesis of aphids, which they consume in huge numbers. They're equally successful exterminators of mealybugs. Praying mantises, because they are green like the foliage under which they hide, and because they look ferocious, may seem to be a danger to your garden; in fact, they

Shown are three of the gardener's best friends (LEFT TO RIGHT): ladybug, adult lacewing, praying mantis.

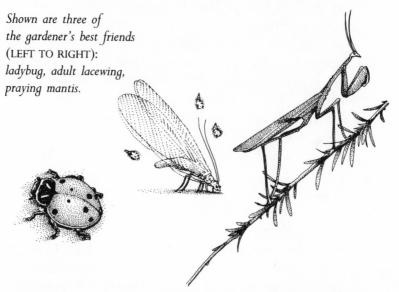

are among its greatest benefactors, by slowly and systematically ridding it of insect pests from early spring to late summer. Last, but far from least, comes the lacewing, that veritable workaholic in its larval stage, when it is also known as aphis lion. But it is just as lethal to mealybugs, whiteflies, spider mites, and insect eggs as it is to aphids. Once the lacewing matures, however, it takes early retirement and lives only on pollen and nectar.

These last three beneficial insects, which can be purchased from several seed houses or gardening research centers, stay in any garden only as long as there are enough pests to feed them. Therefore, in a sense, their presence or absence is a barometer for you to judge the health of your plants. But if their workload becomes too overwhelming, you'll have to help them out— perhaps by including certain plants in your garden which are not only handsome in themselves but also act as insect repellents. By using them, you can enhance *and* protect your flower beds and vegetable patch. Because vegetables are annuals, you might do best to plant repellent annuals among them, and use repellent perennials in the borders. Or, for another effect, you can keep the design of your vegetable bed less constrained by placing several planters or tubs of repellent plants around and among the veggies. The use of these natural repellents is all a part of companion planting (see Chapter 9).

Among the most pungent and powerful insect-repellent perennials are tansy, wormwood, painted daisy (*Pyrethrum*), and any of the allium family. This last includes garlic, onions, and leeks, as well as numerous ornamentals. Feverfew, that favorite of mine, because of its charm and many uses, is another, and so is rue (*Ruta graveolens*) and southernwood. (A sprig of rue, incidentally, mellows when cooked and adds a most delicate flavor to fish.) The mints, too, are repellent to insects, even to mice and moles. But because these plants spread at a furious rate, you might be wise to keep them in large containers, or in a corner of the vegetable bed, where they will not interfere with other plants. Although catnip, or catmint (*Nepeta cataria*), is another useful insect repellent, don't even think of planting it if you or your neighbors have cats. And that includes pet lions. Catnip has been sending felines into a state of purest ecstasy for centuries— nobody seems to know quite why. I planted it once, and watched my cats wallow and stretch and roll in it, nibbling it, tearing it, luxuriating in it, until there was nothing left of the plant. Even then, for days afterward, the cats kept returning to the spot, trying to recapture their blissful high from the last traces of the catnip fragrance still lingering on the soil.

For a show of colors among the otherwise largely unrelieved green of your vegetables, you might consider planting such insect-repellent annuals as petunias, marigolds (the French and African varieties), calendulas, borage, nasturtium, and white geraniums. Please note that the *white* geraniums are lethal to Japanese beetles.

There are also several home remedies I have employed over the years for warding off various pests. For instance, garden snails and slugs became a serious problem in one of my city gardens. Beer was one of the solutions I heard about. Beer! The idea instantly appealed to me, conjuring up some marvelously droll images of a tipsy gang of slimy revelers out for a night on the town. Although I felt a bit foolish doing it, under the ever watchful eyes of neighbors, I set out half a dozen saucers filled with beer. True enough, the evidence was in the next morning. Those topers must have had a rare farewell bash; the saucers were full of dead bodies, all of them victims of drowning. Honey works similarly, and salt dissolves the wretches on contact. But I hesitate to use this last method, because salt also damages my plants.

Besides their value in chilis and other spicy foods, hot peppers are great repellents. Dried and pulverized, they can be sprinkled or rubbed on insect-infested leaves; or sprinkled on corn silks, they make thieving raccoons and chipmunks think twice about stealing corn. But the spray made of a teaspoon of ground hot pepper and two or three large cloves of minced garlic is my favorite. Without harming my plants, it drives the bad-guy insects into mass retreat. Mind you, I don't think that I could withstand a noseful of it, either. You cover the mash with water and let it stand for one or two days, then strain it. Add a little powdered *non-detergent* soap and roughly one gallon of water.

Another potent spray I make is from tobacco. In fact, the tobacco plant has been used as an insecticide for more than two hundred years, and no insect is known to be immune to it. It's the nicotine in tobacco which is poisonous, not only to insects, but also to mammals. For this reason, I strongly recommend not using this spray indoors, and applying it judiciously outdoors, away from children, pets, and beneficial insects. To prepare the spray, use a handful of tobacco—leaves, stems, cigar or cigarette wastes, or chewing tobacco. Let it steep in water for at least twenty-four hours, then strain. Dilute it to the color of a light tea—and go to it. Although poisonous, nicotine is also volatile. This means that it is quickly dissipated from the plants on which it is sprayed. But it is sufficiently effective against the harmful insects on your plants that a second application is seldom necessary, except in the case of major infestations. In such an instance, however, it is often wiser to destroy the infested plant(s).

For a spray against powdery mildew, pick a bunch of horsetail (*Equisetum arvense*) on your next walk in the country. Cover the weeds with water, allowing them to steep and ferment for about two weeks. Strain and dilute, and the spray is ready for use. Or, for off-season use, dry the stems and leaves of the weed. When needed, simmer a generous pinch of the crumbled weed in a cupful of water for twenty minutes, cover until cool, then use undiluted. A strong camomile tea, made from the flowers, is also helpful against powdery mildew.

Finally, although rhubarb leaves are not recommended for human consumption, once boiled in water and used as a spray, they protect roses against black spot. Rhubarb spray is also particularly good for preventing clubroot in the cabbage family. At planting time (seeds or seedlings), simply water in with rhubarb "tea."

When it comes to the various mammals mentioned below, the entire business of pest control becomes less assured. Many of them are wilier or faster off the mark than we can ever hope to be, and all of them seem to think that our gardens—all that careful hard work—were created solely for their collective benefit. And after they've reveled, cavorted, and chomped among our plants, they haven't the decency to show even the slightest sign of remorse or gratitude. On the contrary, I often have the feeling that all my attempts to capture, outwit, or chase off these thieves are being carefully observed and analyzed by dozens of beady eyes, that I'm merely the butt of great merriment, scorn, and pity. Still, I keep trying, just as these four-legged guerrillas keep on ambushing my garden.

For deterring deer, the largest of these pests, I swear that every individual with whom I have ever discussed the subject has had a sure-fire method. As I already showed in Chapter 5, however, if your garden happens to cross an ancient deer path, probably no ploy will ever work. Nevertheless, the list of supposed deer repellents is endless. Take your pick: dried blood, human hair, dirty old socks and assorted underwear, high fences, barbed wire, soap bars, human urine, electric wires, mothballs, bells, tinfoil strips, wood ashes, dogs, and onions. I suspect that all of these have worked at least once, either alone or in combination with others.

Dried blood, human hair, soap, mothballs, and onions are mentioned more often than others. They are said to work best if they are placed in cloth pouches and hung on tree branches. Dried blood may also be sprinkled around plantings you wish to protect. Applications will have to be repeated, however, because rain will wash the blood into the soil. If your dog doesn't mind being tied up in the garden all night, in all winds and weather, his presence and bark will certainly stop deer from approaching. The problem is, how do you program your dog to bark only at deer?

Dogs are also useful in chasing rabbits, but my cats *eliminate* them. I know that baby rabbits are cuddly and adorable, but they have a way of growing into cheeky vandals among my cabbages, peas, lettuce, and beans. So I pretend that my cats are ladybugs and the bunnies are aphids, nature's pest control. For confirmed bunny lovers, there are less violent deterrents. Rabbits hate onions, so that you could plant these among their favorite veg-etables, as long as you remember that some vegetables hate onions (see Chapter 9). Rabbits also retreat from plants sprinkled with hot pepper, wood ashes, or ground limestone.

Of all garden pests, the woodchuck (groundhog) is probably the most despised. The woodchuck has no natural enemies. It is a lumbering, skulking, surly beast, with a rapacious appetite. It also digs burrows wherever it pleases, and always does so with the provision of several exits. Consequently, it does you no good to block the hole you may discover under, say, your delphiniums, because the woodchuck will simply amble in and out of one of the other exits instead, perhaps halfway across the garden, among your blueberries. They say that dogs are a help in keeping wood-chucks at bay. Hah! Only last spring my dog chased and, finally, faced one of them down (from a safe distance). Eagerly I awaited the denouement, and what happened? My dog barked hysterically, the woodchuck chattered its teeth defiantly, and after about ten minutes both of them lost interest and went their separate ways. In fairness, however, I should add that my sister's Labrador retriever stalked, caught, killed, and devoured an entire wood-chuck family. A friend of mine confirmed a similarly successful foray on the part of *his* Labrador.

Squirrels are insolent swashbucklers, quick off the mark and up a tree, carrying away the last of the walnuts they've been stealing for weeks. Try a humane trap primed with sweet corn or nuts, or let your dog chase some of the starch out of them. Such squirrel-proof devices as net covers for fruit trees are prac-tical only on young trees; sticky substances painted on tree trunks may work against earthbound pests but have little effect on aerialist squirrels. Chipmunks, too, can be trapped if they appear in large numbers. In ones or twos, they are sweet and pert, but in groups they wreak havoc among vegetables, fruits, and flowers. My cats also eat chipmunks.

Raccoons are nocturnal and smart. Their first choice is corn, but if you have none, they raid your garbage bin. Oh yes, they know how to open the lid—quietly. And they are omnivorous. You might succeed in trapping them. Or you might forgo raising corn if raccoons are a problem where you live. Opossums are nocturnal and dumb. When *they* open a garbage bin, *every*body hears it. And they are messy. However, they are easily baited into a trap with sweets.

If only skunks weren't so skittish, or didn't express their fear so pungently! Forget about trapping them—one salvo from a skunk and you will be bathing in tomato juice for days to get rid of the stench. Instead, practice magnanimity. Consider the rats, mice, insects, and grubs they eat as ample payment for the fruit and corn they steal from you.

If moles and voles invade your garden, make a repellent spray. In a 2:1 ratio, blend castor oil and dishwashing liquid into a creamy consistency. Blend in an equal amount of water. Then add 2 tablespoons of the mixture to a sprinkling can of warm water and apply over suspected mole and vole habitations, or directly into the burrows. Mice, like moles and voles, can be trapped. Mice are repelled by onions, lemon peel, and mint. Or let your cat roam freely, and be sure to praise it for the "presents" it brings to your door, especially in spring and autumn.

As is true of weeds, it's impossible ever to rid your garden entirely of pests. They, too, are a part of the world in which we live, and serve their purpose in the ecological chain—after all, without them, the good guys would also disappear. Nuisance though they often are, those large and small pests, without them our world would soon be a silent and sterile place. Without them, we'd be truly alone, deprived of much pleasure, of great beauty of form and color, deprived of the myriad sounds that make up nature's deceptive stillness so brimming with the vibrant hum of life.

R · E · C · A · P

1. Learn to distinguish between pests and pals.

2. Discourage insect pest invasions through regular soil cultivation, weeding, and maintenance.

3. Protect *and* enhance your garden with companion plantings.

4. Destroy infected plants that are beyond salvage.

5. Avoid use of all-purpose chemical pesticides.

C·H·A·P·T·E·R 14

Simple Propagation

Ⅱf you have already devoted much
of your love and energy to gardening up to this point, you are
bound to take the next step, if for no other reason than to satisfy
your curiosity. And if you do take this step, it's almost impossible
for you ever to turn back. Suddenly the whole plant world will
have new dimensions, your eyes will see things they never saw
before, and you will recognize—even anticipate—the infinite
number of ways in which you may satisfy many of your gardening
needs and greeds.

In brief, you will be hooked. Hooked on what? you may well
ask. Do you remember when I warned you earlier how easy it
is to be seduced by plants? During your first mad plant-buying
spree, however, you could be excused for falling prey to the
blandishments of plantdom's sirens. In this chapter, I'm suggesting
that you will only too readily act in collusion with those sirens,

163

without feeling even the slightest pang of shame. Your greed will know no bounds, and neither will your sense of possibilities. You will be amazed at discovering all the hidden resources of cunning in your heart—that same heart you had thought so innocent, so untarnished.

From friends and neighbors, you will acquire plants not readily available, plants you had not even heard of or thought you wanted. You will be able to expand your garden with more of the plants you already have, without spending a penny. Even if you have never in your life asked a thing of a living soul, you will now become an unabashed beggar of total strangers. And the people from whom you beg will feel honored that you do! (At least, in most instances.) More than that, they will actually make offers you cannot refuse, sometimes so eagerly that they practically *foist* plants on you. In brief, the sacrifice of what you have always regarded as your impeccably dignified image will be a small price to pay for your gains. The step to this deliciously sinful path is called propagation.

Let me give you just three examples of how it can work:

1. One June day, I arrived at a nursery just as a huge delivery of junipers was being made. Men hauled them unceremoniously off the truck, and in doing so left a wake of broken young branches scattered on the ground. Instantly alert, I asked if I might take some of them. The response was a puzzled look and a casual nod. So I seized a bundle of the best-looking branches and hurried home. There I stripped the leaves from the lower stems, then planted the stems in my hospital bed, firmly tamping the soil around them, and kept them moist until autumn. By the following spring, the tiny pale-green shoots at the tips told me that each of the branches had "taken," or rooted, and was in the process of becoming specimen *Juniperus chinensis pfitzeriana*. At no cost.

2. Friends greatly admired the mass of *Monarda didyma* in my herb garden, and the show of dark scarlet flowers so appealing to bees and hummingbirds. I took out my spade, dug up a clump, and moments later my friends trotted home with their booty. Their clump has since then thrived enough to be shared with numerous of *their* friends. At no cost.

3. My sister has a huge display of *Iris sibirica* which I have long coveted. One day, being an impulsive creature, she decided to reduce the mass dramatically, and turned up at my door bearing a generous contribution of it. By next year, I'll have my own gorgeous display. At no cost.

The list of such examples is endless, as you'll discover yourself once you enter the world of propagation. It is a challenging world, a world full of surprises and wonderment. In the end, the successes by far outweigh the inevitable failures, perhaps not always in number but in your sense of satisfaction. Not least, one of the greatest pleasures comes when you are able to make a gift to someone special of a plant you have propagated and raised yourself.

A great deal has been written about propagation in all its forms—it is an art that has been practiced for thousands of years, and a considerable literature on the subject has accumulated. Some of these writings, in the interests of the scientific ideal, describe propagation in such minute detail, under such perfect conditions, that the chief result is likely to be your utter confusion and dismay. Others lead you to believe that success is guaranteed if you follow every stipulated procedure, and that failure is inevitable if you don't. Still others make propagation sound so playful that you might be tempted to rush out and buy up the nearest nursery and go into business. The truth probably lies somewhere between them all.

Yes, propagation does entail certain steps; there is no arguing their validity. And yes, as you gain experience and confidence, as well as a greater understanding of your plants and their habits, you will probably become increasingly methodical in your approach to these procedures. Even so, success is not always automatically assured. No more is failure inevitable if you vary some procedures. Quite frankly, too, I've found that a bit of luck sometimes plays a role. After all, nature *is* capricious. As an example, I took some cuttings of a *Euonymus alatus* shrub last year, intending to do all the right things. Instead, I was sidetracked, heeled the cuttings in a bit of soil, and forgot about them, only to find them much later, well on the road to healthy growth without my help. Now they are miniature shrubs. (To "heel in," incidentally, means to cover a plant's roots with soil, *temporarily only*, in order to keep the roots moist and cool until they are planted.)

As with everything else we learn, sooner or later we have to start at the beginning. And my object in this chapter is to stimulate you into *trying* propagation. That is why I refer to it as *simple* propagation.

Ideally you will approach this aspect of gardening with a sense of adventure, for the fun of it, and with the prospect of augmenting your garden. The three most essential qualities you should bring to the task are curiosity, *care*, and patience. Almost more than in any other gardening activity, propagation requires the remaining two of my four W's—watching and waiting. You will be doing plenty of both!

The tools you will need, depending on which propagating method you employ, include a very sharp knife, a trowel or spade, a pencil, a small quantity of hormone rooting powder or liquid, a "hospital bed," plenty of moist, rich soil, a watering can, and a crew of bottomless plastic milk bottles.

The only strangers in this list are the rooting powder, which does what its name suggests—it encourages rooting—and the hospital bed.

Like me, you may not have a greenhouse, but even if you do, I strongly suggest you develop a hospital bed. More accurately, I suppose, such a bed should be named a "kindergarten" or "nursery," because the plants you put in it are not sick at all; rather, they are developing—at best, recuperating. However, the first sounds a little too cute and the second too pretentious. At least, at this stage. Call it what you will, but do prepare a hospital bed. Of the three I have, by far the most successful and productive is the one facing east-northeast, where it receives only oblique morning sun. The soil in it is rich, thanks to regular additions of compost (the cold-rot variety), and the location is sheltered against prevailing winds (see Chapter 2) and lies within easy access of the watering hose and can. The object of a hospital bed is to create a mellow, moist, and restful environment, as free as possible from the stresses of the elements.

There are numerous methods for propagating plants, but for the purpose of this book, I will describe only what I believe to be the three most likely to be immediately rewarding at this point in your gardening career. They are: (1) stem cuttings; (2) root division; (3) seed.

Since no book is quite complete without at least a *hint* of the word "sex," here it is. The first two methods fall into the category of vegetative (asexual) propagation. That is, because you will be using an actual part of the parent plant, the new plant you develop from this part will be identical to its parent. You might call it a clone. Raising new plants from seed, however, falls into the category of sexual propagation, and right away we can see the subtle variations in personality that appear in our own families.

Raising new plants from **stem cuttings** is among the most popular methods. Some people also refer to cuttings as "slips." Cuttings may be made from certain annuals, herbaceous perennials, and from a variety of flowering, deciduous, and evergreen shrubs and bushes, even from some trees.

There are two seasons when cuttings may be taken—either in the early spring, when a plant begins its new growth but long before it develops blooms, and after the blooms have faded. You should never take a cutting while a plant is in full blossom, because that is the time when the plant's full energy goes into flower production, with none to spare for vegetative growth. Besides, you would deprive yourself of the color show. Once the show is over and the plant's life force has turned its attention again to vegetative development, the cuttings you take will have the necessary strength and stamina to grow roots and become plants in their own right. Because different plants have different blooming seasons, this means you will be cutting slips of one kind or another through much of the spring and summer.

Although the procedures for stem cuttings are uniformly the same, you may want to try your hand at some of the following familiar plants. These could include annuals like impatiens, be-

gonia, coleus, and geranium; perennials like phlox, chrysanthemum, and lupine; and shrubs like weigela, forsythia, and juniper.

Always choose a strong, vigorous plant from which to take
your cuttings. The pale, wan-looking fellows may end up siring
pale and wan offspring. Depending on the size and growth pattern
of the parent plant, cuttings may be between six and twelve
inches in length. Simply sever the cuttings with a sharp knife, or
with sharp secateurs (pruners). A slanting cut is best. The cuttings
should never be left lying around while you do something else.
They should not be allowed to wilt. Nor should you place the
cuttings with tough, woody stems in water, because this may
have a damaging effect on the cuts. It is also wise to work with
the cuttings of only one plant at a time, so that there can be no
confusion about their identity.

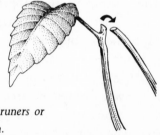

For the health and beauty
of your plants, use sharp *pruners or*
knife to make cuts as shown.

Personally, no matter which plant I wish to propagate, I like
to have reasonable assurance of success through safety in numbers.
Therefore, even if I do not want or need more than one of a
kind, I take between three and five cuttings of the parent, because
not all of them may root. If they do, either I change my garden
plans or I give them away as presents, or I trade them for plants
I would like from somebody else's garden.

Next, remove all flowers and flower buds; then cut the leaves
from the lower portion of your cuttings, up to half or even two-
thirds the length of the stem. Be sure to leave at least three or
four pairs of leaves at the top. The places where the leaves join
the stem are called "nodes"—joints, in other words. If you look
closely, you will see tiny little bumps around the nodes, as well

as in the spaces between them ("internodes"), along the stem. Those bumps are referred to as "calluses"—yes, not unlike the ones you ended up with on your hands after digging your flower beds. And it is from such calluses that roots develop on your cuttings.

In any case, the naked slips are now ready for planting. You may wish to dip the cuts into a hormone rooting powder or liquid, to stimulate rooting, although this step is not essential. Then plant each cutting up to the remaining leaves in the rich, moist soil you prepared in your sheltered hospital bed. Be sure to label each cutting, just as you did during your spring planting. You may also want to include the date, so that you will know, in due course, how long the root development process has taken. This may range anywhere from weeks to months, depending on the kind of plant it is. Keep the soil moist, and if the cuttings show signs of wilting, sprinkle them with water—several times a day if necessary. Shield your planted cuttings from direct sunlight, especially at the start, and from an unexpected cold snap or from high winds by covering them with the bottomless milk bottles.

I realize that the above procedures are a little simplistic, not entirely the accepted norm in horticultural circles. On the other hand, they work more often than not. I learned this from a weatherbeaten old man who had never opened a gardening book in his life. My sister and I found him one day—him and his spectacular small home garden. Of course, he propagated all his plants, and of course, we *had* to know his secret. He regarded us quizzically for a moment, as though he didn't rightly understand the question, while we stood there like schoolgirls, our pens poised over our notebooks. With a helpless kind of shrug, he finally said, "Ain't nothin' won't root if you stick it in the ground deep enough." As an afterthought, he added, "So long as you give it enough time."

No matter how long or short "enough" time may be, few things can quite equal the sense of wonder you'll experience when the first faint hint of new green appears on your cuttings one day. You may need a magnifying glass to see it, but if it's there, you know the cutting has rooted. In short, it worked! And you did it! (With a little help from nature.)

It is best if you let the new plant remain where it is for the present. I rarely move newly rooted cuttings before the following spring, so that they may have a chance to develop strong, healthy root and top growth. By the way, if your new plant is a perennial flower, don't get hysterical when the top growth dies back in autumn. This merely means it is entering its normal dormancy. If the cutting rooted, the plant will reappear next spring.

Incidentally, I suggest you not overlook such opportunities for freebies as when a shoot or twig of an unsuspecting parent plant breaks off during planting. Chrysanthemums are particularly prone to this. Although chrysanthemums bloom late in the season and have, by then, not much time left for rooting before winter sets in, it would surely be foolhardy not to treat such a broken piece as a bonus cutting. Simply disbud and plant it in the hospital bed, and wait for it to emerge next spring—as a new plant! This is not always successful, but I'm quite pleased with my growing (double entendre intended) chrysanthemum collection. Nor am I in the least bit shy about picking up any broken pieces I find at nurseries. After all, if I don't rescue them, they will only be swept away, treated as debris.

Finally, yet another means of simple propagation might be described as first cousin to stem cuttings. It comes from the "true" suckers I referred to in Chapter 9. Such true suckers appear around the base of plants like forsythia, spirea, quince, deutzia, mock orange, and raspberries, as well as species roses and some *Cornus* and *Prunus* species, among others. You can't mistake true suckers. They appear as young, unbranched shoots (whips) around the periphery of the main plant, and with very little effort on your part, they let you increase your stock. In early spring or early autumn, simply scratch away the soil around such a true sucker's base. If roots have formed there, trace the sucker to its source—a root or stem of the parent plant. With a clean cut, remove the rooted sucker at that juncture, carefully probe it loose, and plant it.

Propagating by **root division** applies mostly to a large variety of herbaceous perennials. Among these are the peony, chrysanthemum, phlox, iris, and coral-bell (*Heuchera*). This method involves literally dividing the parent plant into two or more pieces, by cutting or prying it apart, or else detaching babies from the plant's periphery. Each piece or baby is then planted separately, to become a potential parent plant itself.

Divison is also used when the center of a plant has gradually become withered, weary, and woody. This happens with plants like the day-blooming evening primrose (*Oenothera missouriensis*), creeping phlox (*P. subulata*), and some iris, among others. In such an instance, the plant's often wide-ranging offspring may then be further divided to fill the gap and to create strong new plants. Certain perennials like the day lily (*Hemerocallis*), for example, should be routinely divided every two or three years, to stimulate healthy new growth and to stop it from wandering too far afield.

The procedure itself of division is uncomplicated enough. Alas, your tribulations begin when you study how individual plants like to be divided. Suddenly you'll wonder what ever happened to the word "root." Oh, the roots are there all right—it is simply that they are attached to a variety of organs, many of them food-storage vessels, which come with strange-sounding names that may mean little or nothing to you. In this way, you will meet rhizomes, tubers, corms, bulbs, bulblets, bulbils, runners, stolons, and suckers. And, of course, roots. I include the list here only to soften the blow when it eventually (and inevitably) comes. To give you an idea of who has what—and what it looks like—following is one typical example for each of the above terms:

Rhizome*	=	Iris
Tuber	=	Potato
Corm	=	Gladiolus
Bulb	=	Tulip

*This is often referred to as rootstock—not to be confused with the rootstock on which a hybrid rose, for instance, has been grafted (see Chapter 9).

Bulblet	=	Tulip
Bulbil	=	Tiger Lily
Runner	=	Strawberry
Stolon	=	Chrysanthemum
Sucker	=	Red Raspberry

Each of the above represents a means of developing new plants. For the purpose of introducing you to the subject of simple propagation, however, I will describe below only the general principles of plant division.

In temperate climates, plant division works best if it is undertaken in spring or early autumn. The temperatures are cool then, and the air and soil are moist. However, in the Northeast, where I live, as in other more extreme climates, I suggest that you divide your plants only in spring to early summer, so that the corporate-management roots and the food-gathering force I discussed in Chapter 10 may have enough time to become settled and to grow. An autumn division in this part of the country would make that impossible, and your new plants might freeze with the onset of an early winter. No matter which season is right for dividing plants in your region, you should never do so during a hot and dry or a cold and freezing period.

Again, as in making your stem-cutting selections, choose only the healthy-looking, plump and juicy plant candidates for this propagation method. Discard any that are too small or frail. Also cut off any broken roots or shoots before planting. Ideally, you will divide your plants well before they reach full growth for the season, and long before they bloom. *Never* divide plants that are in full flower, for the same reasons I gave you in the preceding section. If your climate is conducive to autumn division, it's best to trim the new plant's top growth to about three or four inches before planting.

As with stem cuttings, there should be as little delay as possible between making a division and planting the babies, in order to prevent the roots from drying out and the foliage from wilting. To spare yourself having to run back and forth, however, making

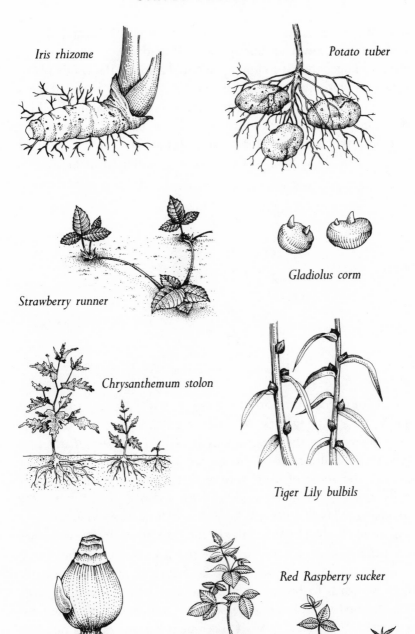

Iris rhizome

Potato tuber

Strawberry runner

Gladiolus corm

Chrysanthemum stolon

Tiger Lily bulbils

Tulip bulb and bulblet

Red Raspberry sucker

divisions and planting them, keep the new plants moist and cool under a wet towel or burlap sack. Provided you don't expect them to linger there too long, you could also put the young plants in a pail with just enough water to cover the roots. It goes without saying that once your new babies are happily bedded down in their new home, they should not only be clearly labeled but also thoroughly watered in and mulched. If the weather becomes suddenly hot, you may have to water them for several days.

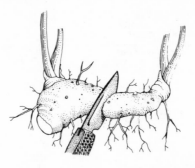

Rhizome sections showing "eyes"

Divisions can be made by hand or with a knife, a trowel, a spade, or a digging fork. Whenever possible, I try to tease the new plants from their parents by hand. This is particularly true when I carefully remove the rooted rosettes that emerge from around the roots of such perennials as yarrow (*Achillea*), coral-bells, and columbine (*Aquilegia*). With a dense clump of day lily or plantain lily (*Hosta*), I take a less delicate approach. Here, I simply spade the clumps apart. In the case of iris, whose rhizomes are often visible on the surface, I use a knife to cut the young rhizome from its parent. If I should forget my knife, however, it does no harm to break the rhizome off. In fact, provided roots are attached to each section, you may even divide a rhizome into several sections, as long as each segment has an "eye," a bud like the eyes on a potato, for next year's growth. To divide ground covers like lily of the valley (*Convallaria majalis*), periwinkle (*Vinca minor*), or sedum, I find it easiest to lift a clump slightly from the soil, so that I can detach some of the offspring. As soon as that's done, I rebed the parent plant firmly. This method also works well with phlox, among others.

Although many young plants like to be grouped together— or at least do not object to it—once they're separated from their parents, *Convallaria* babies are isolationists, they "vant to be left alone." They differ, too, in that their leaf buds are not referred to as crowns or rosettes, but as "pips."

By far the easiest to divide are those creeping perennials that multiply via underground stolons (see above). Among them are evening primrose, bergamot, yellow loosestrife (*Lysimachia*), and "Silver King" (*Artemisia albula*). I love them all dearly, but showy and beautiful as they are, these fellows must be kept firmly in check every spring. So densely packed are their stolons that the soil literally cannot fall out from among them. In desperation last spring, because I've run out of friends who want further such donations, I tossed the dug-up clumps of these plants into the meadow. Frankly, my chief concern was that so much good compost-rich soil was forced to accompany them. You guessed it. Undaunted, those exuberant rascals bloomed anyway, even though they had landed on a thick matting of grass.

There is one final point regarding the above two propagating methods. Many plants raised from division will bloom during the first year, whereas most plants grown from stem cuttings do not bloom until the second year. Of course, that is assuming that they are flowering plants to start with.

Definitely a great favorite of mine is propagation from **seed.**

If ever we needed proof of nature's generosity, that time comes when the myriad seeds ripen all around us, in our gardens and beyond—an unimagined wealth. Their shapes and sizes are as varied as are the plants that produce them. Seeds may appear as minuscule cornucopias or shiny black globules, as tiny specks of dust or tufted darts, or as diaphanous wings, among many others. They are things of great beauty in themselves, if we look closely enough. We may not always recognize them as seeds, or look for or find them, or understand the processes in their formation and fertility, but all together, seeds are nature's promise to us of another year. Of life. For most of them, their transport is the wind; for others, it may be birds or squirrels—or the human hand. Wherever they fall, seeds will find their way to the comfort of the earth, where many of them germinate in their own time and emerge as new plants, sometimes at a great distance from their parent.

That, very loosely speaking, is nature's method of seed propagation. However, unless you want, or don't mind, a wild garden, this method is not entirely satisfactory for your purposes. Consequently, you are well advised to assume the administrative responsibilities of acting as the chief of seed transportation, propagation, and distribution. Only you can know where you want more of a particular plant. Your job is one that requires full vigilance.

Beginning in mid to late summer, you can't help but notice the appearance of pretty little seedlings around some of your plants in the perennial bed. Although they may appear over an extended radius, you will quickly discover the culprit parent in the vicinity. As its flowers faded and the seeds matured, a breeze came long and broadcast those seeds. And now you are looking at the results. Among the most uninhibited seed broadcasters are the poppy (*Papaver*), flax (*Linum*), and feverfew (*Chrysanthemum parthenium*), although I cannot imagine my garden without them. The first two bloom simultaneously, providing a stunning late-spring show of deep orange and pure blue, respectively. The third, feverfew, blooms through most of the summer, and its dozens of small white flowers, single on some plants, double on others, help to unify all the other plant groups as *their* blooming seasons come and go. Nevertheless, all three need strict management. And that means seed collection—or deadheading (see Chapter 15).

Many annuals and vegetables produce seeds that are true to type. It is an easy and inexpensive way to raise new plants. Likely candidates among them might be, respectively: marigolds, zinnias, nicotianas; tomatoes, green peppers, squash. It is best to remove the seeds and let them air-dry thoroughly before storing them. Some of the hardier types among seeds of annuals and vegetables are able to winter over outdoors and turn up as new plants the following spring (see Chapter 9). However, most annual and vegetable seeds—certainly in my Northeastern climate—do best when they are dried and stored, ready for sowing in spring.

Many biennials also self-sow and develop into new plants *without* your help. They include foxglove (*Digitalis*), honesty (*Lunaria*), and hollyhock (*Althaea rosea*), among others. In their case, it's a particularly good idea to gather their seeds, for reasons entirely unrelated to weather. The life cycle of biennials, as the word suggests, spans two years. This means that the seeds they drop this midsummer grow into young plants next year, but these plants do not bloom until the following year. In your garden it works like this: This spring you buy a digitalis. You plant and clearly label it, and the digitalis blooms this summer. When the flowers fade and the seeds ripen, unbeknownst to you, a breeze scatters the seeds across the bed, under your coreopsis, for example. Next spring, when everything else begins to grow, you believe your digitalis must have died (and, indeed, it may have), because all you have left in its place is a bare spot and your label. As the months pass, you weed your garden carefully. Naturally, you don't know that the "weeds" under your coreopsis are new digitalis plants that grew from the seeds the wind scattered there. So you pull them out and throw them away as weeds. And that really *is* the end of your digitalis. Instead, if you'd gathered the digitalis seeds in the first place, you could have sown them around the original parent plant and the new seedlings would have arisen in the neighborhood of your label.

I've already illustrated how at least three of my perennials freely self-sow their seeds. The list, of course, includes many others that do the same, and their seeds develop into exact reproductions of the original plants. The problem arises if a plant you bought at the nursery was labeled as "F_1 Hybrid." In that instance, the chances are very slim that the seeds it produces will grow into more of the same. Hybrids are the result of a complicated procedure in which two strains of a plant are cross-pollinated to produce a plant of exceptional vigor and of reliably uniform growth and flowering performance. Such a procedure, because of the need for rigorously supervised cultural conditions, is generally undertaken only by commercial growers. The seed you gather from a hybrid plant may not germinate at all, because it is sterile, or else it may produce an offspring that resembles one or the other of its progenitors. This same principle also applies to F_1 hybrid biennials and vegetables.

Without doubt, *buying* seeds is by far the simplest means of raising from seed the many plants you want. But "simplest" isn't always "most enjoyable." Therefore, following are a few suggestions for harvesting your own seeds. When the time comes for sowing them, merely follow the guidelines in Chapter 9.

As you begin to study the flowers in your garden, you will surely become enchanted by the truly exquisite array of miniature vessels in which they prepare their seeds for you. These vessels, called "pods," are the fruit of the plants. Pods usually develop from the base of the flower heads, and as the flowers fade, so the pods swell. In some plants, such as zinnias, the flower head seems to develop another within it. That inner "fruiting head" emerges like a hooded monk who wears the dying, fading petals like a fringe around the hem of his habit. Some flowers, like lupines, form fruit like the pods of garden peas, only they are covered with the softest silvery down. On flax, the pods appear as countless tiny round fairy lanterns, swaying gently on the slim, green-feathered stems of the plant. And the pods of iris resemble nothing so much as the armored torso of an ancient knight. And so on, endlessly.

All the various pods will eventually become one shade or another of brown. This means that the seeds they contain are ripening and the pods will soon burst open to let them escape. A browning of the flower stems and the fading of flowers will be additional clues that it's nearly time for you to cut off and gather the pods, before their contents are whisked away by a playful breeze.

If at all possible, try to collect your seeds on a dry day. Keeping each kind separate from the others, spread them on sheets of newspaper, in a warm, dry, airy (but free from wind) indoor area (attic or basement or garage) so that they may finish ripening. Above all, be sure to identify each kind of seed.

At the end of about two or three weeks, the seeds will be ready for storage until planting time next spring. Shake or shell the seeds from the pods, or rub them loose between fingers and thumb. Then place them in *clearly labeled* paper bags, envelopes, small plastic bags, or glass jars, and store them in a cool, dark area, in a container that's secure against rodents and other thieving varmint. After all, what do *they* know about what you went through. To them, one seed is as tasty as another.

Incidentally, besides gathering seeds from your flowers, you may also want to try raising plants from, say, a shrub like spirea, or from a maple or an oak. Or you may want to plant the seeds of a fruit you've just eaten, such as an apple, a mango, or a grapefruit. (The latter two should be considered indoor plants in cold climates like mine.) Be advised, though, that the seeds from these and other fruits are slow to germinate and, more often than not, fail to become fruiting plants in the home indoor or outdoor garden. On the other hand, the plants themselves are so charming and uncommon, some of them growing to considerable size, that their fruiting ability becomes almost secondary. Before planting a hard-shelled mango seed, you can encourage germination if you first and *carefully* chip the shell with a small knife.

With all seeds, there are no rules regarding the length of time they remain viable—able to germinate. Some seeds never do germinate; some may be willing and able for only one year; the viability of others may well outlast the lifespan of your pet dog; and quite a few are known to have survived a century or more of dormancy. I myself *try* not to hold on to seeds for more than two or three years before committing them to the earth en masse. But because being a gardener also makes me a hoarder, trying doesn't always mean succeeding. Besides, who knows, there may be life in the old seed yet—ten, twenty years from now!

R · E · C · A · P

1. Make stem cuttings and root divisions in cool weather only—never at peak blossom time.

2. Depending on parent plant's size, cuttings may be 6 to 12 inches long, severed at a slant.

3. Remove all flowers and flower buds; cut off all except top three to four pairs of leaves.

4. *Optional*: Dip cuts in hormone rooting medium.

5. Plant cuttings in rich, moist soil, in a sheltered location; label cuttings; protect against frost, intense sunlight.

6. Gather stem cuttings, root divisions, seeds from only most vigorous plants.

7. Let seed pods fully develop on plants before removing them.

8. Gather ripe seed pods on dry day; dry in warm location.

9. Shell seeds; store in labeled, secure containers, in cool, dark location.

Garden Maintenance

Strictly speaking, nearly half the chapters in this book are concerned with maintaining your garden and all the plants in it. If you didn't water or weed, compost, mulch, or mow; if you didn't harvest the fruits of your labor, or increase or replace your plants through propagation (or new purchases); if you didn't watch out for unwanted beasties, or entice the beasties you *do* want; or if you didn't prepare your garden for next year by "tucking it in" before winter, quite soon you would end up with a wilderness. A mess. But if you have come thus far in your reading, you already know most of that. You know that regular watering and weeding are at the top of the maintenance list, as is humus-enriched soil. But there is more to it than that. As you know yourself, no matter how carefully you comb your hair, if it has lost its shape, with tufts protruding where they should not, you cannot be satisfied until it is cut and styled again. The principle with plants is much the same.

Therefore, I will now turn your attention to what might be called the refinements, or grooming, of the garden. By far the most immediately visible refinement is called edging. As an illustration, special groupings of trees or shrubs, a flower bed, a lawn or path, a herb or vegetable garden all become instantly striking features once their outlines are clearly defined. Many forms of edging, however, also guard beds and borders against intrusive grass.

True, the moment you have thoroughly dug, composted, planted, and mulched your new beds, they *are* defined—at least for a time—a short time at that. The reason for this is very simply that unless you've dug your garden out of a field of solid rock, gravel, or sand, it is more than likely that you have grass close by. And grass has a habit of creeping to wherever it can gain a comfortable foothold. That includes your flower and other beds. Before long, the grassy invader will siphon off much of the nourishment and moisture in the soil, depriving your plants, while you will be engaged in regular skirmishes trying to weed out the intruder.

Therefore, the time is ripe for creating the gardener's version of a no-man's-land. Such an interruption not only provides a dramatic visual effect but often serves a very practical purpose. It may consist of low-growing border plants, of various construction materials, or of nothing at all except an edge cut and a carefully aimed lawn mower. The alternative to the above is the constant need to weed around the grassy sides of your beds.

Edgings may also serve as "curbs" along paths and driveways; if these consist of gravel, an edging will prevent the gravel from spitting into lawns or beds. Lastly, edgings are often used to retain the soil in raised or sloping beds.

Edge plantings may be formal or informal. They may be composed of a single kind of low, compact-growing perennial like boxwood (*Buxus sempervirens suffruticosa*), candytuft (*Iberis sempervirens*), or box barberry (*Berberis thunbergi minor*).

A massed planting of a single perennial flower like lavender may be another choice—and I can tell you, few edgings have quite the same visual or olfactory impact as massed lavender in full bloom. Or you could alternate lavender with one or more of the following perennials of low-growing habit: *Geranium sanguineum* (reddish-purple flowers), *Saponaria ocymoides* (pink flowers), *Gypsophila repens* (white or pinkish flowers), *Phlox subulata* (purple, pink, and white flowers), or the above-named candytuft.

Your edging could also be devised of annuals, of a single color or mixed. These mean more work for you, of course, because you will have to replace them every year, but annuals add a vividness of color rarely mustered by perennials, *and* they bloom nonstop throughout the summer. Impatiens are good for a semi-shaded area. For full sun, there is nothing quite like petunias densely massed in a brilliant show, or close-set cushions of *Verbena hortensis*. You might prefer a border of sweet alyssum, white or purple, one color only, or both alternating, or perhaps the white of sweet alyssum alternating with the rich blue of ageratum. Geraniums, of course, lend themselves well to edgings and require minimal care. And few plants can match the unflagging stamina, through winds and droughts, of the dear old marigold.

Among construction materials for edgings, genuine, disused railroad ties are popular, although they are more and more difficult to find. Weatherbeaten and often somewhat warped, I like them as natural-looking, rustic borders of otherwise ill-defined driveways, or to contain a small raised bed. Also, I like these ties because they're wide enough to support a variety of planters filled with flowers, to provide a splash of color in what might be a drab or hard-to-plant spot. Weather-treated copies of railroad ties are available commercially. They are neat, symmetrical, and streamlined in appearance, and come in various widths and lengths. They lend themselves well to edgings of narrow or geometric beds, or they can be stacked to create raised beds or retaining walls. But for me, they lack the romance, the mystery, and the sense of adventure that are in the oil- and time-stained old ones.

Available at most garden supply centers are selections of commercial edgings. Although I have tried several of these, I find them generally unsatisfactory for my purposes, which is not to imply that they *are* unsatisfactory. Of these, a fairly wide, heavy metal strip pushed to ground level between lawn and flower bed—a kind of gardener's Berlin Wall—is probably the most efficient. It allows you to mow to the edge of the grass without damaging the lawn mower, and it has the added advantage of remaining in place through a variety of weather conditons. This is not true of the cheaper plastic version of such a strip. First of all, plastic edgings are generally corrugated strips, which makes it impossible for them to hold a neat line. And because they are lightweight and flexible, they tend to heave in frosty winters like mine, or alternatively sink into wet soil. In either situation, they buckle and bend if you try to realign them to the proper depth.

Also sold at garden centers are metal hoops and sections of miniature picket fencing, as well as low chain-link fencing. Because these are essentially decorative and don't even pretend to hold invasive grass at bay, I have never used them. Nevertheless, they look attractive as frames for small beds, or following a path among plant groupings, or as guardians around a focal planting.

Naturally, some gardeners—especially those who are fortunate enough to be or to know a good carpenter—construct a variety of attractive borders and curbs from wooden blocks and cylinders. Others erect miniature post-and-rail fences. Still other gardeners build low stone walls or rock borders, while those

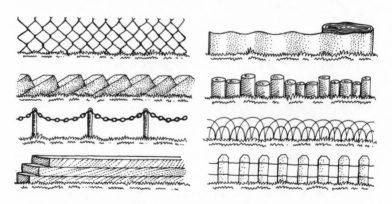

Edgings are a garden's most visible refinement; shown are edgings made of metal, bricks, wood, and plastic.

who have both enough time and enough patience, set borders of bricks in the ground around their beds, or create artfully designed, narrow edging paths, to separate flower beds from the lawn. The owner of at least one garden I've heard about opted for total victory over his grassy creepers. He edged his beds with poured concrete, thirty-six inches deep, topped with a double row of bricks laid end to end at ground level. *He* meant business!

As you may begin to understand from all this, many gardeners view edging as no laughing matter. In fact, it can become a serious and expensive undertaking. And yet none, except possibly the last example, will totally prevent grass from crossing the DMZ. However furtively or arduously, grass roots will find a way to sneak up on your beds, be it from under your defensive installations or over the top of them. Mine, alas, is the cynical voice born of tearstained frustration. Over the years, I've tried at least half the foregoing methods—and abandoned them, disenchanted.

Nowadays, I use the most modest by far of all the edging methods—and just possibly the most effective—the edge cut. That, *plus* some edge plantings. The edge cut lends itself ideally to defining the outlines of freestanding beds, as well as to the grassy verges of any planting. Again, ideally, the edge cut is best made after your plants are in bed but before you mulch.

Wait! Don't slam the book shut in disgust. Don't you see, I *had* to nag you about mulching when I did or you might not have done it at all. Let me hasten to add that this method, too, does not stop grass from making its advances, but it certainly forces it to regroup. Most important of all, its forays into garden beds are immediately visible and can be easily corrected.

If your bed is already mulched, and you decide to try the edge cut, simply clear perhaps two feet around the inside perimeter of the bed by raking the mulch toward the center. (If you decided in Chapter 11 not to mulch—fie! fie!—continue anyway as follows.) Using a spade for this job is easier than a shovel. The commercially available tool called an edger, or an edge cutter, will be most useful as a means of maintaining this edging *after* it has been made. You will also need your garden cart or wheelbarrow and a rake. Your objective is to create a narrow ditch, not unlike the shape of a sloppy check mark.

Make vertical cuts no less than six inches deep all around the edge of the bed. Being careful not to nick this clean line, scoop up at least one shovelful of soil from the base as you go along and put this in your cart for the present. Next, with the *back* of the rake, smooth and gently slope the far side of the ditch toward the plants. Then, again with your spade or shovel, correct any unevenness—nicks and bulges—along the edge cut. The finished edge cut should look like this:

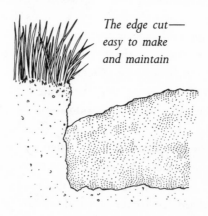

*The edge cut—
easy to make
and maintain*

Spread mulch over the bed and along the bottom of the little ditch, but be sure to keep *at least* three inches of the vertical cut exposed. Finally, use the soil in your cart to help prepare your compost, or for potted plants, or to fill unwanted hollows in the lawn—whatever. And that's all.

If the foregoing edging methods can be termed "positive," there is also another, a "negative," possibility. For instance, if you decide to unify a stand of trees or shrubs by means of a ground cover, you can easily create such a bed effect. As in my description of laying out a free-form bed (see Chapter 7), you may want to couple your watering hoses to obtain a pleasing shape in this instance. Instead of digging the soil, however, now you need only skim off a two- or three-inch layer of sod around your trees or shrubs to get rid of the grass. Then, with your digging fork, loosen the soil of this area, being careful not to damage the roots of the existing trees or shrubs. Spread a three-inch layer of a mulch like bark shavings or leaf mold, and then plant a ground cover like periwinkle or pachysandra, for example. Be sure to water the plants in thoroughly. Within two or three years, the ground cover will have filled out the area, and from then on you need only mow the contours of this bed's "negative" edging.

FOR GENERAL OVERALL MAINTENANCE, I take a walkabout routinely at the end of almost every day, armed with hand pruners and a trowel. Please understand, I do not regard this as a grim "business trip"; rather, I do it for the pleasure of watching my garden grow, and to take care of problems as soon as, or before, they arise. For example, the wind, or a clumsy puppy chasing butterflies, may have broken a twig or flower head; a diseased plant may need digging up (by the way, *never* add diseased plants to your compost; get rid of them entirely); a shoot of one plant may have fallen across another and needs to be pruned or propped up; or a plant may have simply died for any number of reasons, not least because it was not as healthy as it had seemed when I bought it.

Mostly, however, I check for faded flowers, which will have to be "deadheaded." The purpose of deadheading is twofold. Most immediately evident is the fact that the plant looks groomed the instant its faded flowers are removed. More important is the fact that deadheading stops plants from going to seed. If faded blooms are removed, the plant devotes its energy to further growth and development; if faded blossoms are allowed to remain, the plant takes this as a signal to go into seed production and directs its energies to that end (see Chapter 14). This applies as much to certain annuals and biennials as it does to perennials. Small flowers can be easily pinched off between finger and thumb; in the case of larger plants, or those with thick or woody stems— peonies and phlox, for example—it's best to use pruners.

There are plants, like peonies, which have only a single flower show per season—but *what* a glorious show! And there are other plants whose blossoms appear in successive waves, so that it seems as though the same flowers were in bloom throughout the summer. These include, among others, the perennials Maltese cross (*Lychnis chalcedonica*) and feverfew, the biennial foxglove, and the annuals snapdragon (*Antirrhinum*) and zinnia. It will help you, therefore, to have an idea how best to go about deadheading to ensure the continued good looks of the peony and the uninterrupted flowering of the others.

The blossoms of peonies may not last long, but the plants themselves are, I believe, almost indispensable in any perennial garden. From early spring until the first frost, they retain their elegant, upright form, providing a sense of calmness amid the sea of joyous color explosions all around them. And, as the season advances, their large "fingered" leaves assume subtly changing hues, from a rich green to the vibrant tones of autumn bronze. Although the weight of the blossoms will cause your peonies to sprawl, judicious deadheading will quickly correct that once the show is over. Simply cut the stem to about half its length, making the cut a hair above a "leaf axil," the point at which a leaf emerges from the stem. By making the cut just there, in the leaf axil, the leaf becomes the top of the severed stem, and even you will be hard-pressed to find it later. In addition, in this instance of deadheading, you have also pruned the plant, to help it hold its rest-of-the-summer shape.

Before deadheading successive bloomers, look for plantlets in the leaf axils along the stems (or as is the case with coreopsis, amid the low-growing mound of foliage). Such plantlets are largest near the base, and become ever smaller toward the top of the stems. You will recognize them quite easily as small green tufts emerge from the leaf axil, proportionately no larger than a baby kangaroo poking its nose out of its mother's pouch. You will now have to make a decision. If the plant is spindly and rangy, not in the least like the photographs in your gardening books, then you can combine deadheading with pruning. *One at a time,* cut each stem by about one-third to one-half, to just above one of the plantlets. By eliminating the spindly top growth, you will be encouraging the plant to put a little effort into more vigorous growth. If a plant looks perfectly healthy and its shape is full and pleasing, simply take off its faded flowers. In most instances, be sure to cut off the flower *stem* as well, either up to a plantlet or to the next branch.

In the case of such plants as iris, daffodil, tulip, and day lily, however, remove only the faded flowers, *together with the seed pods at their base*. Do not remove the flower stalks. These stalwarts not only support and nourish the flower heads but also serve as the nutrition center for the seed pods. When you remove the seed pods along with the flower heads, the stalks have fulfilled their aboveground duties. They now return the balance of their nutritive inventory to the plant's belowground headquarters bulb, rhizome, corm, etc.—so that these resources may be applied to its own and its offsprings' growth and strength. For this reason, it's important for you to allow the stalks to turn brown before cutting them. Oh, I know, it will be a bit of a letdown for a short time, to see all these naked spikes after the splendid show that came before, but it really is best for your plants. Because they, too, serve as sources of nourishment, the leaves should also be allowed to wilt completely before they're removed.

On all your other plants, if some of the flower seeds have ripened in spite of your vigilance, either prepare them for storing (see Chapter 14) or discard them. If, on the other hand, you *want* to propagate certain of your plants, then allow the seeds of only the healthiest, strongest flower heads to ripen, and deadhead all the others on that plant.

By now, you may be thinking that having a garden is all work and no play, asking yourself, Whatever happened to picking flowers, bunches and bunches of them? You are quite right, especially as having a house full of cut flowers is one of my own main reasons for having a garden. So go ahead, cut your bouquets. All you need do is follow the same procedure as with deadheading. But I would caution you not to denude your plants all at once;

rather, cut them selectively, so that you can satisfy two objectives—an abundance of color and fragrance indoors and well-shaped, groomed flowering plants outside.

Year-round maintenance also means cutting off all broken parts of a plant, and this includes trees and shrubs. Left untended, such damaged members can very easily become host to a variety of diseases or insect infestations. Of course, too, the plants won't win any beauty contests.

In the course of the summer, you may decide that certain plants in your perennial bed do not please you, after all, in the locations where they are at present. I strongly suggest that you make a note about that and wait until autumn or next spring before moving them. In both seasons, the air and soil are cool and moist. If they are transplanted in autumn, the plants will settle down quite comfortably, knowing that they will not be expected to perform until next year. In a spring transplanting, on the other hand, they are already so full of pep, raring to go, that they will hardly notice that you changed stages. Transplant them in midsummer, however, and what you get is . . . a guilt trip.

Spring maintenance includes reestablishing the boundaries of those incorrigible perennials which routinely invade their neighbors' territory. As you already know from propagating them, these plants include *Monarda, Oenothera,* and *Lysimachia.* Deal with them firmly. With your shovel or spade, cut around the bounds you are prepared to allow them (you'll have to do this every spring), and dig up all the roots and shoots outside that line. Then discard this excess, or make presents of it, or plant it in another area of your garden. But beware! Those excess plants will spread there, too.

Only in winter is there very little to do. Even so, I find this a good time to study the form of my flowering and other deciduous shrubs, to determine whether or where they should be pruned. Winter is also a good time to check for true suckers, to decide which of them might be raised into new shrubs or trees, and to mark the rest for removal. The "bad guy" suckers are also more visible now, as are the overall outlines of existing beds, in relation to undeveloped or underdeveloped areas. Winter maintenance includes removing fallen twigs and branches, or cutting those that are broken on your trees and shrubs. Some of your tools might have to be repaired or sharpened, and lists made for replacements or for items necessary for next year's gardening work. This is also the time to scrub all the pots you'll need when you turn your home into a greenhouse in early spring. And you thought you could hibernate?

R · E · C · A · P

1. Define garden beds for a groomed look.

2. Make edge cuts before mulching, if possible.

3. Prune and remove damaged plant portions; destroy diseased plants or plant parts.

4. Support sprawling plants.

5. Deadhead faded flowers; cut spindly tops to encourage new growth.

6. Relocate plants during cool, moist seasons only.

7. Maintain boundaries of spreading plants in spring.

8. In winter, study form of deciduous shrubs for possible pruning; remove broken or fallen twigs and limbs of trees.

9. Repair tools; scrub pots for indoor "greenhouse" planting.

Winterizing Your Garden

T

here comes a day every year when, without warning, the air is suffused with an indefinable sadness. There is a sense of parting that day, of loss. The day may be warm and mellow, or there may be a cool, misty breeze. But it comes, quite unmindful of the calendar date. And every year I realize only when it has passed that it was nature's first day of autumn.

Overnight the mood is gone. It's harvest time, a time when the earth disgorges the last of its riches. And with these come memories. Ever since my earliest years, when I used to watch or help Mother with the annual rituals of preserving the year's glut, I have remained utterly committed to storing food for the cold, dark days of winter. It must be the hamster in me! Consequently, autumn is an especially active season, the time to freeze and bottle vegetables and fruits, to dry herbs and flowers, to make chutneys, vinegars, jams, and soups. Most of all, autumn is the time when the garden needs help to enter its period of rest.

Once you have gathered the last of your harvest, be sure to add all its wastes to your compost heap. Then deeply dig or till the vegetable patch, and seed it with buckwheat or winter rye (see Chapter 3). These will grow into a lush green carpet long before the first snow, well on their way to becoming green manure. When the snow melts next spring, your green manure crop will continue to grow. Let it reach a height of about six inches before thoroughly digging or tilling it under, as you would do in any case, preparatory to a new season of vegetable planting. Not only will your winter crop add and replace valuable nutrients, but it will help to reduce the new year's weeds. By the way, certain vegetables taste better, sweeter, after a frost. This is particularly true of Brussels sprouts, carrots, and parsnips. In fact, Swiss chard and kale may even be harvested from under the cover of snow throughout much of the winter in my area.

In the meantime, the last of your flowers will be fading, their stalks and leaves, as well as their flower heads, turning brown and brittle. Pull up the annuals and add them to the compost. Cut the perennials to about three inches, and be sure that their crowns are covered with mulch. Remember, do not remove the tabs that identify these plants, because, by next spring, you probably will no longer recall where they were. Be sure to harvest your gladiolus corms before the first hard frost (28° F.), cutting the foliage flush with the top of the corms. Clinging to these you'll discover a number of baby corms, called "cormels," no larger than peas. Given enough time and care, these cormels will grow into full-sized corms, to augment your gladiolus collection. For now, however, until planting time next spring, separate the corms and cormels and store them indoors, in a dry, cool, well-ventilated location—I usually keep them in brown paper bags or in cardboard boxes—out of the reach of mice!

Suddenly your garden looks bleak and passive. You cannot bear the thought of the long, cold months ahead, especially when the days of autumn quite often still reach summer warmth. You tell yourself that you should have waited a while before cutting plants down. You may be sure, I used to do the same at the beginning. The fact is, however, there is still quite a lot to be done, and if you delay too long, a sudden snowstorm or plummeting temperatures may make it impossible.

Therefore, cheer yourself up. Think spring. Prepare a festival of brilliant colors for those last restless winter days next March and April. Plant daffodils and tulips, scilla, crocus, and snowdrops, grape hyacinths and star-of-Bethlehem. The varieties are almost boundless. Plant them where you will easily see them from the house on spring days that are too cold for you to spend much time outdoors.

Galaxies of spring bulbs become available in early September. They are offered through seed catalogues and at nurseries, at farm and garden centers—even supermarkets. They are easy to plant and require virtually no care. Best of all, they multiply wherever you plant them, some of them through bulblets alone, others through seed as well as bulblets.

Spring bulbs are best planted in groups, or massed for a showy effect. The depth at which they should be planted is largely determined by the size of the bulbs. As a general rule, set bulbs at a depth two and a half times their size, and slightly farther than that distance apart. Prepare and loosen the soil, as you did for your other plantings last spring, and level the base of the hole. Add roughly a teaspoonful of bone meal and a generous handful of compost per bulb, and mix these lightly with the soil before setting your bulbs into the ground. Then fill the hole and firmly tamp the soil. Presto, that's all. No watering is necessary. In fact, when you finally get off your knees and stretch your back, hardly a trace of your labors will be visible—until next spring.

To help your hybrid roses through the winter cold, especially in northern climes like mine, heap soil around their base, to a height of about one foot. I generally do this in late October. It's best to shield climbing roses with a loose wrap of burlap, plus a mound of soil around their base. Very carefully, and over a period of two or three weeks, my grandfather used to bend his tree roses to the ground, each entire plant wrapped in burlap and attached with string to two bricks, which held it down. Mother did the same with her gooseberry trees. But be careful, if you do this, not to hurry the procedure and to leave a sufficient arc in the stem, so that the weight of snow will not break it. In spring the process is reversed, the tension slowly released, until the stem stands upright again.

Your roses, rhododendrons, and azaleas, as well as most broad-leaved evergreen shrubs—even tender young conifers—will need some protection, too, from winter sun and winds. The reason for winter protection has nothing to do with keeping your plants toasty. They're not warm-blooded creatures like us, needing to be bundled up against the cold. Plants are simply sensitive to extreme changes in their environment. And so the protection you give them serves two vital functions. The first is to minimize the fatal loss of moisture caused by sun and drying winds. The second is to help hardy plants remain dormant through the winter. Protection also lets your plants concentrate on sending their roots down deeply, to avoid the heave-ho's created by temperature fluctuations in the upper layers of the soil. Ecstatic as you and I might be during a warm spell and thaw in midwinter, we would hardly be foolish enough to start romping about in our bathing suits. We know better. Not that our plants are in the least foolish, but lacking calendars and meteorologists, they respond to the weather. Therefore, they would blithely start to awaken and grow, even during a dangerously premature warm period—only to be whacked again by subsequent icy blasts. Very sensibly, the perennials in your flower beds retreat below the surface in autumn. An added cover of mulch not only guards their crowns against sun and winds but keeps the plants evenly moist and cool. Alas, the more sensitive of your larger perennials can't hide under the ground in similar fashion. So by covering or screening them, you spare them what sometimes becomes quite literally a struggle between life and death.

If you have only a few of these plants, you may cover them

individually with burlap sacks stretched over stakes, or burlap sheets loosely tied over the shrubs. This also prevents deer from having a quiet winter nosh when you're not looking—if deer are a problem in your garden. Or you can surround the shrubs with bales of hay or straw. If your garden contains deciduous trees, you can also surround your plants with the fallen leaves and hold these in place with a chicken-wire cage or cover. Next spring, simply remove the leaves and add them to your pile of leaf mold. Some gardeners I know construct a steeply pitched gable roof over their plants, made of two wide boards that are pegged into the ground. Equally useful for low-growing plants are slatted wooden crates and round fruit baskets—provided these are weighted down with bricks or rocks to prevent the wind from moving or carrying them off. For small plants upended clay pots are a very satisfactory solution.

Never wrap your plants in plastic bags or sheets unless you first punch several holes in the plastic. Without these, the condensation that builds up underneath can ruin your plants. To avoid any chance of this happening if all you have is plastic, crumple some newspaper and place it *loosely* around the plant before covering it with a perforated plastic bag or sheet. To prevent it from being blown away, plastic will have to be secured at the base. You can either weight its edges down, again with bricks or rocks, or else loosely fasten them around the plant stem. Remember, your plants *must be able to breathe*.

If you have large plantings in need of winter protection, snow fencing or a screen made of burlap sheeting works best. Most important in the placement of all screens is to shelter your plants not only from frigid winter winds but from the equally damaging effects of the sun to the east and south. All screening should be supported by sturdy stakes placed at ten-foot intervals, in order to withstand the gale-force winter winds that certainly occur in my neck of the woods. To prevent your screen from toppling during such an assault, or during a winter thaw, or too early in spring, I suggest you place the support stakes (or posts) *at least* twelve inches deep in the ground, while the soil is still soft in autumn. Add the screening itself only after the ground is frozen, or even after the first snow, so that you can be sure that the supports will be held in place. Depending on the height of your shrubs, a dense screen of evergreen boughs pressed deeply into the soil is equally effective. And if you have a large planting of roses, mound soil around each plant, as described above, before placing one or more protective screens.

Although the plants are dormant by then, November is the time when I sprinkle a dusting of fertilizer around broad-leaved evergreens like rhododendrons, azaleas, and *Pieris japonica* (often sold as andromeda). By the time the roots wake up next spring, to begin their new cycle of growth, the fertilizer will already be there to serve their needs. I also thoroughly water these plants (and the roses) for the last time in the year. Even if there's a hard frost immediately afterward, and the water turns to ice, that ice will act as both insulation and ensured moisture for the roots, and prevent them from drying or freezing through the variable weather conditions of the winter months.

By now, the last of the leaves will be on the ground. If these are not too densely massed on the grass, I generally give the lawn one final mowing. This shreds the leaves and hastens their decomposition through the winter. Hardly a trace of them will be left next spring, and the shredded leaves will add compost to the grass. But if you have large quantities of fallen leaves, I suggest you rake and remove them to your leaf pile. Heaped in a corner of your garden, or behind a shed, out of sight, they will turn into wonderful leaf mold, ready to be used for mulch or compost next year (see Chapter 11).

This brings you to the end of the season. It is merely a matter of tidying up now—putting away the watering hose and the stakes that supported your tall perennials all summer. Make sure that the lids are firmly closed on fertilizers and any leftover seeds. Above all, thoroughly clean your gardening tools and lightly oil the metal portions before storing the tools for the winter (see Chapter 4). They have earned their rest.

Suddenly, inevitably, you feel quite forlorn as you look around your garden one more time. Gone are the joyous colors, the perspectives and contours which provided you with so much pleasure all through the summer months. The landscape is bare, colored in sepia tones, drowsy, mellow. It seems inconceivable that so much life abounded here such a short time ago. It seems even harder to imagine the power of life merely resting beneath your feet. And yet it's there. Look closely. Next year's buds are already formed on the trees and shrubs and vines around you. The crowns of your perennial flowers and the bulbs under your feet are tinged with the pale-green flush of life. They know that another spring will come. That is their promise to you.

R · E · C · A · P

1. Harvest gladiolus corms and cormels; store in cool, dry location.

2. Remove dead annuals; cut back all faded perennial plants; add refuse to compost.

3. Mulch crowns of perennials.

4. Leave all identifying labels and tabs as guides for next spring.

5. Till or turn over soil in vegetable bed; seed with winter rye or buckwheat.

6. Plant massed spring bulbs near house or in lawn.

7. Heap soil around base of roses; wrap or cover climbers with burlap.

8. Fertilize rhododendrons, other broad-leaved evergreens, young conifers, in November; water thoroughly.

9. Protect individual broad-leaved evergreens from winter sun and wind; for massed plantings, erect protective screens.

10. Rake and pile up (for compost or mulch) large quantities of leaves; shred small quantities in final mowing.

11. Securely cover and store seeds, fertilizers; wash, oil, store all garden tools in dry location.

A·P·P·E·N·D·I·X I

150 Herbaceous Perennials

(BOTANIC AND COMMON NAMES)

ACANTHUS	Bear's Breech
ACHILLEA	Yarrow
ACONITUM	Monkshood
ADENOPHORA	Ladybells
AEGOPODIUM	Goutweed
AETHIONEMA	Persian Candytuft
AGAPANTHUS	African Lily, Lily-of-the-Nile
AJUGA	Bugleweed
ALCHEMILLA	Lady's-Mantle
ALTHAEA	Hollyhock
ALYSSUM	Basket of Gold
AMSONIA	Blue Dogbane, Bluestar
ANAPHALIS	Pearly Everlasting
ANCHUSA	Bugloss, Alkanet
ANTENNARIA	Cat's Foot, Pussytoes
ANTHEMIS	Camomile, Golden Marguerite
AQUILEGIA	Columbine
ARABIS	Rock Cress
ARENARIA	Sandwort
ARMERIA	Sea Pink
ARTEMISIA	Wormwood, Southernwood,

	Silver Mound, "Silver King," Tarragon, Mountain Sage, Dusty Miller, Mugwort
ARUNCUS	Goatsbeard
ASARUM	Wild Ginger
ASCLEPIAS	Butterfly Weed
ASPERULA	Sweet Woodruff
ASTER	Michaelmas Daisy
ASTILBE	False Spirea
AUBRIETA	Purple Rock Cress
BAPTISIA	Blue False Indigo, Rattle Bush, Clover Broom, Shoofly
BELAMCANDA	Blackberry Lily
BERGENIA	Heart-Leaved Bergenia, Siberian Tea
BOLTONIA	False Camomile, False Starwort
BRUNNERA	Siberian Bugloss
CAMPANULA	Bellflower
CASSIA	Wild Senna
CATANANCHE	Cupid's Dart
CENTAUREA	Perennial Cornflower, Dusty Miller, Mountain Bluet, Knapweed, Spanish Buttons
CENTRANTHUS	Red Valerian, Jupiter's Beard
CERASTIUM	Snow-in-Summer
CERATOSTIGMA	Leadwort
CHELONE	Turtlehead, Snake Head, Shellflower
CHRYSANTHEMUM	
maximum	Shasta Daisy
parthenium	Feverfew
CHRYSOGONUM	Golden Star
CIMICIFUGA	Snakeroot, Black Snakeroot, Black Cohosh
CONVALLARIA	Lily of the Valley
COREOPSIS	Tickseed
CYNOGLOSSUM	Chinese Forget-Me-Not
CYPRIPEDIUM	Moccasin Flower, Lady's Slipper, Siberian Orchid

DELPHINIUM	Larkspur
DIANTHUS	Carnation, Pink
DICENTRA	Bleeding Heart, Dutchman's Breeches, Squirrel Corn
DICTAMNUS	Gas Plant, Dittany, Fraxinella, Burning Bush
DIGITALIS	Foxglove
DORONICUM	Leopard's Bane
ECHINACEA	Coneflower, Purple Coneflower, Purple Daisy, Hedgehog Coneflower, Black Sampson
ECHINOPS	Globe Thistle
EPIMEDIUM	Barrenwort, Bishop's Hat
ERIGERON	Fleabane
ERYNGIUM	Sea Holly
EUPATORIUM	Wild Hoarhound, Mistflower, Blue Boneset, Joe Pye Weed, White Snakeroot
EUPHORBIA	Spurge
FILIPENDULA	Meadowsweet, Dropwort
GAILLARDIA	Blanket Flower
GALEGA	Goat's Rue
GALIUM	Bedstraw
GENTIANA	Gentian
GERANIUM	Cranesbill, Hardy Geranium
GERBERA	African Daisy
GEUM	Avens
GYPSOPHILA	Baby's Breath
HELENIUM	Helen's Flower, Sneezeweed, Sneezewort
HELIANTHEMUM	Sun-rose, Frostweed
HELIANTHUS	River Sunflower, Swamp Sunflower, Jerusalem Artichoke
HELIOPSIS	False Sunflower, Hardy Zinnia
HELLEBORUS	Hellebore, Christmas Rose
HEMEROCALLIS	Day Lily
HEPATICA	Liverleaf, Liverwort
HESPERIS	Dame's Rocket, Garden Rocket, Dame's Violet

HEUCHERA	Coral-Bells, Alumroot
HIBISCUS	Rose Mallow, Swamp Mallow, Sea Hollyhock
HOSTA	Plantain Lily, Funkia, Niobe
IBERIS	Candytuft
INCARVILLEA	Hardy Gloxinia
INULA	Elecampane
IRIS	Flag
KNIPHOFIA	Tritoma, Red-Hot Poker
LAMIUM	Dead Nettle
LATHYRUS	Perennial (Sweet) Pea
LAVANDULA	Lavender
LIATRIS	Gay-Feather, Rattlesnake Master, Blazing Star, Prairie Button Snakeroot, Prairie Pine, Devil's Bit
LIGULARIA	Senecio
LILIUM	Lily
LIMONIUM	Sea Lavender, Statice
LINARIA	Toadflax, Figwort
LINUM	Flax
LIRIOPE	Lilyturf
LOBELIA	Cardinal Flower, Great Lobelia
LUPINUS	Lupine
LYCHNIS	Campion, Maltese Cross, Jerusalem Cross, Cuckoo Flower, Ragged Robin, Flower-of-Jove, German Catchfly
LYSIMACHIA	(Yellow) Loosestrife, Moneywort, Creeping Charlie, Creeping Jennie, Willow-wort
LYTHRUM	Purple Loosestrife
MACLEAYA	Plume Poppy
MERTENSIA	Virginia Bluebells, Lungwort, Virginia Cowslip, Roanoke Bells
MONARDA	Bergamot, Oswego Tea, Bee Balm, Red Balm

MYOSOTIS	Forget-Me-Not
NEPETA	Catnip, Catmint
OENOTHERA	Evening Primrose, Sundrops, Missouri Primrose
OPHIOPOGON	Lilyturf
OPUNTIA	Prickly Pear
PACHYSANDRA	Allegheny Spurge, Japanese Spurge
PAEONIA	Peony
PAPAVER	Poppy
PENSTEMON	Beard Tongue, St. Joseph's Wand, Scarlet Bugler
PEROVSKIA	Russian Sage
PHLOX **subulata**	Creeping Phlox, Ground Pink, Moss Pink, Flowering Moss
PHYSALIS	Chinese Lantern, Winter Cherry, Strawberry Tomato, Cape Gooseberry
PHYSOSTEGIA	False Dragonhead, Obedient Plant
PLATYCODON	Balloon Flower
PLUMBAGO	Leadwort
POLEMONIUM	Jacob's Ladder, Greek Valerian, Charity
POLYGONATUM	Solomon's Seal
POTENTILLA	Cinquefoil
PRIMULA	Primrose
PULMONARIA	Lungwort
RUDBECKIA	Black-Eyed Susan, Coneflower, Orange Coneflower, Thimble Flower
RUTA	Rue
SALVIA	Sage
SANGUINARIA	Bloodroot
SANTOLINA	Lavender Cotton
SAPONARIA	Soapwort
SCABIOSA	Pincushion Flower, Mourning Bride
SEDUM	Stonecrop

SIDALCEA	False Mallow, Wild Hollyhock
STACHYS	Lamb's Ears, Betony, Wound-wort
STOKESIA	Stokes' Aster
THALICTRUM	Meadow Rue
THERMOPSIS	False Lupine, Aaron's Rod
TRADESCANTIA	Spiderwort, Wandering Jew
TRICYRTIS	Toad Lily
TRILISA	Carolina Vanilla, Vanilla Leaf
TRILLIUM	Wakerobin, Ground Lily, Jew's Harp
TROLLIUS	Globeflower
VALERIANA	Valerian, Garden Heliotrope, Cretan Spikenard
VERBASCUM	Mullein
VERBENA	Vervain
VERNONIA	Ironweed
VERONICA	Speedwell
VINCA minor	Periwinkle, Creeping Myrtle
VIOLA	Violet, Pansy, Heartsease, Johnny-Jump-Up
YUCCA	Adam's Needle, Spanish Bayonet, Spanish Dagger, Mound Lily, Bear Grass, Joshua Tree

Aaron's Rod	thermopsis	Bugleweed	ajuga
Adam's Needle	yucca	Bugloss	anchusa
African Daisy	gerbera	Bugloss,	brunnera
African Lily	agapanthus	Siberian	
Alkanet	anchusa	Burning Bush	dictamnus
Allegheny	pachysandra	Butterfly Weed	asclepias
Spurge		Camomile	anthemis
Alumroot	heuchera	Camomile, False	boltonia
Avens	geum	Campion	lychnis
Baby's Breath	gypsophila	Candytuft	iberis
Balloon Flower	platycodon	Candytuft,	aethionema
Barrenwort	epimedium	Persian	
Basket of Gold	alyssum	Cape Goose-	physalis
Beard Tongue	penstemon	berry	
Bear Grass	yucca	Cardinal Flower	lobelia
Bear's Breech	acanthus	Carnation	dianthus
Bedstraw	galium	Carolina Vanilla	trilisa
Bee Balm	monarda	Catchfly,	lychnis
Bellflower	campanula	German	
Bergamot	monarda	Catmint	nepeta
Betony	stachys	Catnip	nepeta
Bishop's Hat	epimedium	Cat's Foot	antennaria
Blackberry Lily	belamcanda	Charity	polemonium
Black Cohosh	cimicifuga	Chinese	cynoglossum
Black-Eyed	rudbeckia	Forget-Me-Not	
Susan		Chinese Lantern	physalis
Black Sampson	echinacea	Christmas Rose	helleborus
Black Snakeroot	cimifuga	Cinquefoil	potentilla
Blanket Flower	gaillardia	Clover Broom	baptisia
Blazing Star	liatris	Cohosh, Black	cimicifuga
Bleeding Heart	dicentra	Columbine	aquilegia
Bloodroot	sanguinaria	Coneflower	echinacea
Blue Boneset	eupatorium	Coneflower	rudbeckia
Blue Dogbane	amsonia	Coneflower,	echinacea
Blue False In-	baptisia	Hedgehog	
digo		Coneflower,	rudbeckia
Bluestar	amsonia	Orange	
Boneset, Blue	eupatorium	Coneflower,	echinacea
Bugler, Scarlet	penstemon	Purple	

Coral-Bells	heuchera	False Starwort	boltonia
Cornflower,	centaurea	False Sunflower	heliopsis
Perennial		Feverfew	chrysanthe-
Cranesbill	geranium		mum
Creeping Char-	lysimachia		parthenium
lie		Figwort	linaria
Creeping Jennie	lysimachia	Flag	iris
Creeping Myrtle	vinca minor	Flax	linum
Creeping Phlox	phlox subulata	Fleabane	erigeron
Cretan Spike-	valeriana	Flowering Moss	phlox subulata
nard		Flower-of-Jove	lychnis
Cuckoo Flower	lychnis	Forget-Me-Not	myosotis
Cupid's Dart	catananche	Foxglove	digitalis
Daisy, Purple	echinacea	Fraxinella	dictamnus
Dame's Rocket	hesperis	Frostweed	helianthemum
Dame's Violet	hesperis	Funkia	hosta
Day Lily	hemerocallis	Garden Heli-	valeriana
Dead Nettle	lamium	otrope	
Devil's Bit	liatris	Garden Rocket	hesperis
Dittany	dictamnus	Gas Plant	dictamnus
Dogbane, Blue	amsonia	Gay-Feather	liatris
Dragonhead,	physostegia	Gentian	gentiana
False		Geranium,	geranium
Dropwort	filipendula	Hardy	
Dusty Miller	artemisia	German Catchfly	lychnis
Dusty Miller	centaurea	Ginger, Wild	asarum
Dutchman's	dicentra	Globeflower	trollius
Breeches		Globe Thistle	echinops
Elecampane	inula	Gloxinia, Hardy	incarvillea
Evening Prim-	oenothera	Goatsbeard	aruncus
rose		Goat's Rue	galega
False Camomile	boltonia	Golden Mar-	anthemis
False Dragon-	physostegia	guerite	
head		Golden Star	chrysogonum
False Indigo,	baptisia	Goutweed	aegopodium
Blue		Great Lobelia	lobelia
False Lupine	thermopsis	Greek Valerian	polemonium
False Mallow	sidalcea	Ground Lily	trillium
False Spirea	astilbe	Ground Pink	phlox subulata

Heart-Leaved Bergenia	bergenia	Lily-of-the-Nile	agapanthus
Heartsease	viola	Lily of the Valley	convallaria
Hedgehog Cone-flower	echinacea	Lilyturf	liriope
Helen's Flower	helenium	Lilyturf	ophiopogon
Hellebore	helleborus	Liverleaf	hepatica
Hoarhound, Wild	eupatorium	Liverwort	hepatica
Hollyhock	althaea	Loosestrife, Purple	lythrum
Hollyhock, Sea	hibiscus	Loosestrife (Yellow)	lysimachia
Hollyhock, Wild	sidalcea	Lungwort	mertensia
Indigo, Blue False	baptisia	Lungwort	pulmonaria
Ironweed	vernonia	Lupine	lupinus
Jacob's Ladder	polemonium	Lupine, False	thermopsis
Japanese Spurge	pachysandra	Mallow, Rose	hibiscus
Jerusalem Arti-choke	helianthus	Mallow, Swamp	hibiscus
Jerusalem Cross	lychnis	Maltese Cross	lychnis
Jew's Harp	trillium	Marguerite, Golden	anthemis
Joe Pye Weed	eupatorium	Meadow Rue	thalictrum
Johnny-Jump-Up	viola	Meadowsweet	filipendula
Joshua Tree	yucca	Michaelmas Daisy	aster
Jupiter's Beard	centranthus	Missouri Prim-rose	oenothera
Knapweed	centaurea	Mistflower	eupatorium
Ladybells	adenophora	Moccasin Flower	cypripedium
Lady's-Mantle	alchemilla	Moneywort	lysimachia
Lady's Slipper	cypripedium	Monkshood	aconitum
Lamb's Ears	stachys	Moss Pink	phlox subulata
Larkspur	delphinium	Mound Lily	yucca
Lavender	lavandula	Mountain Bluet	centaurea
Lavender Cotton	santolina	Mountain Sage	artemisia
Lavender, Sea	limonium	Mourning Bride	scabiosa
Leadwort	ceratostigma	Mugwort	artemisia
Leadwort	plumbago	Mullein	verbascum
Leopard's Bane	doronicum	Niobe	hosta
Lily	lilium		

Obedient Plant	physostegia	Pussytoes	antennaria
Orange	rudbeckia	Ragged Robin	lychnis
Coneflower		Rattle Bush	baptisia
Oswego Tea	monarda	Rattlesnake	liatris
Pansy	viola	Master	
Pea, Perennial	lathyrus	Red Balm	monarda
(Sweet)		Red-Hot Poker	kniphofia
Pearly Ever-	anaphalis	Red Valerian	centranthus
lasting		River Sunflower	helianthus
Peony	paeonia	Roanoke Bells	mertensia
Perennial Cone-	centaurea	Rock Cress	arabis
flower		Rose Mallow	hibiscus
Perennial	lathyrus	Rue	ruta
(Sweet) Pea		Rue, Meadow	thalictrum
Periwinkle	vinca minor	Russian Sage	perovskia
Persian Candy-	aethionema	Sage	salvia
tuft		Sage, Russian	perovskia
Pincushion	scabiosa	St. Joseph's	penstemon
Flower		Wand	
Pink Plantain	dianthus hosta	Sandwort	arenaria
Lily		Scarlet Bugler	penstemon
Plume Poppy	macleaya	Sea Holly	eryngium
Poppy	papaver	Sea Hollyhock	hibiscus
Prairie Button	liatris	Sea Lavender	limonium
Snakeroot		Sea Pink	armeria
Prairie Pine	liatris	Senecio	ligularia
Prickly Pear	opuntia	Senna, Wild	cassia
Primrose	primula	Shasta Daisy	chrysanthe-
Primrose,	oenothera		mum maxi-
Evening			mum
Primrose,	oenothera	Shellflower	chelone
Missouri		Shoofly	baptisia
Purple	echinacea	Siberian Bugloss	brunnera
Coneflower		Siberian Orchid	cypripedium
Purple Daisy	echinacea	Siberian Tea	bergenia
Purple	lythrum	"Silver King"	artemisia
Loosestrife		Silver Mound	artemisia
Purple Rock	aubrieta	Snake Head	chelone
Cress		Snakeroot	cimicifuga

Snakeroot, Black	cimicifuga	Swamp Sunflower	helianthus
Snakeroot, White	eupatorium	Sweet Woodruff	asperula
		Tarragon	artemisia
Sneezeweed	helenium	Thimble Flower	rudbeckia
Sneezewort	helenium	Tickseed	coreopsis
Snow-in-Summer	cerastium	Toadflax	linaria
		Toad Lily	tricyrtis
Soapwort	saponaria	Tritoma	kniphofia
Solomon's Seal	polygonatum	Turtlehead	chelone
Southernwood	artemisia	Valerian	valeriana
Spanish Bayonet	yucca	Valerian, Red	centranthus
Spanish Buttons	centaurea	Vanilla, Carolina	trilisa
Spanish Dagger	yucca	Vanilla Leaf	trilisa
Speedwell	veronica	Vervain	verbena
Spiderwort	tradescantia	Violet	viola
Spikenard, Cretan	valeriana	Virginia Bluebells	mertensia
Spirea, False	astilbe	Virginia Cowslip	mertensia
Spurge	euphorbia	Wakerobin	trillium
Spurge, Allegheny	pachysandra	Wandering Jew	tradescantia
		White Snakeroot	eupatorium
Spurge, Japanese	pachysandra		
Squirrel Corn	dicentra	Wild Ginger	asarum
Starwort, False	boltonia	Wild Hoarhound	eupatorium
Statice	limonium	Wild Hollyhock	sidalcea
Stokes' Aster	stokesia	Wild Senna	cassia
Stonecrop	sedum	Willow-wort	lysimachia
Strawberry Tomato	physalis	Winter Cherry	physalis
		Woodruff, Sweet	asperula
Sundrops	oenothera		
Sunflower, False	heliopsis	Wormwood	artemisia
		Woundwort	stachys
Sun-Rose	helianthemum	Yarrow	achillea
Swamp Mallow	hibiscus	Zinnia, Hardy	heliopsis

A·P·P·E·N·D·I·X II

Thirty
Common Weeds

THE HISTORY OF WEEDS closely parallels the history of our country—most of them are descendants of immigrants, largely of European and Asiatic origin. Whether in the treatment of coughs, for such cosmetic purposes as skin tonics, or in the large-scale production of certain everyday commodities, many weeds have served humankind since ancient times. Often they continue to do so today. Very few weeds can be described as outright "no-good bums," although I've indicated these below with the annotation "NGB." Yet I hesitate to malign even these few, just in case one of them is found one day to contain the ultimate cure for cancer, AIDS, or the common cold.

By far the most immediately appealing weeds are those that are edible; some of them are actively cultivated even today for their delectable taste. Therefore, although you'll have to keep chasing them from your garden beds, at least assuage your frustrations by regarding the task as harvesting a free meal!

· INEDIBLE WEEDS ·

Bindweed, Field (*Convolvulus arevensis*): Perennial vine; spreads by seeds and rhizome

Buttercup, Creeping (*Ranunculus repens*)—NGB: Annual; spreads by seeds and rooting at leafstalk joints

Canada Thistle *(Cirsium arvense)*: Perennial; spreads by seeds and rootstocks

Crab Grass *(Digitaria)*—NGB: Annual; spreads by seeds and rooting at leafstalk joints

Crowfoot *see* Buttercup, Creeping

Field Balm *see* Ground Ivy

Finger Grass *see* Crab Grass

Gill-over-the-Ground *see* Ground Ivy

Ground Ivy *(Glecoma hederacea)*: Perennial; scalloped leaves; spreads by seeds and creeping stems

Groundsel *(Senecio vulgaris)*: Annual; spreads by seeds

Heal-All *see* Self-Heal

Horsetail *(Equisetum arvense)*—see Chapter 13: Perennial; spreads by spores and rhizomes

Plantain *(Plantago major* and *P. lanceolata)*—see Chapter12: Perennials; the first has broad leaves, the second has narrow leaves; spread by seeds

Poison Ivy *(Rhus radicans)*—see Chapter 12: Perennial woody vine; sometimes shrubby; spreads by seeds and creeping rootstocks; *poisonous*

Quack Grass *(Agropyron repens)*: Perennial; spreads by pinkish ivory rootstock

Ragweed, Common *(Ambrosia artemisiifolia)*—NGB: Annual; spreads by seeds

Self-Heal *(Prunella vulgaris)*: Perennial; low sprawling; spreads by seeds and rootstocks

Shepherd's Purse *(Capsella bursa-pastoris)*: Annual; spreads by seeds

Sitfast *see* Buttercup, Creeping

Speedwell, Creeping *(Veronica officinalis)*: Perennial; spreads by creeping stems

White Clover *(Trifolium repens)*: Perennial; spreads by seeds and runners

Witch Grass *see* Quack Grass

Yarrow, Common *(Achillea millefolium)*—see Chapter 12: Perennial; spreads by seeds and rootstocks.

· EDIBLE WEEDS ·

ALTHOUGH ALL THE WEEDS listed below are safe to eat, as a neophyte forager you would be wise to observe two criteria: (1) be sure that the weed you are about to eat is indeed the same as named below; (2) begin by eating only small quantities of each weed, to let your system adjust slowly to your new diet.

Beggar's Buttons *see* Burdock, Great

Burdock can grow to 9 ft.; lower leaves are large.

Burdock, Great (*Arctium lappa*): Biennial; fruits prickly, adhere to clothing; deep taproot; spreads by seeds
Uses: culinary, medicinal
Roots: Peel first-year roots, boil in two changes of water, serve as vegetable.
Young Flower- and Leafstalks: Add white pith only to salads, or cook like roots. Taste similar to asparagus.
Young Leaves: Serve in salads, or as vegetable double-boiled like roots.

White-flowered **Chickweed** *can become garden pest.*

Chickweed (*Stellaria media*): Annual; low-growing; spreads by seeds
Uses: culinary, medicinal
Leaves: Young leaves and stems, boiled or steamed, taste like spring spinach. They can also be eaten raw, added to salads.

Chicory's leafless flower stalks can rise 4 ft. from dandelion-like basal leaves.

Chicory (*Cichorium intybus*): Perennial (usually along roadsides); blue, pink, or purplish flowers; taproots; spreads by seeds and runners
Uses: culinary, medicinal, commercial
Roots: Cook, serve young roots like parsnips. Roasted and ground, roots make delicious brewed beverage; best known as coffee additive.
Leaves: Add white underground parts of young leaves to salads, or mix with dandelion (q.v.). Boil young leaf crowns in a little water for an excellent vegetable.
Curly Dock *see* Dock, Curled

*Bright yellow **Dandelions** and their fluffy white seed heads are known worldwide.*

Dandelion (*Taraxacum officinale*): Perennial; spreads by seeds and forked taproots
Uses: culinary, medicinal, commercial
Roots: In early spring, peel and double-boil roots like burdock (q.v.) for superior vegetable. Dug in autumn, roasted and ground, roots make tasty brewed coffee substitute.
Leaves: Season and serve white subsurface leaf crowns as raw salad in spring, or mixed with other salad greens. Cook young leaves like spinach, or use in vegetable soups or stews.
Flowers: Deceptively mellow dandelion wine packs a surprising wallop.

Curled Dock's lower leaves are large; all are wavy-edged.

Dock, Curled (*Rumex crispus*): Perennial; narrow, crisped wavy leaves; taproot; spreads by seeds
Uses: culinary, medicinal
Leafstalks: Cook and eat as substitute for rhubarb.
Leaves: Use very young leaves raw in salads, or cook as vegetable.

Wild Garlic is also called Field Garlic.

Garlic, Wild (*Allium vineale*): Perennial; spreads by bulbs
Uses: culinary, medicinal
Green tops: Raw or cooked, use sparingly, because of strong, pungent flavor.
Bulbs: Though small, bulbs may be pickled like onions.
Goosefoot, White *see* Lamb's Quarters

Lamb's Quarters, their stems and leaf undersides often mealy, can grow to 3 ft.

Lamb's Quarters (*Chenopodium album*): Perennial; spreads by seeds
Use: culinary
Leaves, Leafstalks: Steam young leaves and plant tips for a superior

vegetable—better than spinach. Blanched and packed in airtight containers, Lamb's Quarters can also be frozen.

Seeds: Eat raw, or dry and grind into flour.

*Leaves of **Black Mustard** are less deeply lobed than those of **White Mustard** (shown); flowers are yellow.*

Mustard, White (*Brassica alba*) and
Mustard, Black (*Brassica nigra*): Annuals; spread by seeds
Uses: culinary, medicinal, commercial
Seeds: Known to ancient Greeks; pounded and soaked in new wine, seeds used by Romans as condiment. Pounded with vinegar, mustard was recommended in seventeenth-century England as an "excellent sauce" for meats or fish. Use in pickle recipes.
Leaves: Boiled, young mustard greens are an excellent spring vegetable; add raw young leaves sparingly to salads.
Mutton Tops *see* Lamb's Quarters

*The mature **Stinging Nettle**'s coarse hairs inflict "burn" on exposed skin.*

Nettles, Stinging (*Urtica dioica*): Perennial; spreads by seeds and roots
Uses: culinary, medicinal, cosmetic, commercial
Leaves: Always wear gloves when gathering nettles. If "burned" by them, dock is the antidote; the two plants usually grow near each other. Bruise dock leaves and rub the juice on nettle "burn." (N.B.: Nettle venom is destroyed in both cooking and drying.) Pick only

young leaves and tops; wash and, without adding more water, cook covered for 15 to 20 minutes. Serve as green vegetable or as accompaniment to egg dishes. My mother used to make a superb nettle soup.

This **Wild Onion** *is also called Wild Garlic.*

Onion, Wild (*Allium canadense*): Perennial; spreads by bulbs
Uses: culinary, medicinal
Whole plant: Use as a substitute for scallions; or boil, season, and serve hot as a vegetable. Cook bulbs like creamed onions, or add to stews. Pickle above-ground bulblets.
Pigweed *see* Lamb's Quarters

Prostrate, with succulent leaves and reddish stems, **Purslane** *thrives in rich sandy soils.*

Purslane (*Portulaca oleracea*): Annual; spreads by seeds
Uses: culinary, medicinal
Whole Plant: Known since ancient times, the highly nutritious tender stems, leaves, and flower buds can be eaten raw, cooked, or pickled. Or freeze them, blanched and packed in airtight containers. Native Americans of the Southwest use seeds to make bread and gruel.

Leaves of **Common** *or* **Sheep's Sorrel** *(shown) are pale green, arrow-shaped, sour-tasting; they emerge in clusters from subsurface stolons.*

Sorrel (*Rumex*, various species): Perennial; spreads by seeds and root divisions
Uses: culinary, medicinal
Leaves: Eaten as salad since ancient times, sorrel can be picked through-out the growing season. The chief ingredient in French *soupe aux herbes*; it is also used in ragouts and fricassees. Wash, and simmer without added water, for green vegetable alone, or mixed with other greens. Chewing fresh sorrel leaves quenched my thirst long before I could spell their name.
Sorrel, Wood *see* Wood Sorrel
Starweed *see* Chickweed
Succory *see* Chicory

Creeping **Watercress** *leaves and stems float in running water, brooks, springs.*

Watercress (*Nasturtium officinale*): Perennial; spreads by seeds and stolons, in springs, streams
Uses: culinary, medicinal, cosmetic, commercial
Leaves, Flowers, Seed Pods: An escaped garden plant, this nasturtium is entirely unrelated to the garden plant *Tropaeolum*, commonly known as nasturtium, although both are equally pungent and wholesome to eat. Use only watercress found in uncontaminated waters. Pinch or

cut stems at water surface (below-surface stems are tough). Use fresh as salad, on sandwiches, or as a garnish. Cook like spinach and serve as vegetable alone, or added to other greens. Watercress soup is divine.

Wood Sorrel, *its leaves cloverlike and sour-tasting, is a delicate, low-growing woodland plant.*

Wood Sorrel (*Oxalis acetosella*): Perennial; spreads by seeds and roots
Uses: culinary, medicinal
Leaves and Stems: Botanically, this plant is unrelated to sorrels, but they share a high content of binoxalate of potash, a chemical salt that provides the typically acid taste in sorrels, docks, garden rhubarb—and wood sorrel. It grows mostly in shady areas. Eaten raw as a salad or as a cooked potherb, or used instead of vinegar, wood sorrel has been known since time immemorial. A few leaves chewed raw are an excellent thirst quencher. Long before the introduction of French sorrel, English cooks greatly favored wood sorrel as the basis of Green Sauce.

BON APPÉTIT!

USEFUL READINGS

THOUSANDS OF BOOKS about gardens and gardening fill bookshelves around the world. The wealth of knowledge contained in them surely resembles a gardener's version of King Solomon's Mines. Nevertheless, each of us must pry loose the first nugget, and so at the beginning, we must rely on the "best to start with" readings suggested by a gardening friend, based on his or her own collection. Consequently, the books listed below are from among the most useful or widely recognized works on my own shelves. They inform, guide, and recommend. They describe, explain, illustrate. They are easy to read and fun to browse through. They answer questions you perhaps haven't yet asked or thought you needed to ask. And each book has its own way of stimulating you further to understanding the world of gardening, and to participating in the infinitely wondrous tapestry that is nature.

Browne, Janet. *Growing from Cuttings and Other Means*. Series: Concorde Gardening. London: Ward Lock Limited, 1981.

Cox, Jeff and Marilyn. *The Perennial Garden*: Color Harmonies Through the Seasons. Emmaus, Pennsylvania: Rodale Press, Inc., 1985.

Gibbons, Euell. *Stalking the Wild Asparagus*. New York: David McKay Company, Inc., 1962.

Grieve, Mrs. M. *A Modern Herbal*: The Medicinal, Culinary, Cosmetic and Economic Properties, Cultivation and Folk-Lore of Herbs, Grasses, Fungi, Shrubs & Trees with all their Modern Scientific Uses. New York: Dover Publications, Inc., 1971.

Peterson, Roger Tory, and McKenny, Margaret. *A Field Guide to Wildflowers*. Boston: Houghton Mifflin Company, 1968.

Reader's Digest Illustrated Guide to Gardening. Pleasantville, New York; Montreal: The Reader's Digest Association, Inc., 1978.

Riotte, Louise. *Secrets of Companion Planting for Successful Gardening*. Charlotte, Vermont: Garden Way Publishing, 1975.

Taylor, Norman, ed. *Taylor's Encyclopedia of Gardening*: Horticulture and Landscape Design. Fourth edition. Boston: Houghton Mifflin Company, The Riverside Press, Cambridge, 1961.

Yepsen, Roger B., Jr., ed. *The Encyclopedia of Natural Insect & Disease Control*. Emmaus, Pennsylvania: Rodale Press, Inc., 1984.

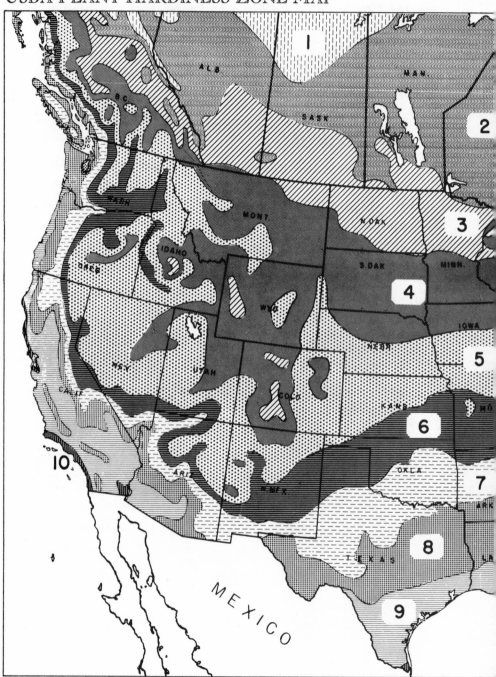

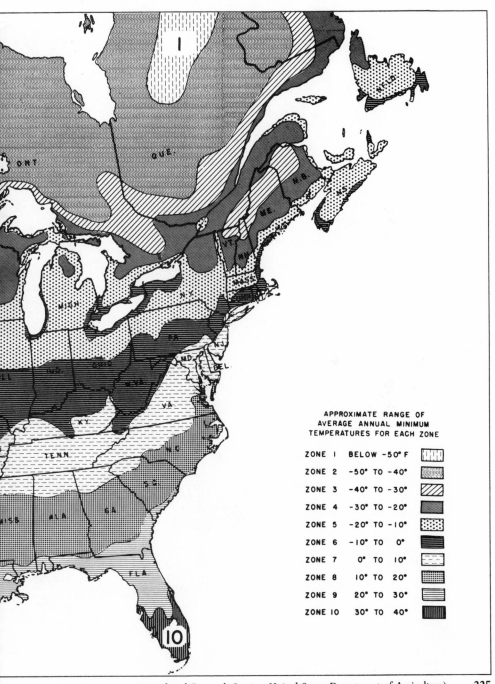

APPROXIMATE RANGE OF
AVERAGE ANNUAL MINIMUM
TEMPERATURES FOR EACH ZONE

ZONE 1 BELOW -50° F

ZONE 2 -50° TO -40°

ZONE 3 -40° TO -30°

ZONE 4 -30° TO -20°

ZONE 5 -20° TO -10°

ZONE 6 -10° TO   0°

ZONE 7   0° TO 10°

ZONE 8   10° TO 20°

ZONE 9   20° TO 30°

ZONE 10 30° TO 40°

(Agricultural Research Service, United States Department of Agriculture)   225

INDEX

acidity of soil, 22–25, 49
aged chicken manure, 55, 62, 132
ageratum, 183
Agriculture Department, U.S.
    (USDA), 10, 20, 25
ailanthus, 24
alkalinity of soil, 22–25
allium family, 157
American pennyroyal, 155
andromeda, 198
annuals, 49
    deadheading of, 187
    for edgings, 183
    hardy, 105
    insect-repellent, 157
    mulching of, 49
    name tabs for, 96

planting of, 96–100
    from seeds, 98
    stem cuttings of, 167–68
    watering of, 125, 127
ants, 154
aphids, 154, 155
aphis lion, 156
apple trees, 14
arbors, 4
asexual propagation, 167
azaleas, 49, 133, 196, 198

bacteria, 152
bark nuggets, 132, 133, 134
bark shavings, 132, 134–35, 187
beach plums, 50
beans, 87, 106, 107, 125

beds:
  angular, 47, 49, 74
  autumn-dug, 71, 76, 78
  center lines for, 73, 74
  compacted subsoil in, 71
  double-digging of, 22, 75–78,
    145
  free-form, 50, 75, 186
  guidelines for, 50
  hospital, 86, 164, 166–67, 169
  marking contours of, 72, 73, 74,
    75
  oval, 50
  preparing of, 69–79
  rectangular, 74
  round, 49, 70, 74
  for shrub groupings, 70
  sizes of, 70
  "spontaneous" groupings in, 97
  spring-dug, 71–72, 76, 78
  square, 72–73
  subsoil for, 70, 71–72
  timing preparation of, 71–72
  topsoil for, 70–71
  vertical digging of, 76
  see also edging
beer, 157–58
bees, 152, 153
beetles, 155
  Japanese, 157
beets, 87, 110
begonias, 97, 167–68
bergamot, 144, 175
biennials, 86, 96, 177
  deadheading of, 187
biodegradable refuse, 56–58, 59,
    95
birds, 12–13
bites, insect, 154–55
black flies, 153
blueberries, 50
blueprints, 46–47

"bolting," 108
bone meal, 29, 58, 62, 195
  for ant control, 154
borage, 157
box barberry, 182
box elder, 24
boxwood, 97, 182
Brassica family, 109, 110
broccoli, 50, 85, 107, 109, 110,
    115, 135
Brussels sprouts, 85, 109, 110, 194
buckwheat, 21, 194
"bud union," 103
bulbils, 171, 172
bulblets, 171, 172, 195
bulbs, 44–45, 171
  from catalogues, 89, 90–91, 195
  deadheading and, 189
  planting of, 195
  spring, 44, 50, 195
burdock, 148, 154, 215
burlap, 95, 195, 197
Butterfly Weed, 97

cabbage, 85, 109, 159
calendula, 147, 157
calluses, 169
camomile tea, 159
candytuft, 182, 183
carnations, 61
carrots, 20, 87, 106, 108–9, 194
catalogues, gardening, 10, 28, 47,
    89–91
  bulbs from, 89, 90–91, 195
  guarantees of, 89
  hardiness zones and, 91
  seeds from, 89–90, 91
  soil-test kits from, 24–25
  symbols in, 48
caterpillars, 155
catnip (catmint), 157
cauliflower, 109

celery plants, 107
chain-link fencing, low, 184
charcoal, powdered, for ant control, 154
Charlotte's Web (White), 154
chemical pesticide sprays, 152
chicken manure, aged, 55, 62, 132
chickweed, 215
chicory, 216
chipmunks, 161
chrysanthemums, 48, 168, 170, 171
city gardens, 69, 157
clayey soils, 18, 21–22, 25
    double-digging of, 78
    treatment for, 22
    watering of, 121
clematis, 14, 100
clothing, 27–28
clubroot, 159
cold frames, 113–14
cold-rot composing, 58, 59–60, 166
coleus, 168
columbine, 174
commercial fertilizers, 62, 64–66
compacted subsoil, 71
companion planting, 107
compasses, 7–8, 27
compost, compost heaps, 53–67, 77, 194
    bins for, 59
    bone meal in, 58, 62
    cold-rot, 58, 59–60, 166
    commercial fertilizer in, 62
    contents of, 56–58
    fish meal in, 58
    hot-rot, 58, 61–63
    household garbage in, 56–58
    lime in, 62
    location of, 57, 58
    sizes of, 58

structuring of, 56–58, 62–63
    tin cans in, 58
    weeds in, 87
conifers, 49
containers, biodegradable, 95
Cooperative Extension Association, 9, 25
coral-bells, 171, 174
coreopsis, 177, 188
cormels, 194
corms, 171, 194
corn, 50, 87, 110
corn husks, ground-up, 132, 133
cottage gardens, 2
creeping phlox, 171, 183
crickets, 155
crocus, 44, 50, 195
cucumbers, 106, 107, 116
cultivators, 29, 37–38
currants, 50
cuttings, stem, 164, 167–71
cutworms, 155

daffodils, 44, 50, 189, 195
dandelion, 148, 216
day lily, 171, 174, 189
deadheading, 176, 187–89
    method of, 188
    purpose of, 187
deer, 51, 197
    repellents for, 159–60
"deer garden," 51
delphiniums, 61, 75, 97, 127, 134
deutzia, 170
digging:
    in autumn, 71, 76, 78
    double-, 22, 75–78, 145
    in spring, 71–72, 76, 78
    vertical, 76
digging forks, 12, 29, 34, 76, 77, 149, 187
dill, 109, 110

dock, curled, 217
double-digging, 22, 75–78, 145
drainage, horseshoe, 19
dried leaves, 132, 135–37
driveways, 45, 70
drowning, 122
dwarf fruit trees, 51

earthworms, 21
ecological balance, 151
edge cuts, 185–86
edgers, edge cutters, 185
edging, 182–87
    annuals vs. perennials as, 183
    commercial, 183–84
    construction materials for, 183
    fences as, 184
    metal hoops, 184
    methods of, 185–87
    rock borders, 184
    stone walls, 184
    uses of, 182
    visual impact of, 183
    wooden block, 184
edible weeds, 215–21
eggplants, 110, 135
English gardens, 2
Euonymus alatus, 165
evening primrose (Oenothera mis-
    souriensis), 171, 175, 190
evergreens, 14, 196

fences:
    low chain-link, 184
    miniature picket, 184
    miniature post-and-rail, 184
    wooden, 3
ferns, 49
fertilizers, 29, 53–67
    commercial, 62, 64–66
    compost, see compost, compost
        heaps

formulas of, 65
    root burn by, 66
    in winter, 198
feverfew, 154, 157, 176, 188
field-grown plants, 86
fish meal, 58
flagstone patios, 4
flax, 176, 178
flies, 153, 156
folding handsaws, 29, 36–37
formal gardens, 2
forsythia, 127, 168, 170
foxglove, 176, 177, 188
frogs, 153, 155
frost pockets, 10
fruit bushes, 50–51, 91
fungi, 152

garden carts, 29, 34–35, 185
garden centers, 28
    commercial edgings at, 183–84
    faulty tool policies of, 41
    insects bought at, 156
    polypropylene bins at, 59
    see also nurseries
garden refuse, 56
gardens:
    birds in, 12–13
    boundaries of, 3; see also beds;
        edging
    clearing of, 13
    "deer," 51
    European words for, 1
    evaluation of, 13–15
    flagstone patios in, 4
    as "framed," 2–3, 4
    Greeks on, 1
    hardiness zones of, see hardiness
        zones
    herb, 4, 15, 44, 147, 164
    house styles and, 3–4
    instant, 2

as outdoor living rooms, 4
planning of, *see* planning, garden
rock, 4
streams in, 3, 4
sun directions on, 8
surrealistic, 4
tools used in, 27–42
types of, 3–4
vegetable, *see* vegetable gardens
walkabouts in, 13–15, 16, 75
wind directions in, 8
yards vs., 1–2
garlic, 85, 107, 155, 157
wild, 217
garter snakes, 153, 155
geraniums, 49, 61, 157, 168, 183
Geranium sanguineum, 183
gladiolus, 194
gooseberries, 50, 196
grafting, 103
grape hyacinths, 44, 195
grass cuttings, 132, 133, 135
greenhouses, 111
makeshift, 112
green manuring, 21, 194
green peppers, 106, 109–10, 111,
115, 135, 176
groundwater, 122–23
groupings, 49, 70
"spontaneous," 97
spread of colors among, 97–98
symmetry of, 97
grow lights, 111–12
Gypsophila repens, 183

hand grubbers, 28, 32–33
hand-pressured spray gun nozzles,
39, 126
hand pruners, 29, 35–36
handsaws, folding, 29, 36–37
hanging baskets, 4
hardening off, 114–15

hardiness zones, 7, 8, 10–12
choosing plants for, 10–11
climatic deviations in, 11
gardening catalogues on, 91
lowest mean temperature in, 10
maps of, 10, 11
hardpan, 71, 75
hardy annuals, 105
harvesting, 93
head coverings, 28
hedge clippers, 29, 39–40
hedges, 39–40, 47
heeling in, 165–66
herbal hand lotion, 147
herb gardens, 4, 15, 44, 147, 164
herbs, 4
for stings and bites, 154–55
hoes, 29, 37–38
hollyhocks, 61, 75, 176
honesty, 176
honeybees, 152, 153
honeydew, 154
hormone rooting powder, 166, 169
horseflies, 153
horse manure, 54, 132
horseshoe drainage, 19
horsetail, 159
hoses, watering, 29, 38–39, 75,
186
hospital beds, 86, 164, 166–67,
169
hot-rot composting, 58, 61–63
humidity, 123
humus, 18, 21, 22, 54, 120, 132
hybrids, 177
hyssop, 154

impatiens, 49, 125, 167, 183
inedible weeds, 214–15
insect bites, 154–55
insect repellent(s):
annuals, 157

insect repellent(s) *(cont.)*
  beer, 157–58
  garlic, 155
  herbs, 154–55
  home remedies, 157–62
  hot peppers, 158
  perennials, 157
  tobacco, 108, 158
  wood ashes, 107
  see also pest control
insects, 151, 152
  as pollinators, 152
  purchase of, 156
internodes, 169
iris, 144, 171, 174, 178, 189
Iris sibirica, 165
iron gratings, 4
ivy, 100

Japanese beetles, 157
jewelweed, 143
junipers, 164, 168

kale, 110, 194
kohlrabi, 110

lacewings, 153, 156
ladybugs, 153, 155–56
lamb's quarters, 217–18
lath strips, 75
lattices, 4, 101
lavender, 182, 183
leaching, 60, 63
leadwort, 86
leaf axils, 188
leaf mold, 56, 77, 136, 187, 198
leaf rakes, 29, 38, 136, 186
leaf-shredding machines, 136
leaves, dried, 132, 135–37
leeks, 85, 157
lettuce, 20, 106, 108, 114
lilacs, 103

lily of the valley, 174
lime, 29, 62, 133
loamy soils, 18, 25
  sandy, 18, 20
low chain-link fencing, 184
lowest mean temperatures, 10
lupines, 22, 127, 168, 178

mail-order plant buying, 89–91
maintenance, 181–91
  by edging, 182–87
  overall, 187–91
  see also mulch; watering; weeding
Maltese cross, 188
manure, 54, 55–56, 61, 62
  aged chicken, 55, 62, 132
  fresh vs. well-rotted, 55
  horse, 54, 132
  as mulch, 132, 133
  root burn and, 55, 56
  well-rotted, 55, 77, 113
marigolds, 49, 127, 157, 176, 183
marrows, 108
mealybugs, 156
mice, 161–62
mildew, sprays for, 159
miniature picket fencing, 184
miniature post-and-rail fencing,
  184
mint, *see specific mints*
mock orange, 170
mold, leaf, 56, 77, 136, 187, 198
moles, 155, 161
Monarda didyma, 164, 190
mosquitos, 153, 155
moths, 155
mulch, mulching, 9, 20, 95, 104,
  120–21, 123, 131–39, 185,
  186, 187
  of annuals, 49
  for fruit trees, 133
  manure as, 132, 133

thickness of, 133
types of, 132
winterizing with, 196
mustard, 218

nasturtiums, 108, 125, 155, 157
natural pest control, 151, 152
nettles, stinging, 218–19
newspapers, 132, 137–38, 197
nicotianas, 176
nitrogen, 54, 59, 61, 65
nodes, 169
nurseries, 81–92
    mail-order, 90–91
    salespeople at, 82–83
    vegetable seedlings in, 87
    see also garden centers

onions, 107, 114, 157, 160
    wild, 219
opossums, 161
outbuildings, 14

pachysandra, 187
painted daisy, 157
parsley, 154
parsnips, 20, 194
patios, flagstone, 4
peas, 20, 87, 106, 107
pennyroyal, American, 155
peonies, 61, 127, 171, 187–88
perennials, 49
    creeping, 174–75
    deadheading of, 187
    dormant condition of, 9
    as edgings, 183
    as field-grown plants, 86
    garden planning with, 49
    herbaceous, 201–11
    hot-rot compost for, 61
    insect-repellent, 157
    planting of, 96–100

root division of, 171
seed propagation of, 176, 177
soil for, 22
stem cuttings of, 168
watering of, 125, 127
periwinkles, 174, 187
pest control, 151–62
    by bees, 153
    burning of plants for, 154
    chemical sprays for, 152
    ecological balance and, 151
    home remedies for, 157–62
    mammals and, 159–62
    natural, 151, 152–53
    by spiders, 154
    by wasps, 153
    see also insect repellents; sprays
petunias, 49, 84, 157
phlox, 48, 96, 144, 168, 171, 174,
    187
phosphorus, 54, 65
pH value of soil, 22–25, 133
picket fencing, miniature, 184
Pieris japonica, 198
pinching off, 84
pine needles, 132
planning, garden, 43–52
    of annuals, 49
    of beds, 47, 49–50
    blueprints for, 46–47
    books on, 43, 51
    catalogues for, 47
    of driveways, 45, 52
    emergency access and, 45–46,
        52
    family traffic patterns and, 45,
        52
    of groupings, 49
    of perennials, 49
    plant heights and, 51–52
    of roses, 49
    septic systems and, 44–45

planning, garden (*cont.*)
  snapshots and, 47, 52
  sun direction and, 48, 52
  of trees, 47–48
  of vegetables, 50–51
plantain, 154
plantain lily, 174
plant buying, 81–92
  budgets for, 81, 88
  from catalogues, 89–91
  by hardiness zones, 10–12, 91
  inspection and, 84
  mail order, 89–91
  preparing for, 81, 82
  see also nurseries; vegetable seed-
    lings
planter benches, 4
planting, 93–117
  in afternoons, 95
  of annuals, 96–100
  with bare hands, 94
  of bulbs, 195
  companion, 107
  drip lines and, 105
  elimination of air pockets and,
    104, 105
  during full moon, 96
  guidelines for, 94–96
  holes for, 95, 102
  in mornings, 95
  of perennials, 96–100
  removal of containers before, 95
  root separation before, 98, 100
  of seeds, 94, 95, 110–16
  spacing in, 97
  by tamping, 99, 103, 104
  of trees, 47–48, 101–6
  of vegetables, 106–10
  of vines, 100–1
  see also transplanting
planting lines, 72
plant-light stands, 111–12

plant stands, graduated, 4
pocket knives, 29, 33–34
pods, 178
poison ivy, 142–43
pollination, 152
polypropylene bins, 59
poppies, 61, 176
post-and-rail fencing, miniature,
  184
potash, 54, 64
"pot-bound" plants, 100
potting soil, 29
powdery mildew, sprays for, 159
praying mantises, 153, 156
pre-weeding, 145–46
propagation, 163–80
  asexual, 167
  from cuttings, 164, 167–71
  by heeling in, 165–66
  history of, 165
  by root division, 167, 171–75
  by seeds, 167, 175–79, 189
  sexual, 167
  slanting cuts for, 168
  tools for, 166, 174
  by true suckers, 170–71
pruning, 152, 168
purslane, 219

quince, 170

rabbits, 160
raccoons, 161
radishes, 20, 87, 106, 108, 114
rain, 8–9, 120, 123, 125–26, 128
rakes, 28, 31–32
  for leaves, 29, 38, 136, 186
raspberries, 66, 170
refuse:
  biodegradable, 56–58, 59, 95
  garden, 56
rhizomes, 171, 174

rhododendrons, 49, 95, 103, 127,
133, 196, 198
rhubarb leaves, 159
rock-garden plants, 4
root burn:
by fertilizers, 66
by fresh manure, 55, 56
root damage, 48
by overexposure, 100
see also root burn
root division, 167, 171–75
rooting powder, hormone, 166,
169
root separation, 100
hand vs. knife, 98–99
of shrubs, 102
of trees, 102
rootstock, 103
roses, 49, 90, 103, 170
hybrid, 103, 195–96
woody mulch for, 133
rototillers, 21, 22
row markers, 72
rue, 157
runners, 171, 172

salt hay, 132, 133
sandy loam soil, 18, 20
sandy soils, 18, 20–21, 25
treatment for, 20–21
sap groove, 40
Saponaria ocymoides, 183
sawdust, 132
scilla, 44, 50, 195
secateurs, 168
sedum, 174
seedlings:
root separation of, 98
vegetable, 87–88, 114–15
seeds:
air-drying of, 176, 178
from catalogues, 89–90, 91

cold frames for, 113–14
growing annuals from, 98
grow lights for, 111–12
guidelines on packets of, 106–7
marking of, 116, 178–79
planting of, 94, 95, 110–16
plants vs., 110
propagation by, 167, 175–79,
189
vegetables from, 87, 91
see also pods
septic systems, 44, 52
settling-in periods, 128
sexual propagation, 167
Shasta daisies, 97
shovels, 12, 28, 30–32, 76, 77
shrubs, 101–6
beds for grouping of, 70
grafted, 103
root separation of, 102
watering of newly planted, 101,
104, 127
silt, 18
"Silver King," 175
silver maple, 24
skunks, 161
slips, *see* stem cuttings
slugs, 155, 157–58
snails, 155, 157–58
snapdragons, 97, 127, 188
snowdrops, 195
soaker systems, 124–25
soil, 17–25
chemical testing of, 23
clayey, 18, 21–22, 25, 78, 121
earthworms in, 21
improvement of, *see* green manuring; mulch
information on, 20
loamy, 18, 25
moisture-retention capacity of,
56

soil (cont.)
  nutrients in, 54
  pH value of, 22–25, 133
  poor, 24
  potting, 29
  rock obstructions in, 14
  sandy, 18, 20–21
  sandy loam, 18, 20
  test kits for, 24–25, 27
  see also subsoil; topsoil
soil line, 103
sorrel, 220
southernwood, 155, 157
spacing, 97
  of vegetables, 110
spades, 28, 30–32, 76, 77, 166,
    185
spading forks, 29, 34
spearmint, 155
spider mites, 156
spiders, 153, 154
spinach, 100, 114
spirea, 170, 179
spores, 152
sports, 116
sprays:
  chemical pesticide, 152
  horsetail, 159
  hot pepper, 158
  for moles, 161
  rhubarb, 159
  tobacco, 158
  see also insect repellents
spring bulbs, 44, 50, 195
sprinklers, 124, 126
  hand-held, 38
  stationary, 38
squash, 106, 108, 116, 176
squirrels, 161
stakes, 75
stake-spools, 72, 74
star-of-Bethlehem, 195
stem cuttings, 164, 167–71

stings, 154, 155
stolons, 171, 172, 175
straw, 132, 133
strawberries, 107
string beans, 106
subsoil, 70, 71–72, 75
suckers, 103, 171, 172, 190–91
  removal of, 103
  true, 104, 170–71, 190
summer squashes, 108
sunlight, 8, 48, 52
sweet alyssum, 183
Swiss chard, 87, 110, 194

tamping, 99, 103, 104, 164
tansy, 155, 157
teasel, 121
temperature, lowest mean, 10
test kits, soil, 24–25, 27
thinning, 115–16
  of carrot tops, 108
thunderstorms, 8–9, 125
toads, 153, 155
tobacco ash, 108
tobacco sprays, 158
tomatoes, 85, 106, 109, 115, 116,
    135, 176
tools, 27–42
  care of, 41, 42
  cost of, 40–41
  hanging of, 42
  for propagation, 166, 174
  storing of, 41–42
  testing of, 40–41, 42
  winter storage of, 42
topsoil, 70–71, 75
trailing leadwort, 86
transplanting, 105–6, 127, 190
  of seedlings, 116
tree pruners, 29, 39
trees:
  dwarf fruit, 51
  holes for, 95, 102

planting of, 47–48, 101–6
on property lines, 3
root separation of, 102
spraying of, 128
watering of newly planted, 101,
104, 127
wrapped in burlap, 95
trellises, 4, 101
trowels, 28, 32, 166
true suckers, 104, 170–71, 190
tubers, 171
tulips, 50, 189, 195
turnips, 87

USDA Zone 4, 11, 49, 91
USDA Zone 5, 11, 91
USDA Zone 6, 11

vegetable gardens, 4
companion planting in, 107
deer in, 51
fruit bushes as borders in, 50–
51
horseshoe drainage in, 19
hot-rot compost for, 61
mulch for, 135
narrow beds for, 50
newspaper mulch in, 137–38
north-south direction of, 50
pest control in, 156–57
planting of, 106–10
sandy soil in, 20
seedlings for, see vegetable seedlings
seed packet guidelines for, 106–
107
winterizing of, 194
vegetable seedlings, 87–88
in cold frames, 114
hardening off, 114–15
insulation for, 88
watering of, 87–88
Verbena hortensis, 183

vertical gardens, 4
viburnums, 103
vines, 100–1
disadvantages of, 100–1
lattices for, 101
voles, 161

walkabouts, 13–15, 16, 75
walls:
as secondary frames, 3
as vertical gardens, 4
wasps, 153
watercress, 220–21
watering, 119–29, 181
benefits of, 121
guidelines for, 124–26
in June, 120
of newly planted trees, 101,
104, 127
over-, 122
after rains, 120, 123, 125–26,
128
of seedlings, 127
of shrubs, 127
by soaker systems, 124–25
tests for, 126
timing of, 124–25
of transplants, 126–27
under-, 122
of vegetable seedlings, 87–88
watering cans, 29, 33, 124
watering hoses, 29, 38–39, 75, 186
watering-in periods, 127
water plants, 121
weed cutters, 13
weeding, 93, 141–50, 151, 181
as continuous process, 144
methods of, 145–49
mulch and, 132
uses of, 149
in vegetable gardens, 106
weeds, 86, 141–42
edible, 214–21

weeds (cont.)
  inedible, 213–14
  taproots of, 148–49
weigela, 127, 168
well-rotted manure, 55, 77, 113
wheelbarrows, 29, 34–35, 77, 78,
    185–86
White, E. B., 154
whiteflies, 156
wild garlic, 217
wild islands, 149–50
wild onion, 219
wind direction, 8–9
windscreens, 9
windsocks, 9
winterizing, 193–99
  against winds, 196
  of bulbs, 195
  of large plants, 197–98
  with mulch, 196
  of roses, 195–96
  of vegetable gardens, 194
winter rye, 21, 22, 194
winter squashes, 108

wisteria, 100
witch hazel, 154
wood ashes, 63, 64, 107, 160
woodchucks, 160–61
wood shavings, 132
wood sorrel, 221
wood thrushes, 12–13
worms, 153, 155
wormwood, 155, 157

yards:
  European terms for, 1
  gardens vs., 1–2
  as paved enclosures, 2, 4
yarrow, 97, 174
YD handles:
  of shovels, 30
  of spading forks, 34
yellow alyssum, 96
yellow loosestrife, 175

zinnias, 127, 176, 178, 188
zucchini, 87, 106, 108